the HOUSE *without* *a* SUMMER

DEANNA KNIPPLING

WONDERLAND PRESS

Contents

THE HOUSE WITHOUT A SUMMER

Historical Note

THE YEAR OF 1816 was known as "the year without a summer." Across the world, temperatures dropped. Snows and frosts lasted until June, interspersed with heavy rain. Sunspots visible to the naked eye covered the sun. Crops rotted in the wet fields. When the fields were replanted, the crops rotted again.

Napoleon had only just been defeated. A plague of typhus spread across Europe, killing more people than the Corsican general had. Merchants bought up what stores of grain there were to be had, increasing prices. Farmers refused to sell their grain outside of their home districts. In Great Britain, what with one thing and another—including the ludicrous Corn Laws, designed to keep the prices of grain high—over a hundred thousand people died of illness and starvation. Food riots happened all across Britain and France.

To some, it was very nearly the end of the world.

The year before, the volcano Mount Tambora had erupted in what was then the Dutch East Indies. It was an eruption ten times as powerful as that of Mount Krakatoa in 1883. The Mount Tambora eruption was the most powerful one known in recorded history, at a seven on the Volcanic Explosivity Index. (Krakatoa was a six; Vesuvius and Mount St. Helens were fives.) So much gas and dust were thrown into the atmosphere that it chilled the surface of the earth for two years. Worldwide famine followed.

Painter J.M.W. Turner caught the strangely miscolored skies after the eruption. His paintings from before the tragedy, in 1814, depict skies of a cool, bluer hue; afterwards, at dawn and sunset, the skies in his paintings burned the color of blood, and in daylight hummed with an almost eerie golden light.

The light remained in its distorted colors for almost the rest of Turner's career; he died in 1851.

The summer of 1816 saw Mary Shelley and Percy Bysshe Shelly in Geneva, Switzerland, telling Gothic tales with the poet George Gordon, Lord Byron, and the doctor John Polidori. The rains kept them indoors most of that summer. Mary Shelly's ghost story was that of a resurrected man, and the mad doctor who brings the creature back from the dead: thus, *Frankenstein* was born. It also saw author Jane Austen beginning to sicken and fade from a mysterious illness, from which she died in 1817.

By September 1816, the snows had begun again. In fact, snow tinted red from volcanic ash fell in some parts Italy all throughout the year.

It was the Regency Era.

While the upper classes held their endless parties, balls, and operas, attended gambling hells, scrambled to make advantageous marriages for their daughters, and obsessed over French fashion, the lower classes rioted and starved.

Many people were convinced the world was ending.

Prologue

The Crystal Palace

IT WASN'T UNTIL MISS Lucy Abbott had attended the Great Exhibition of 1851 several times that she began to truly understand what had happened in the year of 1816.

Decades had passed; the unendurable, mad year of 1816 had come to a close; those who had died had faded from memory for the most part, either disappearing as if they had never lived, or taking on the aspect of the people they ought to have been, rather than the blackguards they were. In particular, the reputation of the Earl of Penderbrook had been much ameliorated.

In Lucy's secret heart of hearts, she suspected that she herself had been changed little by what had happened, although at the time she had felt herself to have been transformed entire. What she had lost seemed the world to her. But, both before the tragedy and after, she was as dark of mind and eye as ever; her heart still dwelled upon the injustices that she saw everywhere. But who might she have been, if events had occurred otherwise? A wife, a mother, and a fine addition to society—if somewhat macabre of humor and a little too interested in novels.

Until the Great Exhibition, she had supposed herself entirely recovered of her peace of mind. And indeed, the first several times she visited the Crystal Palace, home to the exhibition, she felt only wonder, sore feet, and delight.

But as the Great Exhibition progressed, her heart began to leap uncomfortably about in her chest: at the sight of certain too-familiar, yet altogether featureless faces; the smell of mildew and unwashed bodies; even the sound of a laugh, shrill yet commanding, that reminded her of the Earl's.

As she wound her way through the endless exhibits collected by Prince Albert and his committees, she was forced to remind herself more and more often that she was *not* walking through the halls of Penderbrook.

Penderbrook was gone as though it had never existed.

Thank God.

WHEN FIRST THE GREAT Exhibition had opened, she had gone to see it like everyone else: it was a marvel, a wonder, the gathering of all that was brightest and best in the world, the promise of increase and prosperity to all mankind. She went because she had been invited by friends. She went because she had always had more curiosity than sense. She went because she had an idea that she would like to set one of her stories there, or at least to gather the flavor of a hundred different countries around the world, so that she might set her stories anywhere, and at least have some hope of getting *something* right.

She was always in despair that a reader would catch her out in some hideous inaccuracy, although they seldom did, or cared.

The Crystal Palace was a shining edifice, grand and impressive, a hall made of steel and glass. She could see inside it as the carriage approached, the sea of humanity that entered it, and, through the glass, the bustle upstairs, and an endless row of booths. She was handed out her carriage, escorted inside, and treated with all civility. She was not so overwhelmed that she did not understand that she was being treated as visiting royalty in the hopes that she would write something favorable about the exhibition for the Press.

It was everything that she had hoped for, and she promised herself that she would return again and again, and the next time she would attend with a notebook and more comfortable shoes. Later, she remembered little of her first visit but a blur.

She continued to visit the exhibition, to take copious notes, to study, to dream.

This continued into October of 1851, when the exhibition was about to close. The sense of wonder still remained, but it was a frantic sort of emotion now, the kind of feeling that one gets when one stays up past one's bedtime and had drunk just enough brandy to feel a certain amount of strain underneath one's own merriment.

It was a twilight sort of mood.

The exhibits, over the course of the exhibition, became less and less well maintained. The upper tiers of British society began to absent themselves, and the exhibition put on specials for the lower classes to attend more cheaply. The halls were more packed than ever. Little things began to disappear, either stolen by thieves or preventatively removed by the owners, wary of thievery.

She began to feel a certain familiarity, not of the exhibition itself, but of some other place, which she could hardly remember.

Then one day she turned in the hallway around one booth to the next and did not recognize where she was. She was surrounded by pale figures rushing past her, not quite ghosts, but men and women with all the color washed out of their faces, as though they were illustrations printed on onionskin paper. They grimaced at her and at each other, baring their teeth. Her skin rose up in instant gooseflesh, and her teeth chattered against each other several times, shivering, before she clenched them together.

When she glanced back over her shoulder, the hall seemed familiar again. *There* was the new steam engine; *there* was the new type of lock that everyone had been so certain of no-one ever being able to pick! But of course it had been defeated by an American locksmith in a matter of days... In other words, she knew her ground. The phantoms had vanished, or rather been subsumed back into the people surrounding her, who seemed as perfectly ordinary as always.

But upon walking forwards a few steps, she shuddered again.

Penderbrook.

As the word came to her, she jumped back from a pale-faced gentleman who had come forwards to shake her hand. She had no wish to startle the man—he wished only to tell her that he enjoyed her stories—so she forced a laugh and quipped, "You made me think of my editor for a moment!" He laughed, and they chatted briefly.

She hoped that she had concealed her true emotions from appearing on her face.

At any moment, she expected to be snatched from behind, a cold limb twining itself about her shoulders.

Lucy...

You know you must leave, Lucy, before it is too late.

After her admirer had excused himself, she had been solicitously asked by her secretary if she wished him to find her a seat; she had gone quite pale. She clutched his arm, saying that she felt a bit dizzy and did not wish him to leave her side, lest she fall.

Do not let me vanish.

It had long seemed to her that she owed a debt to Penderbrook. Or perhaps *debt* was not the right word. But there was a part of her which belonged to Penderbrook, which she had always suspected would someday be reclaimed as its own.

Her secretary held his arm stiffly at his side, and she clung to it, near to weeping. The halls seemed to spiral about her, wrapping her tighter and tighter until her breath became painful in her chest. The sense of being pulled or called increased. The faces spinning past her seemed to leer at each other, every face turned into a kind of translucent, bloodless clay.

This place is dying, she realized.

The Crystal Palace was clinging to life as a drowning man might cling over-tightly to his would-be savior, causing them both to sink.

As Penderbrook had done.

And she, of all who were present, was perhaps the only one to understand the sensation, because she had felt it before.

She must not let it take her; she must not let it take her secretary. She would linger no longer.

Slowly, carefully, deliberately, she took a step forwards. The Crystal Palace pulled at her. Oh, how it pulled! Like softness, like warmth, like the stupor after lovemaking, like candlelight. But she knew what it was now, knew that it was only winding up its cocoon, tighter and tighter, seeking a place of safety and finding only self-destruction.

Lucy...

You must leave, Lucy, before it is too late...

Her secretary stopped her to ask, "Miss Abbott? Are you quite all right?"

"I have a desperate need of air," she told him, and he led her outside of the Crystal Palace, to which she never again returned.

The building was pulled down soon after. They said it was to be rebuilt on the top of Sydenham Hill, to hold permanent exhibits.

But it was not the same place, and she ever after felt herself having very narrowly escaped indeed.

Chapter One

Return to Penderbrook

October 1816

The year had been, and would continue to be, a bad one, something that was obvious even to a bounder like Marcus.

The weather had been remarkably ill, for one thing. The last frost had occurred in mid-June, and even later in some parts of Scotland. Or so Marcus had been informed. The heaviness of the winter had been such that the roofs of several of the homes in the village near Penderbrook had collapsed from the snow during the previous winter. He had heard similar if unsubstantiated tales from France, but the possibility of it seemed more monstrous, when applied to a place he knew so well. Several people had been smothered to death, sealed in by the snow and killed by their own fireplaces.

While Marcus had been fighting Napoleon in parts abroad, his brother, Barnabas, had sent him neatly-penned monthly letters containing little more than daily climatological data, taken at sunrise, noon, sunset, and often midnight. Marcus couldn't have cared less about the reports but had found his brother's constancy reassuring.

Then his brother had begun to complain of unusual weather patterns, including dropped temperatures and increase in rain- and snowfalls. The winter had been an unusually long one, with snow lingering until the early parts of July. England was not known for its sunny nature, but the flooding that then occurred, between heavy rains and delayed snowmelt, was beyond the ridiculous. Barnabas's meteorological constancy, once reassuring, became distressing. Streams flowed six feet above their banks; ponds flooded; freshly-sown crops were swept away; likewise, fowl, pigs, and cattle; people drowned merely for the sin of having lived too near a swollen creek which had been a mere trickle in years past.

The first frosts had then come in early September. There was talk everywhere of refusing to sell grain outside of one's district. Even in France he had heard such things. He had heard there was rioting in London, too, which he had scoffed at until he had seen it for himself. The poor were starving. And the Earl of Liverpool's government seemed to think that the solution to the problem was that the poor needed to correct themselves from *laziness*.

The wars having ended (*for now*, Marcus added mentally every time he heard someone say it), there was no more market for the goods that the new factories of the United Kingdom had begun producing with such enthusiasm, and tens of thousands of men and their desperate families roamed the land, begging for food. Work? What work? Employment often had to be created entire, with ponds being dredged, bridges built, roads repaired—such was the charity of the English, that they could not simply dole it out, without demanding hard labor in exchange for it. Charity! Call it plain hard labor, for that was what it was, wherever Marcus saw it.

He been quartered with his regiment in Derbyshire when Barnabas's final letter had arrived.

It had expressed no signs of distress or especial trouble, other than that of the weather. It contained descriptions of certain insects that Barnabas had identified in the hopes of having found a new species of some sort of red beetle, sketches included; his final analysis of the harvest, which was extremely poor; and a request for Marcus to come home for Christmas, made by Lucy Abbott and repeated by Barnabas at her instruction.

That last item had stood out to him. Lucy Abbott was a neighbor of theirs, a girl only a year or two younger than Marcus, who had been their playmate when they were children. Why would she want to see Marcus? He had teased her mercilessly. She was dark and morose, too serious to be pretty, although she had grown into her looks as a young woman. She had not married, but had remained at home to care for her father. Had Barnabas formed some sort of connection with her? An engagement? They *were* a matched set, with their long and too-serious faces. If they were engaged, he approved of it. Barnabas would hardly tolerate a wife of a simple, sunny nature; he would treat her as though she were one of his specimens. Lucy Abbott he would treat as he would an assistant, or a fellow man of science. If there were no physical passion there, at least there would be a sort of mental passion to replace it.

Finally, Barnabas had described a sort of sunspot. He said the spot had been quite dark during the first part of the year, then had more or less stopped during the brief thaw lasting from mid-June to mid-September, but had returned with the frosts.

Marcus wondered that Barnabas had not mentioned it previously. Marcus himself had heard every sort of rumor about the sunspots: that they heralded the coming of the Savior, that men had cut down so many trees in America that it had affected the sky itself, that the Earth was moving further and further away from the sun, that the sun itself was going out, that a falling star had knocked the Earth out of its orbit, that the war with

Napoleon had driven God Himself to end His Creation, and that there was an overabundance of men in China, which had caused the rotation of the Earth to go lopsided. He had even heard the implausible theory that a volcano halfway 'round the world had erupted, casting its smoke into the air in such volume that it was affecting the skies of Europe.

It was all madness, rumors spread by impressionable minds.

But it was true that even to the naked eye, one could see that a dark shape had spread across the face of the sun, as though the sun itself were being wrapped in the dark fingers of some monstrous hand. The grip of that hand upon the sun was not steady; some days were brighter, others, dimmer. Marcus had viewed the sunspots through a pair of special glasses that one of his men had had made, which only upset him: with the naked eye, it was possible to tell oneself that the darkness was only in the atmosphere, like a speck of dirt floating on the surface of one's eye. But to see the spots through a pair of dark glasses was to see the sun itself affected. Obscene black spots wandered slowly across the surface, like the terrible suppurations of leprosy.

Marcus had drunk himself into a stupor that night. His doing so was not especially remarked upon; he had always had something of a head for drink, and could be relied upon to pull himself into sobriety by his bootstraps when necessary, in the morning. And they had all gone a little strange after what they had seen in France.

He had promised himself that he would write to his brother, saying that he would come to Penderbrook for Christmas, barring any resumption of the fighting.

But he had not.

Then he received another letter from Penderbrook, this time written by Lucy Abbott:

Marcus,

Your brother has had a terrible accident, and has passed into the arms of his Savior. I beg you to return to Penderbrook as soon as possible. Things are difficult with your father, who, I am very sorry to say, does not seem to comprehend the event of your brother's death. I do not like to speak further on the matter in a letter. You are needed in the most urgent manner. You need only write if you find yourself delayed.

Your friend,

Lucy

Immediately Marcus went to his superior officer and told the man what he knew, which was little enough. He was released from duty, with the assumption that he would sell his commission at a later date, for, with his brother's death, Marcus had become his father's heir.

He took a series of post-carriages back to Daventry, in Northampton-shire, arriving only two days after he had received the letter, then hired a final post-chaise to take him home.

PENDERBROOK WAS PERHAPS THE greatest house in all of England. It had thirty-one bedrooms and twenty-four chimneys. Its carriage-house was the size of other families' palatial mansions.

It was faced in white marble and consisted of one upper storey. It was elegantly proportioned, with two wings surrounding a magnificent entrance. The grounds were likewise of a truly impressive character, with open grounds, orchards, lanes, hedges, a pond, woods, open fields with cattle, even a folly that his father had had built behind the house: the perfectly ridiculous, manufactured ruins of a Norman church, which consisted of half a tower that was open to the weather and two and three-quarters walls, with the front doors still more or less "intact." Stained glass remained, uncracked, in the windows. An altar and several pews remained within; the altar was often decorated with posies by the Earl's guests.

As Marcus approached the house, he was overcome by emotion. *Here* he had climbed a tree. *There* he had swum in the pond. And *there* he had slept in the field, dreaming of becoming a general, a leader of armies, a master strategist.

Every memory of his involved the tall, dark, sombre shadow of his brother, rarely intrusive, always present.

Yet now gone.

Happier memories of summers past had been replaced by a limp, gray sort of autumn. Icy drizzle disappeared as it touched the wet earth. The grass, which generally lingered with a faded greenness until the snows covered it, had turned brown. It was clearly sodden through, drowning in the standing water which lay everywhere about the property, seeming to reflect nothing but the leaden sky. The oaks clung to their yellowish, rotting leaves. The leaves on the elms had turned brown but clung to the branches as though they feared to fall. The marble walls of the main house looked the same color as the sky; they needed cleaning. The windows were streaked with water. Black stains had collected underneath them, as though each glazed pane had begun to weep. The small fish pond had flooded over its banks, and, further downstream, the level of the lake was also very high. At any moment, the temperature could sink, and the icy rain could become snow.

Within the house, a few of the candles had already been lit, even though it was not yet sunset; he could see their dull light from behind the window-panes.

The driver pulled the post-carriage to the front of the house, where a man waited for Marcus: Barton, his father's valet. It was tactful, if not entirely regular, that Barton be waiting for him. Barton had always been like a sort of uncle to Marcus, a guiding star in the senseless heavens of his father's orbit, but was of no direct relation whatsoever.

Marcus climbed out of the carriage and shoved a sovereign at the driver.

"Sorry to hear about Lord Barnabas, m'lord," the man said. He had said so previously.

Marcus said, "Please drink to him, if you are a drinking man." He strode towards the door of the house. From the corners of his eyes, he saw servants moving towards the carriage to collect what few possessions he had brought with him. Within moments—as though to escape Penderbrook as soon as might be possible—the post-carriage turned in the drive, and hurried away.

Marcus reached Barton and shook his hand heartily.

Barton was one of those small, compact Irishmen who are deadly in a brawl, and seem built of spite, gristle, sullenness, and loyalty. "My lord."

The statement would have been insufficient greeting for anyone other than Barton, who managed to convey both trouble and sympathy with those plain two words.

"Barton. Is my brother truly dead?"

"Aye, my lord. More to it than that. Miss Abbott will tell you the whole story...I'll fetch her. She's the one for telling tales."

Barton wasn't wrong; Lucy Abbott had fancied herself something of a lady-writer, of distinctly dark and foolish tales—or at least she had when Marcus had left to join up with his regiment.

Marcus said, "Let's go in, unless you have something you need to tell me outside while we stand in the freezing rain."

He turned towards the door, but Barton put a hand on his shoulder. "Your father's mad," Barton said. "Talks as though Barny's going to walk back into the room any time now."

"Good God. Is Barnabas buried yet?"

Barton shook his head. "Down t' the wine cellar."

"*What?*"

"Miss Abbott. She'll explain."

MISS ABBOTT—LUCY, THAT WAS—WAS not at Penderbrook at the moment, but was quickly sent for. Barton took Marcus's coat and hat and boots, and gave him a second, drier pair of boots to wear indoors. It was a strange season.

"Barton, will it do me any good to speak to my father before I get the tale from Lucy? Miss Abbott, I mean?"

Barton made a face. "Better speak to him now. It'll not be any easier, afterwards."

"Then take me to him, if he is available."

Barton led him upstairs. Not to his father's usual bedroom or even to the usual wing of the house where it was contained—the west wing—but to the east wing, upstairs and down a long hallway.

"Don't tell me that he's not in the *nursery*," Marcus said abruptly.

Barton gave him a look that said, *I won't tell you, then*, and continued forwards. At the nursery door he stopped, knocked, and, hearing some soft answer, let himself inside, closing the door behind him.

Was his father in such a state that he must be discreet with his own son, then?

Marcus put his head against the door. It was a thick door—deliberately so—and he could not hear much, if anything, only murmurs. Then he heard the floor creak, and he stepped back.

Barton emerged. "He'll see you now."

They entered.

The nursery had not changed. It was still the room that Marcus remembered: the battered furnishings; the sturdy, simple paintings on wood panels bolted to the walls, completely unmovable; the dingy curtains; the table and chairs by the window where he had been made to study; the trunk that had once been full of old toys.

Now, however, it contained also a small, low cot, upon which sat his father. He was fully dressed.

The Earl watched Marcus enter. He began to smile, at first in a haphazard sort of way, and then more broadly. "Marcus, my boy! You've come home! I'm shocked that your regiment gave you leave to join us!"

Marcus gave his father a formal bow. "Hello, Father. How are you? How is the house? How is everything?"

"Oh, nothing of importance," his father said. "Barnabas is out, of course, although he expects to return soon. I have everything all ready for him."

Marcus restrained himself from letting his surprise show upon his face. "I've missed a few letters," he said. "I'm afraid I'm not entirely caught up with the news."

"What! Hasn't your brother been writing to you this entire time?"

Marcus gave Barton a glance, but the Irishman's face was made of stone.

Marcus said, "He has, but of course he places far more importance on his daily temperature measurements than he does upon anything else. I hardly know what has been going on at all, unless someone else chooses to write of it."

His father nodded. "You'd be better off speaking with Miss Abbott to get *that* all straightened out."

"So I've heard," Marcus said.

The entire situation was so strange that, for a moment, he had trouble remembering or believing that Barnabas was dead. In fact, Marcus caught himself questioning whether Barnabas was dead at all—but he had learnt not to trust his father's assurances. He trusted Lucy's letter; he trusted Barnabas.

The Earl was merely worryingly convincing.

Marcus was unsure of how to proceed. More than anything, he desperately wanted to escape this childish room and the presence of his father, and yet something further must be said. He resorted to the coward's and the dullard's topic of conversation: the weather.

"How fares Penderbrook in this terrible weather?" he asked, anticipating nothing more unusual than a list of complaints.

Instead, his father's face went pale, his shoulders hunched towards themselves, and he stood, practically leaping up from the cot, screaming, "It fares as well as ever! It fares as well as ever! It fares—"

Marcus found himself forcibly removed from the room.

BARTON SAID NOTHING AS he led Marcus away from the nursery; behind them, he could still hear his father screaming.

"What's wrong with him, Barton?" he asked as they walked—or, rather, fled—down the long hallway to the great staircase near the entrance.

Barton stopped at the top of the stairs. "'E's not well."

"I can see that. Is he mad?"

But Barton only made a face.

Marcus could hear the sound of quick steps across the floor below, two women crossing the entry hall. "Lucy! Is that you?" he shouted over the rail.

The footsteps stopped. "Marcus?"

Marcus whooped once, then pushed past Barton and ran down the stairs, laughing. He felt giddy. Lucy was a rock, a small, dark, polished pebble that lay upon the shores of all this madness, strangely unmovable. She had always been that way, the kind of girl that it had been impossible to bully.

She stepped into sight, waiting for him to rush down at her. He caught a glimpse of her face, a mask of sympathy: the situation, then, really was terrible; it was all terrible; and he suddenly didn't want her to explain to him just how terrible it was.

She was wearing the severest black, a day dress recently dyed. He swept her up in his arms and swung her about, still shouting: "Lucy!"

She allowed him two loops, then said, "Put me down, Marcus, you're making me ill."

If her looks were any indication, she had already been ill. "If you like," he said, setting her on her feet. She was as delicate as a doll.

He promised himself that he would say nothing, he would wait for her to tell him that it was time to discuss all of it. Then a second later he said, "Everyone tells me that you're the one to make sense of all this."

She shook her head. Her dark hair had been pulled back into a bun at the nape of her neck.

"There is no sense to be had," she said. "You will not believe a word of what I say. But it is true that Barnabas is dead."

Marcus put his hand over his face. Something creaked on the roof, the house seemed to shiver. Lucy's slight hand took his and led him out of the entryway and into a nearby drawing room. The room seemed to swim around him, as though he had suddenly been struck by a fever. Without transition it had come to him that his brother *was* truly dead. He now knew nothing but the crushing weight of it.

He was led to a chair. A few moments later, Lucy handed him a glass of Scotch whisky. Her hand was shaking.

"Marcus," she said, then stopped.

"It's not a joke, then?" he asked, not with any real hope.

"He's gone."

"It was an experiment, wasn't it? It was some kind of terrible experiment with his chemicals in the boat-house. He blew himself up."

The old boat-house on the lake had been converted over to a laboratory for Barnabas after several of his experiments had caused remarkably ill odors in the house, and eaten through the nursery's sturdy oak table.

Lucy inhaled sharply. "No, nothing like that. Although it may have been a different type of experiment entirely. No one is certain."

Marcus sipped his whisky. It tasted strange, although he could not have said how so. "What is this?"

"Your father's, from the cellar," she said.

"It's deuced odd."

She didn't respond. Ye gods, she looked wasted, as though she had been used ill and left empty.

"Is it true that you were engaged?" he asked. "Barnabas didn't tell me. It was just something I put together."

"Yes. We were planning to wed over Christmas. I had been just about to write you, to ask whether you would stand with us."

"I would have," Marcus said. "Probably."

The small drawing room was all gilt borders on the ceiling and gold-framed portraits and mirrors hanging from fine chains along the walls. French doors led out into the gardens. The room was awash in gray, weak, cloud-covered sunlight. It felt an underwater sort of retreat. Lucy moved to sit in a divan next to his chair, and he saw her reflection in one of the mirrors: she seemed to ripple as she passed.

Lucy said, "I don't know where to begin."

"How did Barnabas die?" Marcus asked.

She shook her head. "I don't know whether I can answer that question. I can tell you what I know of it, but it will only leave you as confused as ever."

"And he—Barton said he was in the cellar. He hadn't been buried?"

Lucy bit her lips. "With your father as disturbed as he is...I hoped, we all hoped, that he would recover his wits before any funeral. I wanted to wait for an inquest, but of course we had to send for someone and no one has arrived...the servants are all being strange about it, too. It almost seemed natural to leave him there. We all feel as though we are waiting for something, but what that event might be, no one can clearly say. It's all a series of excuses, this waiting."

"You might have been waiting for me to come home."

"That would have been like waiting for the rains to stop," Lucy said. "They might, they might not."

"Ah, a hit," Marcus said. "But I *did* come as soon as I could."

"Thank you." Lucy took a deep breath. "I'll try to tell you what happened. But I can't promise anything sensible."

Marcus started to take another sip of the whisky, then leaned forwards and set the glass on a side-table. "I didn't know whisky could go bad," he said. "But this certainly seems to have."

She flashed a thin smile at him. "Then you're doomed to sobriety while you're here," she said. "It's all gone strange like that, even the stuff that was bottled twenty years ago."

Biting a thumbnail, Marcus said, "All right. Tell me what you can, and we'll see what sense we can make of it before I become completely sober."

"I warn you," she said, "it is unpleasant."

Chapter Two

The Red Fungus

Lucy's Tale

I had known that there was something amiss with the weather some time ago. I had become convinced of it last fall, in November of 1815. It was a feeling of disruption. The birds seemed to turn in strange patterns, as though they had suddenly become unable to find the direction of the wind. The insects hatched late, so that flies buzzed even as the snow fell. Spiders' webs were tangled, ants crawled all over the floors in every house in the village, the mice would run out in front of the cats as if on purpose, and there was a terrible season of rabid dogs and bats. Several children were bitten and died during Christmastide. Disease seemed to be everywhere.

The sun began to darken about then. None but Barnabas would believe that its color had changed. He said that he doubted that it would prove to have much meaning, scientifically speaking, but he believed me. There were such things as sunspots, he explained, that would appear and disappear from the face of the sun. He set up an arrangement so that we could see the sunspots for ourselves, a *camera obscura*, which was in actuality a small hole that he had cut into a wall of one of the sheds, and hung a white sheet at a certain point against the back wall, so that when the sun shone through the hole during a certain time of day, we would be able to view the sun, inverted, upon the sheet. He cautioned me that I should not stare at the sun itself, for it is easy to harm one's eyesight that way. There were things, he said, that the eye was not meant to witness, at least for any length of time.

As though the sun itself wished to taunt us, the day was clear enough for the experiment, far less overcast than usual. At the proper time, the sun pierced the small hole in the shed, and gradually the image of the sun was cast, upside-down, onto the sheet.

What we saw was no mere sunspot.

The pattern on the face of the sun was not that of a spot, or even several spots, but a lacy sort of filament, stretched across the face of the sun, like a spiderweb. But to tell the truth, the pattern did not truly resemble a spiderweb, or at least not those of any spider I have seen. It more appeared to be a kind of growth, a system of roots or fine hairs sprouting from a node. Your brother said it reminded him of a certain red fungus he had been studying, a type of ergot. He cursed the weather, saying that the rain must have caused the fungus to sprout over the hole he had cut into the shed, and so what we saw was this red fungus, greatly magnified.

But when he had cleared the hole using a stick, the filaments remained. Later, he showed me illustrations of sunspots from his books. None of them resembled what we saw.

I wish, now, that I had never mentioned it to him. The study of the filaments growing across the sun became an obsession with him. His research and study grew to encompass the study of his red fungus, which he said had begun to grow more plentifully in the area than it had previously.

As the filaments thickened, the sky began to take on an ever more reddish hue. I suppose you must have seen it, even in France. I have heard it said that it is a sign of the end of the world.

Meanwhile, your father's cotton mill was being built. Did Barnabas think to mention it? Your father has become something other than a landowner. Between the war with Bonaparte and the terrible weather, he has turned an immense profit now. He had gone from being teased about his new factory, to being worshipped. Not only has he employed all those in the district who were in want, but he absorbed many others who had left their situations in order to escape destitution elsewhere.

Your father, who was ever considered one of the least lights of a formerly renowned family, suddenly became more than the sum of his inheritance. People spoke of him as a great man and philanthropist, a lover of humanity and an ameliorator of the human condition. Even women who found themselves in reduced circumstances due to ill-chosen behavior were allowed to take up work there. Because of that, and due to the cloth they made being shipped the whole world 'round, your father was identified as more than a mere man, but an ambassador for peace.

At first, your father seemed to revel in his change in station. Your family's fortune has always been such that he had never to think of its increase or decrease, but, as you know, he has ever been sensitive to his reputation.

Then, he began to change.

We both know, I think, that the face which your father presents to the world is not the true one. Many men have the skill of appearing to be that which they are not, but your father is the master of such things. However, of late, the shifting face of your father has become more and more obvious to those around him.

It began after the opening of Parliament.

Your father had gone to the townhouse in London. We heard, even here, that he had begun to lash out at the servants there. He wished them to follow the same rules as the men and women at his mill, and would become irrational with rage when they did not. Then he began to be rude to his guests, insisting that they follow the same rules as well. Every suggestion of vice was forbidden. Even tea and coffee were to be spurned! He began to hold religious services in the front parlor in the evenings, which featured the addition of strange prayers of his own devising. Finally, he gave a speech in Parliament that was sheer madness, calling first that everyone in the House be required to purchase his cloth, and second that coffee, tea, alcohol, and other inebriants be completely banned.

He was laughed out of the session, and returned to Penderbrook in a violent fury, harming one of the maids, and had to be dragged off her by Barton.

That was in early June.

Then stores began to run low, and your father began buying up all the grain he could obtain, saying it was for the sake of the millworkers. But soon no one would sell their grain to anyone. With no new growth this summer, stores of grain were being used at a prodigious rate, and what grain there was, had taken on a taint of rot. The red fungus had infected not only your father's granaries, but every one of the granaries in the district. The bread that is made from it is the color of dried blood, and it leaves many people ill.

Meanwhile, your father grew ever more disjointed. He would leave off speaking in the middle of a sentence during dinner. He would often forget my name, or Barnabas's. He would stand in the fields and take off his shoes, squelching around in the mud with his hands in the air. He spent more and more time at the mill, and it was said that he had taken to relations with the millworker women.

Then came July, and he began to disappear for days at a time. We could find him *nowhere*, although often he would be found at his folly, unclothed and raving.

August was a quiet month, and we all had hopes that both the chill season and your father's strange behavior had come to a gentle close, and would soon be forgotten. He was seen more at the house, although many evenings he spent at the mill. He was "developing a new type of fabric, which would become more fashionable in high circles than any fabric had done previously." How this was to be accomplished was not spoken of. There were no orders, and no additional supplies.

In early September, your brother and I became engaged.

Upon hearing Barnabas's announcement, your father claimed to have been preparing to breed us to each other since before our births. He spoke of a family breeding-book, a thing which had never before been mentioned, but which he showed to Barnabas: lines of descent, intermarriages, records of children having been "disposed of," due to defect. Your father had kept up the book over the decades, and showed your brother how it was to be completed. I found it perfectly foul. Barnabas seemed at turns both disgusted and fascinated.

I'm sure you're curious as to the reason for our engagement. I have always thought your brother would suit me well as a husband, if a husband I must have; but I had no suspicion of his thinking likewise, when he abruptly proposed.

One day, he seemed to be pale and withdrawn, and spent most of the day in bed, in fear of having caught a fever. The next, his eyes were bright and eager, and he went down on one knee and proposed, appealing to me to help him stand against the inevitable progress of time itself. He wanted me at his side as a helpmeet—he wanted to know if I could tolerate him—he wanted to know if I wanted children all at once, or later, when it might be more convenient—and I wouldn't mind handling his correspondence for him, would I? And other questions of a similar nature. I'm sure you can imagine.

I answered all of his questions agreeably, for it was in my mind to agree with them, but they struck me as strange. At the time I assumed your brother had worked himself into an excitement. He can be *very* awkward and dear. But now I wonder if there was more to the matter.

As for myself, I found myself in bliss; what one wants best in life is to be known, and understood, and to have the support of a companionable mind in times of trouble. Your brother was those things to me, Marcus, as he had always been. *You*, Marcus, are the adventurous one; but your brother was quiet, and funny, and intelligent, and kind, and I will mourn him forever.

Chapter Three

The White Creature

Lucy's Story Continues.

Soon after our engagement, the snows returned. It felt as though the end of the world had paused for a month. We had all breathed a sigh of relief, but then the end of the world had resumed its progress, and our mourning for all that we would lose was redoubled. In fact, in my case, the risk had only become greater, for Barnabas and I were not to marry until Christmas, when it was hoped that you would condescend to return to Penderbrook.

How can I describe that time? Your brother threw himself back into his research as the cold settled in again, and the frosts began to do their deadly work. Your brother's inquiries into the red fungus took on a seriousness that I could not comprehend. I begged him to explain it to me as I assisted him in his laboratory. "We must discover what sort of organism this red fungus is," was all that he would tell me, "and determine what affects that it has upon that which lives in nearness to it."

He fed rats grain tainted with the red fungus; he grew the red fungus on small plates, which he studied under the microscope and in other manners. He preserved bits of red fungus in alcohol. He tested various admixtures upon it, everything from sugar to arsenic, attempting to increase or halt its growth. He burned it; he ate it; he cut his flesh and rubbed it against the wounds.

It was the last, I think, that caused his death.

He had previously discovered that the red fungus served as a kind of preventative of infection in his rats and other animals upon which he experimented. A wound which would kill an untreated rat would only injure a treated one, and those wounds never turned septic. A dose of poison that would cause an untreated rat to die in agony would cause distinct suffering, but not death, in a rat which had been treated. It was the same with every thing which causes death, distress, and sickness: the rats which had been treated with the red fungus could be killed, but it required more severity than an ordinary rat in order to do so.

However, the infected rats began to behave strangely. One of them would watch Barnabas and myself while the others disported themselves, but it was not always the same rat, and the particular watch-rat would change as soon as one was seen to have looked. And then, if one rat would perform a task well, then another would perform it correspondingly poorly, so that a consistent average was achieved. Barnabas said that their behavior appeared to be natural, and random, but that the results of true randomness would spike and dip. The behavior of *these* rats was such that it appeared natural, but was quite calculated to appear so, and suggested an intelligence far above what was normal in rats. But he was unable to discover anything further; he said the rats were too clever for him.

In frustration, he began to experiment upon himself.

After I found him cutting himself one day in the boat-house, I berated him. He admitted that he was unsure of his own behavior of late. He showed me some of the scars on his body, which he had made about his torso and thighs in order to hide them. The scars were knobbed and twisted, quite raised, but already pale. I am sure that you are aware of the behavior of normal scar tissue on the wounded, and how long it takes before the red coloration fades. In Barnabas's case, the fading had already begun, although the easing of the scar tissue back into the rest of the ordinary flesh had not occurred with similar rapidity. In fact the scar tissue had grown, overspilling the original cuts.

I touched some of the scar tissue; it was of a rigid character, not the least bit supple. He could feel pressure upon it, but only faintly. If he held his scar tissue to a flame, the flesh would begin to smolder before he felt it. Once, he said, he had held a bit of the strange tissue on his arm over the flames for so long that he felt himself removed from his own body. His spirit, he said, seemed to have found itself on the other side of the laboratory, lingering near the ceiling, watching himself as he calmly removed his arm from the flames and bandaged his own wounds.

He seemed perfectly rational at the time that we discussed the matter. It was the first week of September. However, by the end of the second week of September, he had lost his mind, or had lost the key to his mind—I am unsure of which.

His behavior began to change. Once I noticed that all of the rats were looking away from the two of us as we worked. They ate, or slept, or played, but none of them watched us, which was unusual. I thought to remark upon this to Barnabas, and turned to do so, only to notice that *he* was watching me out of the corner of his eye, as though *he* were the one who had the duty.

I froze in place, and he turned back to what he was doing. It was then that one of the rats stopped its play within its cage and turned to look at me, as if taking over your brother's duties. In fact, it watched me rather curiously. It seemed to wonder what one such as I was thinking, or rather what I *could* think.

I shivered and made my excuses to return home for the evening; I wished to attend my father, I said. But I think Barnabas knew—or whatever controlled him knew—why it was that I had, in truth, fled.

To speak to him directly was to suspect nothing. He seemed perfectly the same as always. His public behavior, when observed, was simply no different than it had been. It was the events that occurred out of the corner of one's eye that showed any change. When questioned about them, he would claim that he had a rational reason for each of them, reasons that sounded perfectly legitimate. It was only *in toto* that they appeared strange.

For one particular example, his handwriting changed. If I was watching him, his hand would be the same as ever, but when I reviewed the rest of his notes later, the strokes were different, with a lighter touch. He wrote more rapidly, and certain characters began to emerge that had not existed before. A *th* would become a single, crossed loop. Two repeated characters would become one. He ceased to dot those letters which required it, then left out all punctuation, and then all spaces between the words, so that they almost seemed to run into a single line of mysterious characters. It *was* more efficient, and when I asked him about it, he said that he was attempting a new sort of handwriting that would allow him to more rapidly scribe his thoughts upon the page. He teased me about it, saying that I was worrying too much, and I should spend more time with my own projects. He asked about the state of the novel that I was attempting to write, and listened with interest, providing several suggestions as to this or that element. I was pleased and flattered that he should take my endeavors so seriously, and promised—as he requested—that I read him my pages as I wrote them.

But he had never taken an interest in my tales before; you were always the more interested of the two.

Later, I realized his behavior for what it was: a redirection of my attention.

His experiments in handwriting continued, until I could interpret nothing of what he wrote. I have been working through the evolution of his writing and making notes of its changes as it transformed, in the hopes of being able to eventually assign the characters some sort of meaning. The concepts that he is writing of become ever more foreign to me as well. What, for example, is *laros*? Does it come from another language? Is it an abbreviation of some other, more recognizable word? I do not know.

By the end of September, your brother seemed to split into two personalities: the first was the man I saw, the man whom formerly I knew. The second seemed stripped of every other trait but curiosity. His fascination with the red fungus consumed him.

Then, suddenly, your father called him away to the mill; the two of them traveled there on the first of October, returning late at night. I knew nothing of their return until the following morning. The servants said that, upon their return, they had gone straight to the old nursery, and spent the rest of the night there, and slept.

Your father slept for three days. A physician was called to attend him. It was found that your father had similar scarring upon his torso and limbs, of a similar character to the scars upon your brother, although the overspilling of the scar tissue seemed less advanced. The doctor was puzzled, and spoke of the case to several of the servants, who later mentioned it to me.

We received a report that a tragedy had occurred at the mill, and that several men had been killed; one of the machines had broken. Its springs had been under such stress that it had torn itself apart, and the pieces had killed several of the men and wounded others. Your father and Barnabas, although nearby at the time, were not harmed.

When Barnabas awoke, he rose quickly and went to his laboratory. I was informed, and traveled to join him there. I was anxious, as you can imagine, to discover what had happened at the mill. When I arrived, for a moment he seemed not to recognize me. He had developed some sort of red film over his eyes, that seemed to reflect a metallic, blood-colored light.

"What is it?" I asked. "Oh, Barnabas, what has happened? And what has happened to *you*?"

He said, "Lucy," and seemed to return to himself. He embraced me tightly.

When he released me, he said, "There was an accident at the mill with one of the machines. I got a variety of the red fungus in my eyes when it happened—a new variety, it seems. Many of the folk who work at the mill have been similarly infected—it is a thing that gets into your eyes and face, and you breathe it in."

"Have they shut down the mill?"

He shook his head. "You know they cannot, for if they do, then the families who work there will starve. The season is so poor, and many folk have nowhere left to go. For their sake, my father has left it running—although he is taking steps to have the fungus removed and the machines cleaned."

"He could pay them without making them work in such a poisonous atmosphere," I cried. "And what will be done for *you*? Are you not blind?"

He only laughed at me. "Do not worry yourself so," he said. "My eyes are already clearing, and I can see, if somewhat blurrily. Of course it shall take time to discover whether the fungus damages the lungs or any other part of the body, but the workers at the mill are well, and seem healthier than ever. Except for their eyes, of course, at the moment."

I shook my head. "This is madness."

"You are always saying that," he teased me, in a kind tone. "And it *is* always madness, until the sense of it emerges."

Then Barton came to the laboratory, knocking upon the door, calling out to Barnabas to hurry and attend him.

"Is it Father?" Barnabas asked.

"No, it is something the men have found in the woods on the other side of the pond."

We both followed Barton across the grounds to the woods, although Barton protested that I should not be allowed to come, saying that a man's body had been discovered, and was not fit for women to see. But Barnabas said, "Come now, this is Lucy, who has dressed rabbits and doves and helped deliver lambs in the field with us, when we were children. Did you think she had forgotten? Death has no terror for either of us." Barton seemed as though he would argue the point, but several men came out of the fields and waved at us, calling to "hurry, hurry, the red fungus is spreading."

We all began to run, and soon arrived at the edge of the woods. Once again, Barton importuned Barnabas to make me turn back; he knew that it was useless to request it of *me*. But Barnabas ignored him, either to forestall a dispute that would have no happy resolution, or simply because he was consumed by curiosity at what might be before us.

We reached the location that the men pointed us to.

It was a sodden, wet area. The leaves on the trees were a dull shade of yellow, and many of the branches had turned black and rotten. You know well the particular tree the body was discovered under, for it was where our old tree-castle was. A few old boards are still affixed among the branches.

Underneath them lay a mass of red fungus. Near the outer edges, it seemed a bit of cotton fluff that had been dyed the color of blood, but in the center, a solid mass. The men had begun clearing it away, and, peeling the red, spongy mass away, found what looked like human flesh underneath, entirely unclothed.

As we arrived, one of the men squatted next to the body, prodding the flesh between the ribs—which were clearly visible, and only a little bloody—with the tip of a knife.

Then the body under the fungus began to move.

It swung an arm, knocking the man with the knife aside, then pulled the layer of fungus back over its ribs, much the same way as a child will pull its blanket back in place. Then it rolled onto its side, and then its knees, and, with a disgusted-sounding wheeze, began to stand.

It lurched towards your brother, raising its "hands" towards him, as if to embrace him. Your brother, in turn, seemed hypnotized. He took a step forwards, then raised his hands as well.

"Barnabas! Get away!" I called. Your brother looked towards me; it seemed for a moment that the other figure did as well; both of them hesitated in concert. Then both turned towards each other once more.

Barton ordered the men to take your brother away from the red fungus. Two of the men heeded him. The man with the knife had already been lifted onto his feet by another of the men.

Quickly, Barnabas was dragged away from the body.

Barton said, "Miss Abbott?" and held out his hand to me.

The fungus-covered figure had turned towards myself and Barton, still stretching out its arms, and began to lurch towards me. I screamed.

Barton shouted the word "No! Down!" as though he were disciplining one of the dogs.

The figure halted where it was, and lowered its arms, then crouched so its arms were wrapped around its knees, and rocked back and forth, keening.

Barton took my head and began to lead me away. However, behind us, we heard a ghastly sort of sucking sound, and both of us, as one, turned to look.

The figure had once more risen to its feet. The filaments melted away as we watched, leaving behind a pale, tall figure, broad through the shoulders, but quite wasted away in its limbs. It was entirely unclothed, although its nakedness was of no moment, as it retained no semblance of either male or female characteristics. Most of the red fungus lay upon the leaf-mold, clods of red vegetable matter surrounded by red dust, all of which began to turn dull brown, then black.

The figure's keening had stopped, although its pale, featureless face had not stopped watching the two of us for a moment. I was reminded of the behavior of the rats. It had no mouth, no nose, no ears, no eyes. It had nothing with which to sense us. And yet, unerringly, it strode towards us, its feet squelching in the damp leaves.

"Stop!" Barton shouted, but this time his words had no effect, and it was I who pulled upon his arm, for he seemed stunned with horror.

"Barton, you must save me!" I cried, unwilling to flee without him.

He cursed, then took my hand and began to run.

The white creature strode after us, walking quickly.

Other men were running from the house towards us and towards the men dragging Barnabas away from the woods. Two of them carried loaded muskets. Barton shoved me towards one of them, then took the man's musket away from him. He turned and aimed the musket at the white creature, which was still striding inexorably towards us, and fired.

The white creature was struck full in the chest. The figure burst as though Barton had fired into a statue made of powder. In one instant, it was as though the figure had never existed. The powder scattered.

But it was of no use.

The men who had taken Barnabas with them shouted, for he had gone limp. When they lowered him to the ground, they discovered he was dead.

Your brother was brought back to the house. When your father saw him, he said, "Take the body to the cellar; we shall await his return." And that was when your father became what you see now: mad, and waiting for your brother's return, in the nursery.

I have viewed Barnabas's body several times where it lay in its coffin amongst the bottles: and it appears just as fresh as though he had breathed his last breath. I have looked at the scars; they seemed to have swollen a little, though they are just as pale as ever. It is as though he were in an enchanted sleep, in a nursemaid's story, just about to awake.

Chapter Four

Down in The Wine Cavern

THERE WAS NO SENSE to be made of Lucy's tale, at least not at the moment. Marcus's glass had long since gone dry. He thought of asking Lucy to refill it; if ever there were a time that a bracing draft of whisky were required, it was then. But the thought of gulping the ill-tasting liquor, which might be infected with the same disease that had scarred his brother, was not appealing.

Marcus wished to know, not unreasonably, that if he should feel his guts burning, whether it was due to drink or something of a more fatal nature.

He rose, finding himself less steady than he might have wished.

"Are you all right?" she asked.

Drily, he said, "You've had several weeks to comprehend the incomprehensible. In addition to which, you have always had more sense than I. Forgive me a few moments, while I attempt to convince myself that it will be impossible to understand what is going on here."

"I am not lying to you," said Lucy hotly.

"I had not a single thought that you might," he replied. "Good God, Lucy. What else could explain Barnabas's death and my father's madness, but some sort of wild tale such as this?"

"What will you do now?" she asked.

"I will see my brother."

Lucy remained silent as he led her towards the wine cellar door: it was locked, and she went to Cook to obtain the key. She had not yet become mistress of the house, he realized, even though it almost seemed she had. She gave an air of control that spread all about her, like a cloak. In a moment she returned with the ring of keys and a lantern to light their way.

Marcus opened the door then took it from her, trading her the keys. She tucked them into a pocket, where they made soft tinkling sounds as the two of them descended the stairs.

Penderbrook had been built on limestone. In years past, the cavernous underbelly of the house was dug out and replaced with heavier stone, and sealed against the damp. One archway of the original limestone remained, surrounded by heavy blocks of granite. In the archway a black, wrought-iron gate had been placed. This, too, was locked: it was where the wine and brandy bottles were stored. Outside the gates, a corridor was filled with large barrels of beer and smaller casks of whisky. He remembered many a time, as a young man, when he would find the cellar door carelessly left open—much to his delight—but the gates to the wine were always locked.

Lucy plucked the keys from her skirts, selected a key, and handed it to Marcus. He winced: he was the heir now. One day, all of this would be his, a fate he had been working diligently to avoid.

He unlocked the wine-cavern gates, joking, "If we're wrong, and Barnabas wasn't dead when he was brought down here..."

The light shuddered. He looked back at Lucy; tears stood in her eyes. He muttered an apology and traded keys again for lamp. He pushed half the gate inwards. It creaked in the damp.

He carried the lamp into the wine cavern. It was like stepping into a sort of family enclave or mausoleum, where each of the bottles were one of the beloved dead, a voice echoing down from past years, enrobed in dust, spiderwebs, and tradition.

In front of him he saw the shape of a rough wooden coffin lying on the corking table. The lid had not been screwed or nailed down, but only rested loosely atop the boards of the coffin. The damp had begun to buckle the wood, and it was possible to see a gap beneath one edge of the lid.

Marcus hung the lantern on the hook over the table, then lifted the lid of the coffin and set it on the floor, resting it gently against a rack of bottles containing the fruits of summers past.

It was true, what Lucy said, that his brother's spirit seemed to have only just passed from this world to the next. His cheeks were pale, but not of the waxen temperament that betokened death. And, although he had lain in this state for several weeks, he had not begun to fall prey to the forces of decay. It was as though time itself had looked away from him.

Marcus said, "Where are the scars?"

"All over him."

Barnabas wore his loose, everyday clothing, including his boots, which were still besmirched with mud. "Has he not been prepared for burial?" Marcus asked.

"No. We were not...at first we were not sure that he had not simply fallen unconscious. We banged blocks of wood together next to his ear, we pricked him with pins under his fingernails, we gave him smelling-salts... When there was no change to his state, he was placed in the coffin, but left in his room for three days. Then he was brought here, because it disturbed the servants too much to have him lying there. Barton comes and goes here regularly, to ensure that your brother had neither awakened nor begun to...to smell."

Marcus snorted. "You were all hoping that I would come home and tell you what to do."

"Yes."

He shook his head. "I wish I could tell you." He pulled back the collar of his brother's shirt. Underneath the linen undershirt were several ridges of pale scar tissue. The tissue was just as Lucy had described it, raised and firm to the touch, quite stiff in fact. "And this is all over him?"

"Yes."

"You stripped him to check, didn't you?"

She didn't answer. Marcus leaned forwards and sniffed. He smelled nothing. Not decay, not bile, not even a faint hint of garlic or pepper or wine from a final meal. He pressed on his brother's chest. Marcus knew himself to be no doctor, but he had acquired a sense of death's offices while he had been in France. Either in death or in life, the body would have filled up with gasses; the smell of them would tell him much.

But when he pressed down onto his brother's chest, nothing was emitted. In fact his brother's chest felt solid.

"Something is inside him," he said.

Lucy shivered, retucking her shawl more tightly around her waist.

He pressed again, putting his head directly against his brother's mouth and nose. There was nothing: it was as though he pressed against a block of wood, covered by a thin layer of flesh.

"Is it the red fungus, I wonder," Marcus said. "You said he'd infected himself with it. It might have kept growing within him, until it filled him up."

Lucy pulled on his shoulder, trying to urge him back away from the body. "Oh, get away, get away," she said. "What if it should come out of him suddenly? What if it should fruit?"

That was the term, Marcus remembered, that was used when a fungus sprouted—whether in the form of mushrooms or in some other way—in order to release its spores.

He lowered his head once again to Marcus's chest. "A moment...I thought I heard something..."

Lucy inhaled sharply. He pressed on his brother's chest again, meeting with the same result. Then he twitched and reached for his ear, sticking a finger into it. "I think I...I think I felt something go into my ear!"

Lucy hissed between her teeth, and drew back.

"Lucy...you must look for me. Do you see it? I feel it, well, I feel as if it were moving!"

She pulled his head towards her and obediently peered into his ear. However, his head was placed between the lantern and her eye, and she could see nothing.

Suddenly, he straightened up and clapped both hands to the ear, bellowing, "It is crawling deeper!"

He did not intend to find himself slammed down onto the corking table, his head pinned to the wood at his brother's feet, but that was what ensued: Lucy had acquired a sudden, monstrous strength, the strength of any woman faced with a terror that could not be defeated by the damned fool of a man next to her. She half-climbed onto the table and grabbed the lantern from its hook, then held it down to his ear.

"I cannot see it," she said. "Can you still feel it moving?"

He could barely breathe. He wheezed. "I...cannot...help..."

The keys rattled, and he caught sight of something swinging towards his ear: the entire ring of keys.

In an instant he writhed away from her, holding both hands up in front of him in defense. "I was only teasing!" he cried.

She threw the lantern at him, full force. Which fortunately wasn't much; her strength in anger was far less than her strength in fear. "How dare you!"

He caught the lamp. "You should see your face!"

She shrieked, "He is your brother!"

Marcus knew that he should apologize, but a lump had risen in his throat. He shook his head. Lucy pushed past him, storming out into the hallway and up the cellar stairs.

"Keys," he said to her back. In a moment they flew through the air and landed at his feet. Her black-clad form soon disappeared into the darkness. She was gone.

He stood there with the keys to the cellar in one hand and a lantern in the other. It was more power than had been entrusted to him before, including in France, when he had been entrusted with the lives of men. What did mere lives mean, to the Penderbrooks? He could drink anything, steal anything, smash anything. He could bring a doxy down here, push his brother's coffin to the side, and make love to her on the corking table—if he could find a doxy, that was. His father had always been something of a Puritan with regards to the women who worked that trade, especially after Marcus had discovered a taste for it.

Instead, he put his head against his brother's chest and pressed down upon it again. He increased the pressure until his brother's ribs should have been creaking with the strain, but there was nothing. He half-lifted his somewhat limp brother, discovering that either rigor mortis had passed or had never reached its onset in the first place, and found that the fluids of his brother's body had not collected themselves along his backside, and neither had his flesh bruised or suppurated while it lay at rest for so long in the coffin. Either living or dead, it should show some damage or at least change in color. But there was none.

Marcus looked around him to make sure that Lucy had not slipped back down the stairs. She was always at one's elbow when one least expected it. But he did not see her. He reached into a pocket and took out a small blade, then nicked his brother's skin, underneath his shirt.

The wound did not bleed; it did not ooze. The cut remained dry and pale, the flesh within a very light pink, the same color as the skin.

Marcus lay his brother back in his coffin, straightening his clothing as well as he could. He opened his brother's mouth. If the joints at his brother's waist should be able to bend, then why not the ribs, which were attached to his spine? The jaw opened with some pressure. Inside the mouth there was nothing more unusual than tongue and teeth. He closed his brother's mouth again, then lifted his eyelids.

He had forgotten about the red eyes that Lucy had described. They startled him.

Red films completely covered each eye. They were as round as ever, and even slightly moist: no fishmonger could have been prouder of his wares.

Marcus had seen more of death than it could rightfully be judged wise to see; he had long since passed the bounds of propriety when it came to the handling of a corpse. Likewise, he had lost the sense that the dead would get up and move again, either due to the angel's trumpet call at the end of time, or from some sort of horrible uprising, more infernally driven. He was too familiar with the dead to think that they could return.

But in Barnabas's case, he wondered. His brother was not alive; that much was obvious. But was he *dead*?

Marcus put the lid of the coffin back into place, pressing down upon it for a moment, as though to will it to nail itself shut.

Then he took the lantern and the keys, closed and locked the wine-cavern gates behind him, and stood in silence. He thought he heard something, but not from behind him: from the long hallway where the casks were stored. He lifted the lantern and the shadows jumped among the casks. He began walking forwards.

Then he saw something small and white dash from one shadow to the next: a mouse.

Marcus started towards the stairs, then stopped. He did not like to leave his brother down there in the dark.

But he was sure that whatever had happened to his brother, it was not some sort of enchanted sleep, and if his brother rose, it would not be to wish them a good evening.

Shivering, Marcus climbed the cellar stairs.

Chapter Five

What Is to Be Done

Cook kept her head lowered as Marcus returned the keys. "Miss Lucy left some time ago, Lord Marcus."

Marcus knew Cook was biting her tongue; before his brother's death, she would have scolded him freely. Now, however, he was the heir, and was expected to assume his father's roles and responsibilities, as well as his attitude of mastery and arrogance.

Barnabas had been the kind of man who could treat others around him with decency as a matter of course; Marcus had to think it through, often after he had done something he regretted. But if he, Marcus, was not to become the man his father was, he would have to change his ways.

Marcus steeled himself and faced Cook until she looked up at him. "She left because I said something cruel to her. It was pure folly. Any temper on her part is entirely my fault."

Cook said something under her breath; Marcus chose not to ask her to repeat it. There was only so much humility he could swallow at a single sitting, and he hadn't eaten yet. He said, "Send someone to bring Barton to the drawing room to speak with me, and have something brought to me for supper. Is it time for supper? I don't know. I'm famished."

"It's four o'clock, my lord."

"Time for tea, then, if you will forgive me for asking for it early. It would be a mercy."

Cook bobbed a curtsey to him, looking far less as though she were swallowing a distasteful necessity than when he had first ascended the stairs.

Marcus returned to the drawing room and sat in the chair that Lucy had led him to earlier. He stared into early darkness. Time seemed to have slipped. Was it night already? Hadn't he only just arrived, at midmorning? He felt as famished and exhausted as though he had been awake for days. His thirst was strong. He poured himself a whisky from the bottle at hand, wishing he could add a little water but not willing to call someone to bring it to him. The strong alcohol seemed to burn with unusual strength down his throat.

A girl arrived with a tray of sandwiches, which she put upon a small table beside him. Tea was ordinarily to be had at five o'clock, not four, but Cook was not one to refuse man or boy a bite to eat, no matter the hour, and no matter how rude the request. Marcus thanked the girl and took up a sandwich of cold beef and drippings, eating it with wolfish abandon. The girl returned with a pot of steaming tea, which she poured for him.

God, his head ached. He gulped at the tea, which burned his mouth, then returned to the sandwich. He was ravenous.

Barton appeared, and Marcus waved him towards the tray, which was over-plentiful, even for Marcus's appetite. Barton shook his head, but allowed himself to sit next to Marcus on a chair. He used only the front edge of it, not the slightest bit of relaxation or informality in his frame.

"I've spoken with Lucy," Marcus said finally, pouring himself more tea. "I've heard the tale. It's incredible."

"That it is, my lord."

"Is it true? Did you see some sort of white creature in the woods, emerging from a cocoon of red fungus? Did you shoot it, and see it turn to some sort of powder?"

Barton paused. "My lord, if I knew how to tell the tale myself, I would not have directed you to Miss Lucy in order for her to tell it."

"Come, man, give me a simple yes or no!"

Barton took a breath, then shook his head.

"What do you mean?"

Barton said, "I know what Miss Abbott saw. But that was not what I saw."

Marcus took another sip of the burning whisky. "You will have to explain yourself. I cannot imagine Lucy telling a falsehood."

"I do not believe she did, my lord. I believe that we were all under some sort of madness. If you were to question the rest of the men who were present, I think you would come to much the same conclusion. Whatever happened, no two of us agree on the sense of it, or the details, other than to point towards your brother down in the cellar, and to say, 'There lies Lord Barnabas.'"

"What did you yourself see?"

Barton shook his head again. "I do not know."

"You cannot even describe your delusion?"

"It seems all fragmented, as though I were in a fever." Barton paused. "I thought I saw *you*, my lord."

"Me? Where?"

"You had come home to us somehow, and had been living in the woods in secret. We found you, and it seemed as though you grew wings and ascended into the air. I...I shot you, which caused your brother to faint dead away, but you were unharmed. You rose further, bathing us all in brilliant white light, which somehow caused your brother's death."

"Well," Marcus said, unwilling to consider himself in this image of an angel.

"One of the men saw his own wife, who had been dead two years gone, attack your brother and sup a flow of blood from his throat. Another man saw the trees around us strangle your brother, growing roots up through the ground, which sprang at him and forced their way down his throat. The others—"

Marcus raised a hand, unable to countenance any more of the wild images. "It is impossible to determine what any of you truly witnessed, then."

"Yes, my lord."

"In short, you called Barnabas and Lucy to look at *something* in the woods, did you not?"

"I did. That much I remember. But after that, I am not sure."

"I wonder what it was that happened. It does not seem probable, does it? That a white, faceless creature should emerge from a red cocoon? Or that I should become the Angel of Death?"

Barton only shrugged. Marcus finished his meal and his whisky in silence, then supped at the tea, which had gone tepid.

"You have said your farewells to your brother," Barton said after a time. "What do you wish to do with him? Shall we bury him?"

"If he were not the one who had died, I would ask him to investigate the body for having died so mysteriously. But who else is there?" Marcus said. "Is there some man in London, some physician, who might be able to look inside him and determine what the cause of his death might be, and what keeps him in such an unnatural state of preservation? I think there is not, and, further, I have no wish to think of Barnabas laid out on a professor's table in a gallery, for the edification of a room full of students in the tiers, or having been pulled out of the ground by a corpse-thief and sold to a college of surgeons. Also, the ground is wet."

Barton said, "My lord?"

"We should have him burned, Barton. In whatever secrecy we might find. We can bury an empty coffin, for all I care. I have seen enough death to know that whatever awaits us after death, it cannot be stopped by damage to a man's frame. There are no cripples in Heaven, and in Hell they have better tortures planned for us. It's only on earth that we must suffer such things. I say we burn him, and lie to anyone who questions it."

Barton was making a pained face.

"We shall say that he was diseased," Marcus said, "and that he was burned to prevent the spread of it. It does not matter what we say. But we *shall* burn him, and soon. Tomorrow."

Barton nodded. "We cannot tell your father."

"I know it."

"I will make plans for it, and speak to the vicar, who I think shall agree with you."

Marcus shook his head. The vicar was the kind of man who had cursed him, Marcus, as a godless fool when he was young. To agree with the vicar on any matter whatsoever seemed a bad sign indeed.

"Is my father still awake?"

"It is uncertain. He seems to move to the call of a different star than the sun, of late."

"He is being watched?"

"At all hours, my lord, even when he is supposed to be asleep."

"Good. My preferences are that he continue to be watched, and for any letters or messages that he attempts to send to be first given to me."

"As you like, my lord."

"I am exhausted, Barton. I am going upstairs to my room to seek some quiet. Do not let anyone disturb me but for Miss Lucy or yourself—and then only if you must. Prepare what I need for tomorrow for me, and wake me at whatever time it is that ordinary people begin attempting to make sense of the madness around them."

"Yes, my lord."

Marcus rose. Barton rose with him. Barton gave him a little bow. Marcus walked from the room, Barton behind him, his footsteps almost in time with Marcus's own.

It would be easy enough for the man to slip a knife into his back, or shoot him down, or poison him, or a hundred other things. And yet it was impossible to imagine it. Marcus was the heir; his father was insane. Marcus was, therefore, the last boundary between order and chaos; after Marcus, there was only some distant cousin, who had long since gone to America to make his fortune, and who knew what had become of him? Theirs was a family that had increased its wealth and weight of consequence until it had begun to crush itself.

Marcus yawned. He was falling asleep on his feet at half past four o'clock in the afternoon.

Damn it! Why was he so exhausted? And where had the rest of the day gone?

Chapter Six

The Shapes That Move Beneath

THE NEXT MORNING, BARTON awakened Marcus as the sun was rising, with a doubtful look, as if to ask whether he, Marcus, was sure that it was what he wanted, to be wakened at an early hour, like a man who had an immense property to manage, plans to make regarding his father's madness, and a brother to burn.

But Marcus, no longer the wastrel of his youth but a military man, had often been wakened earlier still, when he was in the field. In the hours before dawn he would rise, to meet with his officers. He was not the spoiled boy that Barton had last known.

He asked for coffee, dressed himself, and went into his father's empty study.

"Barton," he said, "explain to me what it is that I must do. Not in the way that you would have explained it to my brother. He understood the reasons for all this—the management of Penderbrook. I do not, and my father would never trouble himself to speak with me of it."

Barton said, "Miss Lucy...?"

"If she will consent to tell me, I will let her, gladly. But I was an ass yesterday, and I doubt she'll speak to me for a while yet."

Barton made a face. "I will attempt it, my lord."

The conversation did not go well. Marcus finished it less sure of what was needed or expected of him than before they had begun. Barton had an excellent head for many details, but he was a practical man, a valet—not a secretary with a head for numbers. Even the Earl had had to rely upon the services of several secretaries and managers, to do what must be done for the earldom. But now there was no-one. In fact the servants of the house were few in number, and Marcus learned that most of them had been sent to the mill to assist in its success, and were not expected to return. His father had not entertained over the summer, nor had he planned to host any friends for the shooting season, and there were not even any plans for Christmas.

Penderbrook was one of the biggest houses in the country; certainly, one of the wealthiest. It was as though the Prince Regent had rolled over in bed one day, said, "I don't feel like seeing anyone today," and shut down the Government, or near to.

Marcus knew in some vague way that the entertaining that his family did was meant to facilitate all sorts of public functions, but he did not know what they were, nor was Barton able to explain them. What he did understand was that the morale of the people in the care of Penderbrook would suffer, if Penderbrook was not seen to exert its largesse towards them.

Finally, Marcus admitted the truth: "Barton, I don't understand a word of what you are saying. It makes my head ache. Where are the men who are supposed to be in charge of this sort of thing? Where are all the secretaries?"

"At the mill," Barton said.

"I want them to return."

"But the mill?"

"I need at least two. Have word sent that I want the two best ones back here immediately. The Earl has been too long up in the nursery to leave affairs like this, and if the mill is in such a shambles that it cannot spare anyone for us, then we are in worse trouble than I thought."

"I will send word, my lord."

"Now, my brother's body. How will we burn it without alerting the countryside? Perhaps I ought to have done that task first, and let the finances go hang themselves. I suppose we might burn him tomorrow, if it would be more discreet."

"There are many things which need to be burnt on an estate, my lord; as long as the body is concealed, we will not attract attention, unless we burn it at night. It will, however, take several hours. Do you wish to attend him?"

Marcus put his hand over his face.

He suddenly remembered one summer, when he was twelve and Barnabas thirteen. Lucy hadn't been with them; the two of them naturally gravitated to more chancy endeavors when she wasn't around.

They had decided to sail the pond. They had gone out on a poorly-built raft, built from wood they had dragged from the trees, and lashed together with old rope. It was barely sturdy enough to support both of them at the same time. Barnabas had fussed over the arrangement of the branches, trying to find the most efficient way of binding them with their too-short piece of rope. Marcus had rushed him when he hesitated, stepped onto the raft, and pushed off with the pole. Barnabas had leapt to join him from the shore.

We are pirates! Marcus had declared.

We are two boys testing a raft design, said his brother.

The pond was ten feet deep at most, but well-filled with small, delicate water-weeds that dangled into the muck below. It was habitated by a pair of ducks who, every spring, hatched a brood of ducklings. Frogs sang from its edges. Insects skated over the surface, and a few cantankerous trout lay in the depths to eat them.

They soon reached the center of the pond, where Marcus had swung around a stick, playing at sword fighting, and Barnabas had lay flat on his stomach at the edge of the raft, looking at the shapes which moved beneath it.

The rope, as it must, came loose by degrees, and finally they were forced to try to pole themselves back to shore, before the rope unloosed itself entirely.

That which comes undone on its own accord always begins slowly, then finishes in great suddenness. At the point it would be easiest to make repairs, it always seems the least necessary—at least, in Marcus's experience, it did.

The raft came to pieces all at once.

Marcus, standing, slipped and fell as the pieces of wood turned underneath him. He threw out his arms. His pirate-sword stick flew free. His feet sank into the water, lost in a tangle of branches. He hit his head on a piece of wood, not enough to knock him into insensibility, but more than enough to stun him for a red, ringing moment. The water-weeds, shining and green, closed up around him.

He struggled under the water, but it felt as though the sirens of the deep had hold of him and wished nothing more than to drag him under. He knew that he should stop struggling and allow himself to float, that he was doing nothing more than entangling himself even further in the weeds. But he could not control himself.

The air in his lungs burned until he must release it, or be poisoned by it. And then, as it exploded from between his lips, there was no more of it to be had.

He gasped. He *must* gasp.

The water rushed in, and with it, mouthfuls of thin, weedy tendrils, sudden and slippery down his throat. They wished to choke him. They wished him dead.

He seemed to fall even deeper into the water. The water became more than water; it became an infinity of darkness, sparkling with sudden flashes, which seemed to be the distant, uncaring stars. He heard a hissing, crackling sound in his ears. The weeds still bound him and worked their inexorable way down his throat. Above him, he seemed to see the shining blue-and-white pearl of the earth itself.

He was falling deeper and deeper; in a moment he would tear through the stars and fall somewhere outside of Creation.

He looked below him: underneath him was, of all things, Penderbrook itself, attached to the weeds, a weight dragging against his feet.

Penderbrook was surrounded by ghostlike, thin figures with pale, grinning, yet somehow mouthless rictuses on their faces, tall figures that dragged their long, thousand-jointed fingers through the house, twisting and turning it until it was nothing more than a tiny pebble. They were destroying the house, making it as though it had never been.

If once they touched him, Marcus knew, he would be lost, infinitely lost, eternally folded up and tucked into a place worse than Hell, worse than Death.

He kicked off his shoes. He still felt Penderbrook's weight upon him, but it was less, and he was able to kick his way upwards, until he plunged up to the surface, and somehow found himself back in the pond, and then being dragged backwards to the shore, his brother's arm around his neck.

Now he could go limp. *Now* he could suppress every instinct.

Once upon the shore, he was turned onto his stomach and his back was pumped, so that a river of water came out of him. Later, Barnabas would carefully measure the quantity of water-weeds which had worked their way down Marcus's throat, and determine that, by volume, they occupied more than two pints.

"It was almost as if Marcus had been trying to eat them," he said later to Lucy, who had reacted with the appropriate amount of horror and revulsion.

Marcus had never said anything to anyone about his vision under the surface of the pond. The moment he had come back to himself, coughing up blood and weeds and vomit, was the moment he knew that he must free himself of Penderbrook.

Not his father, not his family, not his inheritance: simply the house itself.

It was a weight, vulnerable to those grinning, horrible *things* that had grasped onto it and begun to fold it into impossibility.

And yet, here Marcus was, still pacing his father's study, with Barton watching him concernedly.

Barton cleared his throat. "My lord? Do you wish to witness the burning of your brother?"

"I do," Marcus said, although he fervently wished the opposite. "But I have remembered something. I have seen the things Miss Lucy described earlier, the pale human-like forms without a face. It was when I almost drowned in the pond, if you remember that day. I had a vision of them."

"My lord? You were ill, if I remember, and raged with a fever. You said many things without sense."

"And yet I saw them," Marcus said.

Barton shook his head slowly, spreading his hands.

Marcus shrugged. "It doesn't matter. Let us spirit Barnabas out of the wine cave and burn him, before something worse happens."

Chapter Seven

That Which Has Rewakened

THE TWO OF THEM descended into the cellar together. Barton had offered to arrange things without Marcus's assistance—the man had a set of keys, after all, and was the Earl's most trusted man still left at the house—but Marcus knew that he himself must be present. When the truth of Barnabas's ugly cremation emerged, and it would, then it must be known that Marcus himself had been present, and that he himself had lit the byre. The man who chose the manner of his brother's burial must be responsible for its execution. No question of Barton acting behind Marcus's back must be allowed to surface, for all their sakes.

They descended the steps, Barton carrying a lantern and holding his set of keys. He stopped suddenly, hissing through his teeth.

Marcus asked, "What is it?"

"The wine-cave gate is open, my lord."

The two of them descended. "The upper door was locked," Marcus said.

"Yes, my lord."

"And the gate cannot be opened from within?"

"If one had the key, it might. But all the keys are accounted for."

They reached the cellar floor. The panels of the gate had been burst open, from the inside out. The rest of the cellar, other than for the standing rows of beer barrels and whisky casks, was empty.

Marcus pushed past Barton and stepped into the wine-cavern, walking directly to the table.

His brother's coffin, and the corpse within it, were gone. A thick red smear lay on the surface of the table, and the substance had furthermore dripped onto the floor. The edge of a boot heel had trod upon the stain; a half-vanished trail of dry red prints led out of the wine-cavern.

Marcus took the lantern and followed the trail which disappeared in a long scuff on the stone floor just outside the gate. Whoever had stolen his brother's corpse had paused to clean his feet. Marcus strode down the corridor of casks and barrels, holding the lantern over his head, to check between them.

Between the barrels there was nothing. There was a second cellar off the kitchen, where such things as potatoes and apples were stored for the winter, and there was a cellar for coal, so that they would not have to burn the woods about the house. But neither of those cellars had any access to this one. It was meant to be a secure, sealed place for the storage of valuable wines, ales, and whiskys, with only the butler and the family able to enter it—and Cook, now, for she held the other set of keys.

Marcus could not conceive of his brother's being removed from the cellar via the stairs. One of the servants would have seen or heard it. The doors were locked at night, and, in the morning, the women would be bustling about, running errands and busily cleaning—and therefore watching.

According to all logic, the only man who could have removed the body was standing directly behind Marcus.

"This isn't some sort of trick, is it?" he asked. "You're the only one who could have moved him."

"I did not, my lord."

"Does Father still have his keys?"

"He does."

Marcus swore. He would have to question his father this morning as well. "At what hour does he rise?"

Barton shook his head. "The maids tell me when he does. He is not yet awake."

"And they have been with him all night?"

"Outside the room. I do not feel it proper for them to be in the same room with him, at night."

Marcus made a face and kicked the wall in front of him, and was rewarded with a dull throb in his toes. "Where did he *go*? And what burst out of the gates?"

They returned to the doors of the wine-cavern. The metal was twisted, torn, and rusting.

"I do not recall that the metal was in such poor condition when I saw it yesterday," Marcus said, putting the lantern on the floor and squatting next to the metal. He prodded the torn hinges with a finger. The metal crumbled to his touch. "That's deuced odd. If the iron had been this fragile yesterday, the gates would have fallen off the hinges."

Barton said, "I will have the house and grounds searched, my lord."

"Go ahead. I have my own set of keys, from Miss Lucy. I'm going to take another look around, and see whether I can make anything of this."

AFTER MARCUS FINISHED LOOKING over the cellar, no wiser when he had finished than when he had begun, he locked the cellar door and went upstairs to the nursery to wake, then question, his father. The day was bright, or at least as bright as such a day, gray and overcast as it was, would become.

One of the maids greeted him outside the nursery door, giving him a curtsey. "He has not yet called, my lord."

"I will wake him," Marcus said. He opened the door and stepped into the room.

The curtains were closed; the room was dark. But Marcus could hear his father creeping about in the corner, as though trying to hide behind an old table. Marcus opened the curtains. The day was the sort that one wished to fill up with loud women and bright whisky, yet also the sort during which one always seemed to be prevented from doing so. His father appeared in the sudden light, raising his hand to cover his eyes. He was near his cot now, having moved from one side of the room to the other in complete silence.

In Marcus's mind, his father was still larger than he, Marcus, was—stronger and wilier, too, not to be thwarted. The man in front of him now seemed too small to be his father; he was wasted and slight; he had lost weight and become quite pale. He had lost a great deal of his hair, not in the usual way of its receding backwards into a widow's peak so much as a general thinning. The pink of his scalp was easily seen under the wispy hairs.

His father asked, "Barnabas? Is that you?"

"No, Father, it's only me, Marcus."

"Has Barnabas not returned yet?"

"No, Father."

"I dreamed that he did."

Marcus said, "Father, did you go down to the cellar yesterday, or this morning?"

"No," his father said.

But Marcus had already seen a smear of thick red paste on his father's cot. He looked around the room for his father's boots, or slippers, or whatever the women were letting him wear in his madness. The boots lay just inside the doorway. Marcus picked one of them up; it was untouched by the red paste. Yet a few red boot prints appeared in the center of one of the nursery rugs. Someone else must have tracked it there—a man, by the shape and size of the print.

Again the signs pointed towards Barton.

"Barnabas will be back soon," his father said. He yawned, then curled his fists into balls and rubbed his eyes. "Whatever it is that concerns you, no need to rush into anything until then."

"Where *is* Barnabas?" Marcus asked.

"Out," his father said. "On business."

"Out where?"

His father tilted his head to the side. "I'm sure that he'll be back soon, and able to explain."

"Is he in London?"

"He is not in London."

"Is he at the mill?"

"He *was* at the mill, but he wasn't able to find what he was looking for."

"What was he looking for?"

His father yawned again. "He'll tell you himself. It was some sort of project of his, the sort of thing he normally gets up to in his laboratory."

"What was he researching?"

His father shrugged. "The red fungus still, I suppose. He said it was a fascinating subject. Where is Miss Lucy?"

"Oh," Marcus said, "I played a trick on her yesterday, and she's still angry at me."

"She would know what Barnabas was working on. Apologize and ask her." His father's voice suddenly turned childish. "I do wish that you would let me go back to sleep. It's far too early to be awake, you know. Barnabas never would have disturbed me this early."

For some reason, that gave Marcus a stab of annoyance. "Even if he were back?"

His father's face opened up eagerly. "Is he back?"

"No."

His father's face fell. "He should be back by now."

"I've asked some of the secretaries to come back from the mill to take care of business while Barnabas is away," Marcus said.

"Oh, you can't do that," his father said. "They're needed at the mill."

"I'm sure they have everything arranged at the mill by now. And you know that I have a terrible head for figures."

His father looked at him pityingly. "That is true."

"*You* could do the accounts," Marcus said, the idea coming to him in a flash. "Then we wouldn't have to call back the secretaries."

His father harrumphed. "I can't possibly. I'm needed here. Are you sure that Barnabas didn't come back yet? He might have come in and seen that I was sleeping, then left again to come back later."

Marcus found himself pacing the length of the nursery. He had to stop himself from agreeing with his father; he could almost see Barnabas stepping into the room *there*, in the middle of the rug, appearing as if out of nowhere. The prints strode towards his father's cot, then faded away, as red paste was trod from the bottoms of his brother's boots. The red smear on the cot must have been Barnabas bending or kneeling over his father, bracing one hand on the side of the cot to steady himself.

But Barnabas was dead, and his father was mad.

Worryingly, Marcus had to keep reminding himself of those things.

He said, "Barnabas is not in his room, or anywhere else, and Barton hasn't seen him."

His father chortled. "He's in his laboratory, of course. You know how he is, when he's in the middle of a project."

Marcus did know. He also knew that he had seen his brother's corpse the day before. But what he said was, "Yes, father. I'll go there and look."

One did not argue with a madman. No argument could penetrate the fog of true madness; mere words, no matter how fervently spoken, could not break its spell.

"You look thin, Father," Marcus said. "Have you eaten? How is your appetite?"

"Not what it used to be, alas," his father said, patting his stomach. "I feel as though I have swallowed a lead weight that draws me ever inwards, spoiling the taste of every thing, so that it tastes only of metal."

"What has the doctor said about it?"

His father shrugged. "I have no doubt that he would prescribe for me a series of nourishing broths, which Cook already supplies in good measure. She and Miss Lucy have been in close consultation about what would be best." He chuckled. "Your brother is a lucky man: he has found the only woman who would have him, and deuced conveniently close at hand as well. She even joins him in the laboratory to take notes for him! One would almost think that her interest was unfeigned. *What* he shall do when she has children and he loses his helpmeet is almost not to be thought of!"

"Yes, Father," Marcus said. "You really ought to have held a ball to celebrate their engagement."

"Alas," his father said. "Too many of the folk were needed at the mill. We could not."

Marcus shook his head. "Go back to bed, Father. I will wake you if Barnabas comes."

His father yawned again, an enormous stretching of his face that almost seemed to split it in two. "Send one of the girls with some tea at noon if he does not. I shall sleep until then, I am certain." And then he climbed into the nest of blankets on the little cot and turned himself about like a dog before the fire, until he was nestled up in a bundle, perfectly content.

A mixture of bitterness and contempt filled Marcus like a simmering potion in a glass retort: his father had become smaller in both body and spirit. It was difficult to imagine him as Marcus remembered him from childhood. His mind was gone.

Or was it?

Marcus stepped backwards out of the room, leaving the curtains open. One thing was certain. Even if his father was lying and had stolen Barnabas's corpse, he must have had help. The man had become old and frail in Marcus's absence.

Surely, even in his madness, he could not have lifted Barnabas on his own.

Chapter Eight

To Have Become Someone Else Entirely

Marcus spoke again with the girl outside the nursery door. She denied having slept; she denied anyone having come to the Earl's room since Barton had left the night before; she denied having heard the Earl moving about during the night.

Marcus returned to his room. He was tempted to pull off his boots, lie down upon the bed, fold his hands over his chest, and pretend to be dead. Or at least asleep. Penderbrook had its claws in him again, more firmly than ever. It felt as though it would never release him, now.

He could slip away in the night, flee to Belgium, join a company of mercenaries, get himself signed up as a sailor on a merchant ship, sail to China. He could fake his own death and leave behind him the theoretical problem of Penderbrook's future inheritance. In his absence, the estate would settle upon some cousin in another branch of the family, a distant one—the only known heirs were living in America somewhere, if they had not been murdered by savages or each other, that was. The family line had always been maintained by the slenderest of threads; the property was entailed, which always seemed to mean that one could never be sure of one's children inheriting anything at all, if one were the younger brother.

He, himself, had intended never to have legitimate children, so that they would not become entangled in the fortunes of the house.

Damn it all!

Marcus tossed restlessly in bed. He had once been a great proponent of running away from one's problems. It was what had landed him in the Army in the first place, attempting to flee a cock-up. He could hardly remember what it had been, now. He was going to have been arrested for something involving a drunken night in London, a theater actress, a few dozen games of cards...

It was no use. He could not remember exactly what it was that he had done, and he could not settle himself to return to sleep.

He abandoned his bed, straightened his clothing, and determined to face the day as if he still had men under his command. What else did he know how to do, now?

But endure?

BARNABAS WAS ALREADY AT the bottom of the stairs, as though he had been expecting Marcus to appear. The clocks were striking eleven, but the house was as still as if it had been before dawn.

Barnabas asked, "How fares your father, my lord?"

Marcus said, "The girl says that my father did not leave his room last night, and that he had no visitors. Is that true?"

Barton said, "My lord?"

"If there is something going on in this house, Barton, you are well-placed to have a hand in it. I must have it from your lips that you know nothing of any ordinary sort of affairs, scandals, or goings-on."

Barton nodded. "I swear that I know of no earthly disturbances within, or without, the nursery last night or any other, my lord."

Marcus felt his throat tighten. "Thank you, Barton. I am sorry to have had to question you."

"I understand, my lord." He paused. "My lord, I feel that I must speak to you of several uncomfortable matters. Would you follow me to the study?"

"Are these things secrets, then, that the household doesn't know about them?" Marcus asked.

Barton shook his head.

"Then, instead, let us go to the kitchen and obtain tea, which I feel more in need of than privacy."

Barton told Cook that tea was wanted, then brought Marcus to the portrait-filled drawing room near the entrance, the same one that he and Lucy had used the day before.

"Well?" Marcus asked, after the tea had arrived and been poured; until then, Barton had merely paced the room distractedly, like a general planning a battle he knows he cannot win.

Barton seated himself beside Marcus, again sitting on the very edge of the seat. "I have known that your father's health has been deteriorating for some time. Not only is it clear to those of us who must observe him, but his doctors have spoken to me of it as well."

"What is his trouble?"

"They do not know, my lord. Only that it draws strength from him, and acuteness of mind. It worsened much when your brother died. I am sure you have remarked upon how shrunken he seems."

Marcus nodded. "I have."

"Recently, it has become evident that he is unable to manage the affairs of the estate."

"I have noted this as well. What else?"

Barton looked to the side. "The mill, my lord. There is trouble at it."

"What sort of trouble?"

"With the end of the war with France came the end of the orders of uniforms, my lord. Many of the folk who worked there had to be turned off, or else the losses would have dragged the estate down with it. Your father has spent many hours trying to acquire new business and find other measures with which to save it."

"And now he does nothing of the kind. I see," Marcus said. "What would occur, if the mill were simply closed?"

"Many would starve," Barton said simply. "It has been a year of which tragic tales will be written by such as Miss Lucy. You have been in France, and in a war. To you, our suffering must seem as nothing. But there has been nothing but cold, and hunger, and wet, and winter, and sickness."

"People starved in France," Marcus said, "but I supposed it to be because of the war."

"That may be, but here it is the weather, my lord. Last summer's stores have been used up, and we face a winter ahead with little but the last dregs of moldy red grain."

"Red grain?"

"The fungus has infected what stores remain," Barton said.

Marcus ran his hands through his hair, feeling the widow's peak creeping steadily backwards under his curls. "Tomorrow, I must go to see the mill. The secretaries must go through the accounts here, and we must see how many we can feed, and at what cost. 'An army marches on its stomach,' Napoleon was said to say. So, then, does Penderbrook. A damnable time for my brother to die and my father to lose his mind."

"Yes, my lord."

"Ask a few of the men who can be trusted to search for Barnabas's corpse. Let me know if anything turns up. I will be in my brother's laboratory, looking to see if there is anything there to be found. Notes on what to do with the grain—something. If Miss Lucy decides I am fit to speak to, bring her to me. If anyone could find order in this disarray..."

"Yes, my lord."

It was soon arranged. To-morrow they would go to the mill.

THE AIR BIT AT Marcus's skin, not viciously, but with the taste of snow in it. He set off towards his brother's laboratory, which had formerly been the boathouse, down by the side of the lake. The path was winding and indirect; Marcus cut across the loops and whorls of the picturesque gravel path, feet crunching on the dry, half-frozen grass as he took his usual shortcut. At first the boathouse seemed to be in good repair, but that soon proved to be an illusion as Marcus approached closer to it.

The boathouse had gone unused since a previous generation's fashion for boating had faded with its members. Marcus's father's generation had had a madness for follies; therefore, his father had built one, a ruined Norman church. Marcus supposed that *his* generation's madness lay with the Prince Regent at Court, in an endless series of balls and fêtes. That madness had passed Penderbrook by, for the most part. Marcus had gone to London to disport himself after he had returned from France, although he had had to take care not to be trapped by mothers desperate to marry off their daughters to one of the few eligible bachelors of the Season.

Even if Marcus *was* only a younger son, at least he had all his limbs.

The door of the boathouse was locked. Barton had given him a key, but it would not go into the lock: there was another key turned inside it on the other side. He knocked on the door but received no answer.

The laboratory had a peculiarity: having begun as a boathouse, it had a second entrance facing the water, for the use of the boats. Marcus circled the building, waded into the icy lake, and tested the pair of wide doors. They were locked, but it was possible to push and pull them so that he could slip between the halves of the doors, and inside.

The lower room was dim and full of rotting wood, rusting machines, and thin tendrils of the red fungus, which at first he took for spiderwebs as he climbed out of the water. The boat doors were chained together with a well-rusted padlock. The air in the boathouse smelt foul and stagnant, and was much higher in level than it ought to have been.

He looked around in a cupboard and found an oilcloth coat that had long been left behind; it wasn't so savaged by rats and moths as to be useless, so he put it on over his clothes. He had already spoiled his breeches with the water and mud, and the chill of doing so had left him near to shivering.

He walked to the door which had earlier thwarted him, and unlocked the door, tucking the key that had been left behind into his pocket.

His brother's laboratory was upstairs. Marcus trod carefully on the steps, fearing that the old wood would buckle under his weight, but they only creaked. Another door lay at the top of them, but it had no lock, only a bolt.

It was bolted.

But Marcus knew a trick for that, too; above the door was a thin piece of tin, which he used to worry back the bolt. Barnabas had had a tendency to lock himself away, not wanting to be disturbed. But Marcus had always had a talent for disturbances, and had countered his brother's wishes at every turn. It had been a sort of game to them, most of the time.

The bolt creaked as he worked at it, and he heard a gasp from the other side of the door. Lucy's voice spoke with strained loudness. "Who is it?"

"Marcus, for my sins," he said.

She said something unintelligible but not inaudible. Then: "Stay out!"

"What are you doing here? I'd like to read his notes."

"Why?"

Marcus chewed the inside of his cheek. If he told her about Barnabas's disappearance, she would think that he was continuing to tease her. "I have spoken with Barton," he said. "The mill is doing so poorly that Father is struggling to keep it in business, for the sake of the workers there. I think he sent Barnabas to the mill in truth to determine what could be done to save it, and I hope to see his notes upon the matter."

"He has no notes upon the matter," Lucy said sharply. "Go away."

"I *will* enter, Lucy. Barnabas's journals do not belong to you, and neither does this laboratory. Any claims you make upon my brother's possessions have no legal standing. Open the door."

It was a cruel thing to have said, but Marcus had known Lucy too long to be able to spare her.

Footsteps approached, the bolt slid back, the door opened. She was neatly dressed in black, with dark circles under her eyes. "There, you have entered." She swept one hand towards the long table that served as the base for Barnabas's experiments, and his table to write them up afterwards. "There, you can see that I have not moved his journals. They are all there."

"I'll have to check," Marcus said. She did not answer. "Have you discovered anything of note?"

She pressed her lips together; her nostrils flared.

He said, "Would it do any good to apologize?"

"Not in the slightest."

"Very well. Then help me read these. I have to go to the mill tomorrow to try to work some sort of miracle with Barton, and I need whatever knowledge or insight into the situation I can obtain. Barton says one of the main troubles of the season is that we shall suffer a shortage of grain, and that it might be difficult, with all the cold and flooding, to get more at any price. Barnabas may have been working at a method to supplement our supplies, or at least to do something about the red fungus infecting the granaries."

"Aren't you supposed to be halfway to Africa by now? Isn't that what you do?" she asked.

"I thought about running away," he admitted. "But I could not. I have run so far away from Penderbrook that I have become someone else entirely, and now I cannot run away again."

Chapter Nine

Within the Laboratory

THE COLLECTION OF HIS brother's journals was extensive, a fact that Marcus had known—Barnabas had always been writing in one or another of them—but not one that he had comprehended.

Barnabas's journals were a series of nearly-identical, cloth-and-leather bound journals, with leather along the spine to reinforce them, and the green canvas cloth and dull brown leather brushed with glaire-wash to help seal them. Labels had been gummed to the spine, with Barnabas's inelegant, yet precise, handwriting on each. A dingy glass-fronted case along one wall was stuffed with them, each of the shelves completely filled with journals, and the spaces above the regular rows stuffed with more of them.

Lucy had pulled out a dozen of them and laid them out on the long table running along the center of the room that served as Barnabas's workbench. It was covered with gouges, scars, burn marks, and other damage, and showed evidence of the presence of mice.

One of the journals was open. Lucy handed him another. "If you wish to discover for yourself what is in his journals, here it is, then, the final volume."

"Thank you," Marcus said. "Your assistance is valuable to me."

"Of course it is," she snapped. "You read cards like a genius, but of anything else very little."

He snorted, but swallowed back a reply. He opened the journal, then squinted at it: the letters were illegible.

"Is this written in code?"

Lucy said, "As I told you it would be."

Marcus sighed. "Lucy, tell me what it is that I need to know."

"How should I know what that is?"

"Because you are intelligent, and because you know what is needed, and because you are not so proud that you cannot set aside your dislike of me for the sake of the people here."

"I don't dislike you," she said. "But I am very near to."

"My brother is dead. I can only grieve in all seriousness for a moment or two at a time, Lucy. Put a musket in my hand and a sabre at my side, and an army in front of me, and I will weep for the whole world entire. But this business of grieving for Barnabas, well, I cannot, not until I understand what happened. Until then, I can only caper and jape."

She softened, as he knew she would. "I will read it to you."

"Please do."

"To tell you the truth, I cannot say whether or not these volumes contain anything of use to you. I *know* what should be in them, and I cannot understand them. Your brother seemed to think thoughts that went beyond what he discussed with me, of a genius that I cannot comprehend."

"Read them to me. Please."

She folded her hands in front of her and went still as a doll, then murmured, "Where to begin?"

Marcus left her to consider the matter: from long experience, he knew it would be useless to try to hurry her. He stood up and looked around the room; soon, he would have to decide what to do with the boathouse, that was, whether to tear it down or try to restore it.

The single room ran the length of the boathouse, with a bare and creaking wood floor underfoot. Where his brother had commonly trod, the boards were darker from his footprints. Red fungus grew in the upper corners of the high roof.

The north wall was entirely covered with apothecary's drawers and shelves and cases, porcelain jars, wood boxes, screws of paper in a wineglass, a rat's skull on a string. The drawers were only half-labeled, and one of the drawers, marked *Saltpeter*, instead contained a vial of mercury, which silvery fluid rocked back and forth in its tube.

The scarred main table that ran through the center of the room was big enough for a nobleman's feast. It was high and narrow, however, so all the guests must stand to take their victuals, or else sit on one of a pair of tall stools, one of which now held Lucy, still thinking.

The south wall contained a few glass windows, as yet unshuttered. He opened one, cleared away the strands of fungus and spiderweb growing across it, and looked out across the lake, to the woods and fields. The ground glistened wetly. Everywhere there was the smell of mold and rot, and the air itself was cold and damp and biting; it woefully promised snow, like an old soldier with a weather-wise ache in his leg where the surgeons had cut it off at the knee. The trees were gray; the earth was a sodden dark brown; the lake was a piece of tarnished silver.

He walked to the end of the boathouse, the east end which directly overlooked the lake, and looked down from the window there. In the water he saw discolored, pale weeds under the surface, where he had walked only a little while before. He started—then breathed a sigh of relief. For a moment he had thought he saw his brother under the water, dead, but not quite still.

Abruptly, Lucy said, "We should begin where he started to become strange."

"We should start at his first entry as a child, then." Marcus looked over his shoulder to see her wave a dismissive hand at him.

"More recently," she said. "After I pointed out the sunspots."

"After the sunspots, before the fungus?"

She frowned at him. "The fungus has always been here, although it has only been recently that it has begun to behave in such an unusual manner. But Penderbrook has always been troubled by it."

"I don't remember seeing it until my return from France," Marcus said.

"I suppose that we would have thought it was some sort of spider's web, if we had noted it at all," Lucy said. "But Barnabas said that he found reference to it in the record books for the house."

"Odd," Marcus said.

"It isn't always red," Lucy said. "That was it—that was what he said. 'It isn't always red.' Sometimes it is white, often black; at times it will mimic the gray of stone, or a dull sort of green."

"A strange sort of fungus," Marcus said. "Quite Protean."

"Indeed," Lucy agreed. "He said it might change to brighter colors when it was more poisonous."

"If it is poisonous, that might explain why my father is mad," Marcus said. "At any rate, there was some of it in his room this morning." He shook his head. "Lucy, I do not like to tell you this, but I cannot think of who else to ask for advice. Your brother's body was not in the cellar this morning when Barton and I went to check it."

"To prepare it for burial?" she asked.

He did not answer; she was already looking into the distance.

She said, "Was the cellar door unlocked?"

"It was locked, but the gates of the wine cave were smashed open, the hinges rotted."

"The hinges on the wine cave are perfectly in order."

"They were yesterday," Marcus said. "But this morning, they were rusted through, and puffed into powder when I touched them."

"I do not understand."

"There we are agreed."

"What happened to him?"

Again, Marcus did not answer her.

She said, "He was taken? He rose up and escaped? He carried no keys, Marcus; even if he had risen from the dead on the last day, he should not have left the locked cellar door behind. Was the door damaged?"

"Not that I noticed."

She threw up her hands. "Someone with a key to the cellar but not the wine cave went down to it, pulled open the gates, spirited the body away, and locked the cellar door behind him."

"Who?"

"Who has the key to the one, but not the other?"

"Cook," Marcus said. "Butler has both sets of keys. Or it might have been old Mrs. Andrews, whom I have not seen, now that I think of it. Is she not still the head housekeeper?"

"Mrs. Andrews passed while you were away in France," Lucy said. "And was replaced by a Mrs. Symons."

"Mrs. Andrews cannot possibly be dead!" Marcus exclaimed. "But no wonder everything is in such chaos. Mrs. Andrews would never have allowed it."

"She was buried in the yard by the chapel." Lucy wrinkled her nose. "Near where the dogs were buried."

Marcus choked back a laugh. It must have taken his father a great deal of mental effort to appear so thoughtlessly cruel. He shook his head. "But to return to my brother. Where could he have gone? None of us would have taken him. Would no one have noticed a stranger in the house?"

"Penderbrook is very much abandoned. If the body were moved to a spare parlor, then taken away after the doors had been unlocked in the morning, perhaps."

"And no-one to see my brother's body being carried?"

"It might have been disguised in some fashion, covered over."

"But why?"

Lucy had no answer for him.

Marcus sighed. "I shall speak to Mrs. Symons."

Lucy made a pensive noise in her throat. "Mrs. Symons was named Miss Beale when you knew her; she was the upstairs maid when you were here last."

Marcus had a flash of a pleasant-faced, middle-aged woman, a silver cross at her neck and handkerchief over her hair. "Miss Beale? I remember her—but only just."

"She married a Mr. Symons and was promoted to housekeeper after the death of Mrs. Andrews. And then Mr. Symons, who lived in the village, died of a fever."

"She seemed pleasant enough, from what I remember," Marcus said.

"Pleasantry is no recommendation in a housekeeper. One wants order, not facile familiarity," Lucy said. "And it was said that the marriage, although short, was a most unhappy one."

"And that Mr. Symons's death a bit too convenient?"

"The rumors faded quickly. I think it was only gossip."

"And yet you repeated it."

She made a small smile. "It is something that you might use to pry open the gates of her reticence. You are, after all, no longer young and charming enough to seduce *every* woman you meet."

Chapter Ten

To London Those Souls Must Go

AFTER A TIME, THE rest of Lucy's anger passed, as Marcus knew it must, and she invited him to supper away from Penderbrook, at Bramble House. Her father, she acknowledged, wished to speak to him on some matter, which he would not tell to *her*.

It was a short journey across the grounds to reach Bramble House, which once had been the residence of a long-ago reeve in the Earl's service, but now was a private residence entailed upon the Abbotts for services rendered by their family in a previous century. Between the lake and the pond there was a small creek; leading to the creek was a footpath, and a small stone bridge. After the bridge, the footpath continued through some woods and up a hill. This was the place that the three of them had played as children, for the most part. Barnabas had died on the near side of the bridge, if Lucy's story was to be believed. Just past the crest of the hill, the footpath led to a clearing, a tended lawn with a kitchen garden and several flower beds near to the house, and the house itself: a squat, square building completely covered in rose brambles, all but for the doors, windows, and chimneys.

At first glance, Mr. Abbott seemed a squat, square sort of man, a man in perfect harmony with his own dwelling. But to stand next to him was to discover how tall he really was—taller than Marcus, in fact. However, even close by, Mr. Abbott never gave the impression of dominating the company he was with; the petite femininity of his daughter always seemed to loom larger in Marcus's mind than the honest mass of her father.

They dined comfortably, with Mr. Abbott offering his condolences as to Barnabas's death, without becoming fulsome in his sympathies, or intrusively curious as to the date of the funeral. Mr. Abbott also did not ask any questions about France, for which Marcus was grateful. Mr. Abbott, having fought in his youth in the American War of Independence, seemed to have no taste for such matters.

Mr. Abbott's reticence loosened Marcus's tongue, and he found himself relating most of what he knew, or suspected, about the situation at home. Mr. Abbott did not protest any disbelief, and his questions tended towards the clarifying rather than the doubtful. After a time, Marcus found himself wondering how Mr. Abbott could accept such strange events with equanimity, and even apparent belief. But the supper did not proceed solely in seriousness, but soon changed to a great deal of laughter at memories of Barnabas and Marcus and Lucy, as children. Marcus felt a sharp ache in remembering his brother, to have him remembered, to have himself once again defined in relation to his brother, and his brother to him. It was good to hear his name, and to remember, even if more than once he must dash a tear from his eye, mingled with the laughter.

After supper, Lucy excused herself, saying that she was "done in." Marcus and Mr. Abbott drank brandy that tasted only a little of the fungus.

Mr. Abbott said, "What do you plan for Penderbrook?"

Marcus grimaced. "I plan to go to the mill tomorrow, and learn what there is to be learned. Until I discover just what is going on there, I cannot plan any further. Every thing that has been related to me about that place raises my hackles."

"I, too, have wondered what goes on at that place," Mr. Abbott said, refilling their glasses. "But, Marcus, you must leave here. You *must* leave. You must give in to whatever impulse has always driven you from Penderbrook, and follow it as the divine guidance that it is. Take Lucy with you, in whatever capacity you will. If you but take her to London in shame and abandon her in some garret, penniless, it is still the most fervent desire of my heart. She will not go, otherwise."

Marcus's skin turned to ice, and his heart seemed to stop in his chest. "I do not understand."

Mr. Abbott shook his head. "Nor are you like to. We have never spoken of the reason that I hold your father in such contempt, although I suspect that you know I do."

Marcus waved a hand: he had grown up knowing that Mr. Abbott was not to be spoken of in front of the Earl, and vice versa.

Mr. Abbott said, "You have never heard the true story of the reason that my wife Mary died; nor do you know the reason I was never surprised at your father's hidden nature, the difference between the fair and foolish face that he turns towards the world, and his true nature. And I suppose I should tell them to you now, but I find that I cannot. If you wish to know them, if someday you should find a moment's rest that you wish to have disturbed, then ask Lucy of them. But do not ask them of me now."

"That is what everyone tells me, to ask Miss Lucy. But you must tell me," Marcus said, "why it is that you wish me to go, and to abduct your daughter."

"I cannot. To my regret, I cannot," Mr. Abbott said. He finished his brandy at a gulp, and put the glass down in such a way that it punctuated the finality of his statement. "I can only say that Penderbrook is damned,

Marcus. And I would do *anything* to ensure my daughter is not drawn into its depths."

THE NEXT MORNING MARCUS wakened at the unhealthy hour of four a.m., monks' hours. He had lived long enough in France to have known more than a few monks; whatever other sins they had, they paid with the penance of rising at the hour of nightmares and regrets.

Barton rode with him in the carriage. They brought with them a leather satchel packed with papers. The early hours crept along with them, first in complete darkness and silence, and then with a thin gray gruel of light to break their fast. The sky was clouded over again, but thinly, and looked to burn clear later in the morning. They planned to attack the mill as early as possible, in order to better discommode whatever defenses they found there.

When Marcus was able to see, he saw that the fields were swampy with wetness. The drainage had not always been so poor. Everywhere he went, he saw rot in the fields, and wetness. At one point, they had to exit the carriage to cross a wooden bridge. The coachman climbed down from his seat, and led the horses across. The water of the stream below did not quite overflow the wood, but it was clear from the bridge's creaking and swaying and rotten softness, that it must be immediately replaced.

The horse crossed safely—this time—and they re-entered the carriage.

When they were within a mile of the mill, Marcus saw an enormous tangle of red strands of fungus, which spread from a nearby wood and into the fields. Several men walked there, carrying guns; they had covered their faces with handkerchiefs, to keep from breathing in the spores.

Marcus exclaimed, "Barton, what is that? The fungus? It is enormous!"

"It has begun to appear like that, my lord, here and there, as it did when your brother…" Barnabas fell silent for a moment, then added, "Men seem to go mad around it, seeing visions."

"Have there been any deaths? Serious illnesses?"

"None that I have heard tell of. Only the madness."

"Keep me apprised."

Marcus watched the fields and pastures pass them by. The fungus grew more freely past the bridge as they followed the stream, often covering one or two trees entirely; mounds of it loomed in the fields, large as haystacks.

"We are here," Barton said suddenly.

The mill had been built after Marcus had purchased his commission; before it had been a cotton mill, it had been a small village. The original mill, quite small, had once been a humble flour mill in service of Penderbrook.

Little Millwich was now a startling collection of buildings, both large and small, most of which had been built from fresh-baked bricks that were already starting to crumble. The woods around the mill had long since been cleared, leaving open ground that had been worked into fields.

Marcus swore. "How many reside in Little Millwich now? A hundred?"

"Almost five hundred, my lord."

Long brick buildings with steep, plain roofs lay next to the pond, both above and below the new, strong dam that had been built. The high-risen water was controlled, more or less, with sandbags that lay along the millpond, near the buildings, and even to barricade the water from flowing down some of the streets. The two largest mill buildings roared with noise and activity already, and none of the workers were about. Boards had been put down here and there to aid in walking, and were covered in muddy, ice-rimmed footprints. The air smelled thick and musty.

They arrived at the mill manager's house. It was two storeys, narrow windows shuttered on the ground level, but all of them open on the floor above. Marcus had no feeling that he was being watched, strangely; it felt as though there wasn't a single living soul about the place. Little Millwich lacked dogs, children, and other animals. No cocks crowed; no babies wailed.

The door opened, and a man stepped out to greet them. Barton introduced him as Howe, the manager; he was a blunt, open-looking man with the coloration of an Irishman but a slight Prussian accent. He would show them about the mill himself; he knew of the Earl's difficulties and Barnabas's death, and wished to provide Marcus the information he needed to judge the fate of the millworks, which were—he nodded several times as he spoke, as if to reassure himself—fine and extensive.

Howe led him indoors, to begin the tour. The secretaries were upstairs at work, but could of course be disturbed at Marcus's merest wish. Upstairs, the five secretaries scribbled busily at heavy, angle-topped desks near the windows, reminding Marcus of the monks he had known in France. None of the men seemed to notice their approach up the creaking stairs, so busy were they at their work.

Barton introduced him to the two men who were to return to Penderbrook to manage the accounts there. They seemed the most perfectly dull men of Marcus's acquaintance, and sounded indifferent as to where they would be performing their duties, whether in Little Millwich or Penderbrook. When Howe told them they were to be transferred, and the sooner the better, they merely closed their account-books mid-entry, stood, and left the room, to gather what little they needed and await Marcus's pleasure.

It was uncanny.

Marcus was shown the rest of the house. He inquired whether the red fungus were present in the house. "Oh, no," said Howe, "it was found once or twice in the cellar, but it has since been cleared." Marcus asked to see the place where it was found and was duly escorted down a set of clammy stone stairs. He was shown the coal cellar, and where the red fungus had been found in the far corner. Marcus saw no sign of it at present. He looked about the rest of the cellar and noted that the stores were low. "How fares the village for food?"

It was a subject upon which Howe had much to say. The quality of grain was poor, and often infected with red fungus; the bread that was baked with it tasted ill; the workers complained of their diet with great frequency, and it was only the arrival of those who were worse off than they—a flood of the desperate washed through Little Millwich on most days, Howe asserted—that kept the workers from rioting. The desperate brought with them such tales of starvation as to stifle outrage, if not complaint.

Then they were shown the mill. From outside its walls, the sound of the machines could be heard quite clearly; within the mill, the noise was nearly deafening. The force of the water flowing into Millwich Pond had been cleverly harnessed to power the machines. There were so many of them! Rows and rows of machines to perform every task. What a hundred women could do with their spindles and spinning-wheels over a winter, the machines of the mill could conclude within a few moments. The cotton was cleaned and teased into threads; the threads were spun into the desired thickness, with perfect evenness; cloth was woven of the thread, and the cloth dyed or printed with various patterns.

Howe spoke of efficiency, and of the support that the British cotton industry provided the nation, and the excellent fabric that they provided for the world.

He did not speak of the workers; a more miserable lot Marcus had never before seen. It was such misery as could not comprehend itself. Each person that Marcus questioned spoke of being content with their lot, for so many had lives of want, and they did not. And yet they seemed to have been suppressed, entirely so: the children who worked at the machines did not laugh; the women who looked over their shoulders did not gossip; the men who lifted bales of cotton or directed the women did not brag or tell filthy jokes, even when Marcus was not looking. Their faces were pale in the semi-darkness. The roof of the mill building was interrupted by windows, and let in what pale daylight could be snatched from the weak and watery season. Even during that bright morning—for the clouds had indeed burnt away in the sun—the light was so thin on the mill floor as to seem as though the day had never proceeded past the dawn.

Howe seemed proud of the windows, and of having them regularly cleaned, and of the bright and clean conditions of the mill, and often said so.

"What is it that you do with the desperate ones who come to the town?" Marcus asked. "Surely you cannot house them all."

Howe said, "We take the best of them for workers. But many of them work here for only a week or two, then disappear elsewhere, to find easier work on a farm or in a house, or to join the Navy. Other than that, we encourage them to move on."

They had left the mill floor so that they might speak to each other without shouting. Marcus felt as though he must take to stuffing his ears with cotton if he lived in the town, for some sort of surcease from the incessant noise. He had seen many of the workers do so already.

"In truth?" Marcus asked. "You turn away those who beg for charity?"

"In truth," Howe said. "We have little enough food for the millworkers and their families; we cannot support the influx of the thousands of men and women and children who come begging at our doors."

"Thousands of them?" Marcus asked incredulously, thinking of the empty streets. "What do they do, when they leave here?"

"They continue towards London, for the most part. It is a great sinkhole of humanity, into which the indigent and infirm can disappear as quickly as anyone might wish."

Marcus shuddered. "It is inhuman."

"Yes," Howe admitted freely, "but you have not seen the beggars in their steady streams, and counted the stores in the granaries against those you are already pledged to feed, and have not made those rough calculations for yourself."

"Of course not," Marcus said, feeling unaccountably stung by the man's words. "I have been too busy in France fighting Napoleon to have any matter as serious as *that* upon my mind."

"We must station men on the west side of the village, the direction from which their onslaught arrives. My lord, we cannot feed all the strays that pass through the district, and to do so would only encourage them to linger here, more arriving daily, until Little Millwich were just as starved, and as degenerate, as the countryside from which they come. If Little Millwich is to feed itself, it is to London those souls must go."

Chapter Eleven

The Cellar

After the mill-buildings, they toured the entire village, and saw no-one about.

"And that is everything, my lord," said Howe.

Marcus knew it was not: "Where was my brother working, when he was here in July?"

Howe said nothing for a moment, then blinked and said, "In the cellars of the mill, my lord."

"I wish to see where he went. I have his journals."

"The cellars are ill with the fungus, my lord. They have been sealed up, for the workers' safety."

"For what reason?"

"For the reason that they are full of fungus."

"And no-one has cleaned them out, or fumigated them?"

"It would mean closing down the mill, my lord."

"Very well, it means closing down the mill for a time. Why, then, has it not been done? Has the Earl not directed so?"

"No, my lord, he has not communicated on this matter. We sent word to him, but he was indisposed."

"Then you may consider that word has been received: clear the cellars of the fungus. It cannot be for the sake of the workers' health that you have kept the cellars sealed, but rather the opposite."

Howe trembled, and bit his lip. It was the first sign of any sort of emotion other than smug obsequiousness that Marcus had seen from the man.

"My lord, perhaps you would like to see them first."

"Perhaps I would."

He and Barton were led to the cellar doors and given thick cloths soaked in water and vinegar to cover their mouths. Howe had covered his entire head with the cloth and could barely breathe behind it, he had wrapped it so tight.

The three of them were accompanied by two other men, very large and strong in appearance, with their heads and faces also thickly swathed in wet vinegar cloths and carrying heavy oak truncheons. Howe and the two men carried lanterns with them; the man in front of Marcus seemed to shiver as they reached the cellar door.

"My lord, I beg you not to step inside the room," Howe said. "You will only be putting yourself, and the mill, in danger if you do. You will be able to see the extent of the infestation from outside the doorway, I assure you."

"I have noted your request," Marcus said. "Now, open the door."

Howe pulled out a large ring of keys and laboriously selected one of them. He placed the key in the lock and turned it, but had difficulty opening the door. One of the men was forced to assist him in shoving the door inwards. The wood of the door dragged loudly across the cellar floor, which was made of stone.

Howe paused to listen for a moment. The man was holding his breath! Marcus turned his head also to listen, and heard the slight scuttle of rats.

After a long moment, Howe stepped across the threshold, placed the lantern carefully on the stone floor, and stepped backwards to the small landing where they all crowded.

Marcus stepped forwards, holding one hand up to shield his eyes from the lantern's light.

In the dark and gloom of the windowless cellar, he saw a dark red haze stretching from floor to roof. At the bottom of the cellar were the dark, lumpen shapes of coal. Above that was a mass of red fungus that filled the entire cellar.

"It must be cleared," Marcus said.

"My lord…"

A sound came from within the cellar, and they both hushed. Howe looked at the burly man standing next to him; the man raised his truncheon in readiness.

It was a subtle noise that nevertheless raised the hairs on the back of Marcus's neck.

"Close the door?" the burly man asked.

"We cannot," Howe said. "If he does not see it, he will never believe."

The burly man nodded, and leaned forwards to reach for the handle.

"Stand back," Howe snapped. "Do not touch the door until I tell you. Remember Mairs."

The man stood back, and raised his truncheon. The flame in the lantern flickered.

"Not much oil in the lantern," Howe said. "It will put itself out, soon enough."

They waited; for what, Marcus did not know. Then a flash of something white moved among the strands of fungus. Barton hissed between his teeth; Howe said, "Wait."

It was low, no taller in size than a large dog. But it was long, about five or six feet in length. It crept along the ground on long, slender white limbs—five or six of them—and moved sinuously, as a lizard might.

It approached the lantern, scuttling sideways like a crab. It was white, white as the moon, white as a woman's skin under her clothing. Smears of red and black showed along its lower half, from resting on the fungus and the coal.

It was a man, or what was left of a man, the last lumps of his face and his sex turned upwards to face the ceiling. His limbs had been broken backwards, his joints reversed. His eyes were closed. The hair of his head had almost fallen out, and a blank space at the top of his head appeared to watch them past the dull glow of the lantern light.

"Do you see it?" Howe asked.

"I see it," Marcus said.

The burly man leaned forwards, grasped the handle of the door, and began to pull it back.

Then a thing with long, white fingers reached around the door, snatching the man's wrist. The man shouted: "Mother of God!" and disappeared around the door, hitting his head solidly upon the wood as he was dragged.

Marcus stepped into the doorway, snatched up the truncheon from where the man had dropped it, and lay about himself with it.

Slender, white limbs tried to grasp him. He beat at them, and kicked them and jumped on them. The limbs were stronger than they looked, like the roots of a live tree that must be chopped away, in order to clear new fields.

The fight was a blur. He soon found himself further and further away from the lantern, being pushed and drawn and beaten deeper into the dark.

"Barton!" he shouted.

"Here, my lord!"

"To me!"

Then Barton was beside him, and they somehow fought their way back to the doorway. The second man and Howe were outside the room waiting for them, covered with bloody scratches and streaks of coal and red fungus.

"Where is Tompkins? Did you see him?" cried Howe.

"We only just managed to escape," Marcus said.

"Wait!" cried the other man, lifting his lantern.

A limp hand and forearm were dragged across the doorway, almost at the far edge of the light. Marcus leapt forwards, dove, and caught Tompkins's arm a moment before it was too late.

He was jerked forwards, onto the coal, then someone caught his feet and began to pull him backwards. The pull doubled in intensity, and Marcus nearly groaned in agony, from his arms nearly being wrenched out of their sockets.

And yet he managed to hold on to Tompkins's arm.

He was drawn back to the door of the cellar, pulling the unmoving Tompkins behind him. The man's head was covered in blood from a cut on his temple, but he seemed—at least, in the dying, flickering lamplight—to be still breathing.

Marcus's feet were dropped, and Barnabas stepped forwards to close the door, then jerked his hand away, as the white fingers reached around the door again.

Howe screamed and threw one of the other lanterns into the darkness. The glass shattered, the lamp burst, and oil was spilled on the floor of the coal cellar. The lantern's flame leapt across the oil. The fungus sizzled and hissed and popped and smoked. The cellar was quickly filled with smoke, but not before the light of the fire revealed dozens—hundreds—of pale white figures.

Howe cried, "The door!"

Barnabas reached forth again, and this time closed the door un-molested. Howe locked it, and they fled up the cellar stairs, dragging Thompkins with them.

Their only hope was that the lack of air would cause the fire to smother itself before it could burn its way through the floor and spread—and that its smoke would kill whatever crept in the depths of the cellar.

AFTER HOWE HAD HAD a short, whispered argument with one of his mill managers, they left the mill-building, carrying Thompkins with them back to Howe's house. Thompkins was not conscious, but moaned loudly, his face covered in sweat. By the time they reached Howe's front parlor, the man was dead. Marcus tried to rouse him, laying him out on the floor and beating upon his chest, and trying to inflate the man's lungs with his breath, but it was as if Thompkins had turned to stone at the moment of his death. His chest was solid, allowing for no air either to be taken in or expelled.

The similarities between Thompkins's body and Barnabas's was not lost upon Marcus.

The six of them—Marcus, Barnabas, Howe, the other man who had accompanied them to the cellar, and the two secretaries, who had been awaiting their journey in Howe's parlor—sat in stunned silence. After a moment, Barton stood and fetched them all brandies from a bottle on the sideboard.

Upon Barton filling his third brandy, Marcus said, "The body must be locked away."

Howe looked at him, startled. "My lord?"

Marcus did not wish to explain fully; he did not wish to consider the state of his brother's missing corpse. "This man's body must be locked away, and made sure that his family or anyone else cannot get at it. He may carry a deadly infection now."

"As you say."

"After three days, if there is no change, have him burnt. If any change occurs which is not in the natural way of death, send word to me, and I shall..."

His throat tightened, and he finished the brandy in his glass, then stepped outside to look at the mill buildings as they rose above the houses and buildings of Little Millwich.

The streets, so recently empty, were now filled with shivering folk, who stood and watched to see whether the building would burn, and whether they would be sent, with the rest of the hordes generated by poverty, to London; or if it would be nothing, and they would be sent back to work, their pay docked for the time they had been idle.

"It might be better to let it burn," Marcus murmured.

Howe and Barton had followed him out of doors. Barton said nothing, but Howe said, "Do not jest, my lord. Excuse me. I must see to the workers."

It turned out to be nothing, more or less: the lantern oil that had been spilled in the cellar had indeed burnt itself out, for lack of air. The cellar coal-hatch had been sealed over by the manager that Howe had spoken to earlier, and the chinks in the cellar stuffed with mineral wool, the door guarded by men with truncheons and muskets.

The scent of smoke slowly dispersed; the mill floor above the burning cellar remained cool; no white creatures emerged from the darkness.

The workers returned to their work.

It would have been wisest—in any other circumstance—to open the cellar door and make sure that none of the supports of the floor above had been weakened or burnt through, but not even Marcus was foolhardy enough to suggest it. A man had died, or worse, because of Marcus's insistence on opening that door. For his suspicions, another must pay the heaviest price.

Tompkins had no children, having lost them to a choleric fever in a previous year, when he lived with his wife in Claverdon. She still lived, and worked at the mill.

"What will become of her?" Marcus asked.

"She has employment," Howe said shortly, as though that would be enough.

Chapter Twelve

This Damnable Fungus

ANY IDEA OF WHAT Marcus might do to repair the situation at the mill—and at Penderbrook itself—was, after the death of Thompkins, beyond his mental capabilities. In addition, he could not imagine what was to be done about the infestation of creatures in the cellar, either, unless it was to burn down the mill entire: burn what *could* be burned, and return to topple whatever stones remained.

If only they had a Romish priest, to say an exorcism!

Marcus sat in Howe's downstairs front parlor, trying to keep himself from shivering. Barton poured him another brandy.

"Howe," Marcus said, "Did you fight against the French?"

"No, my lord," said Howe.

"The creatures in the cellar remind me of something."

"My lord?" Howe asked, shocked.

"I saw many unusual things in France. I told myself I was imagining things. Then in 1809, near Antwerp, I saw something I could not deny. I was a mere boy, a leader in name only, a danger to myself and to my men."

Marcus closed his eyes. He had never spoken of the matter before, but now he found he could not help himself. The loss of Thompkins had brought it all back, the ice in his vitals, the dryness of his mouth, the feeling that he was sinking, sinking—

"We were camped in a wood that was abandoned: no villages, no farms, no sheep. The sergeants told me that it was because the woods were haunted, and I laughed at them. They told me that the place had once been the site of a massacre of Belgian Protestants, and that the woods were covered with bones. I kicked up a few piles of leaves and called them liars.

"Nobody liked to be there, not even myself. It was too quiet. But orders were orders.

"One night I wakened to the sound of voices, singing sweet hymns. I woke one of the sergeants, who hissed, *Hush, my lord, the French will hear you.* But the voices were not singing in French, but Dutch.

"I slipped out of the back of my tent and followed the sound of the voices into the woods. I was alone. Under the trees there was movement; shapes rose up out of the forest floor, the ancient bones of men.

"They faced the moon and raised their long arm-bones towards it. It was they who sang those old hymns.

"I was tempted to join them, but only for a moment. I heard the sound of a man's voice singing, from the direction of the camp. As though they were cats after a mouse, the old skeletons turned towards the sound as one, and bounded through the forest towards it.

"A moment later, I heard the man scream—then go silent. It was a sound that I heard several times that night: the inhuman singing, then a human voice joined in chorus, then screams. I stuffed the front of my shirt into my mouth, to muffle the sound, should I begin to sing.

"Then a thin cloud covered the moon, and the bones stumbled home again, and crawled back under their blankets of leaves to rest. After a time, I tiptoed back to the camp, where the sergeants saw me and caught me, saying I must stay away from the woods. It was too late by then. I pushed them away and returned to my tent.

"In the morning, about a dozen of the men were gone, the ones the sergeants had been unable to keep from singing. And, after that night, I have always been able to see the bones, pale under the moon."

Howe said, "I am sorry about the men, my lord."

"I am, too," Marcus said. "And I am sorry about Thompkins."

Marcus was beginning to understand that he had not returned to the place of his birth in a time of peace, but a war, one which he could not understand, and which might consume them all.

BEFORE MARCUS AND BARTON left to return to Penderbrook, Marcus told Howe to do whatever he thought best for the moment, to keep the mill running or to close it down. He warned him that sudden changes might come, that anything could happen. "Keep the fungus from spreading, at least," Marcus said. "Send men on patrol to do it. The houses should be checked as well as the mill. Do not trust any householder to guard their own house, for the fungus seems to cause madness at times. Make the men go in pairs, and if their reports differ, send another pair of men to look."

Howe agreed with the seriousness of the situation; he agreed easily with everything that Marcus said. Marcus was tempted to leave Barton behind, to ensure that his instructions were carried out, but did not dare do so. Barton was invaluable; he was the only one left who knew Penderbrook's business in any kind of way, and Marcus could not afford to lose the use of him until the secretaries had resumed their work.

It was with a conflicted heart that Marcus directed the carriage to return to Penderbrook.

The secretaries' possessions made the carriage a little heavier, and they chose to unload everything and carry it across the decaying bridge before driving the carriage over it. It was past sunset when they arrived at Penderbrook. The house had not been brightly lit since Marcus had arrived, but it was almost completely dark that evening.

"What do you think has happened now, Barton?" Marcus asked. "Why has the house gone so dark?"

"I do not know, my lord."

They were greeted by Lucy, who was waiting for them inside the main doors. The secretaries were directed to the rooms that had been prepared for them, to begin the work of determining the true status of the estate upon the morrow.

When the men had gone, Marcus said, "Tell me."

Lucy had said little since their arrival.

"It is the folly," she declared. "The sounds of screams and moans have been coming from it, and many of the servants have left to sleep in the village. The sound has echoed through the house all day long."

Marcus shook his head. "What is it coming from? Has anyone looked?"

"Several of the men went to the folly. No one was seen. It was as though the horrible sound—"

A scream rent the air.

Lucy gasped and swayed on her feet. Marcus took one of her arms; the other, she threw over her face.

"That is how it has been almost the entire day," said she. "I had hoped that it had finished, for it has been over an hour since the last one."

The scream did not sound as though it were coming from outside, but from under the floor itself. And although it sounded as though the one who made it were indeed in agony, it could not be said that the throat which made it was conclusively human.

Marcus barked a command at Barton: "The cellar keys!"

They ran for the door, unlocked it, threw it open, and charged down the stairs in the darkness. Wavering candlelight came from behind as Lucy descended the stairs after them.

The scream had ended by the time they reached the cellar floor.

The gates to the wine cave had been taken from the floor and neatly laid against the wall. Within, the corking table remained stained by fungus. The fungus appeared to have spread into broad pools across the corking table and all across the floor.

Marcus heard some slight noise from the corridor. He waved at Barton to follow him.

There was nothing to be found.

"Have the stains cleaned in the morning," Marcus told him. "Tell the girls not to bother with laying fires that no one will burn or dusting rooms that no one will enter, or polishing silver that no one will admire. We will eat plain and live in dust, and fight this damnable fungus instead."

Chapter Thirteen

The Unworthy Son

THE SCREAMS WERE NOT repeated.

From the cellar, they proceeded to the folly, the ruins of the Norman church that the Earl had had built for the amusement of himself and his guests, and then briefly searched the woods. They heard no suspicious noises, found no bodies—not even Barnabas's—and saw no lurid bloodstains. Although the red fungus that had grown under the trees had been cleared, it had begun to spread again.

The night had thickened, and the air smelled of snow: even though they were all desperate for additional days of warmth and sun, Marcus found himself glad of the deepening chill. A hard frost would kill the fungus that lay out of doors, and drive it underground and into dormancy.

He returned to the house and ate a humble and solitary supper. Lucy was still at the house, holding watch outside the nursery; one of the girls had fled back to her parents, and another was ill: there was no one else to keep watch on his father.

After he had finished his supper, Marcus brought up a tray of food for his father, and to relieve Lucy from her duties.

Lucy sat near the door in a chair, writing by candlelight at a tiny writing-desk that had been brought for her.

"If you bend over the paper like that, your hair will catch fire," Marcus teased, putting the tray down on a chair.

"My hair has been so singed by that candle that it can no longer burn," Lucy said.

"We discovered nothing at the mill."

She finished her sentence, cleaned the pen, and returned the cap to the bottle of ink. "I did not think you would."

"Lucy, your father said something odd last night after you had gone to bed. He wished to see you leave this place and go to London. He put it in the strongest possible terms."

She snorted. "And you?"

"I think you should go, too. Something ill plagues Penderbrook, and I do not wish to see you hurt. I have friends you can stay with—you have friends you can stay with. Why do you not leave in the morning? Tomorrow?"

"What happened today, Marcus?"

He shook his head; there was no need to tell her anything; it was only necessary that she should go.

"I do not know what is happening to Penderbrook, but it seems worse than what is happening to the rest of England. You could go to France. I would send you to Italy—to America. To anywhere away from here that it is possible to go."

"What if it is not possible?" she asked.

"To leave Penderbrook? It is the easiest thing, I assure you. I did it myself this morning, and set out in a carriage, arriving at Little Millwich in good time."

She pointed towards the ceiling, or rather through it, towards the sky. "You have forgotten the weather, which by all reports is ill everywhere one might go. And you have also forgotten the web covering the sun. It is no small doom that is upon us; whatever is happening is not limited to Penderbrook."

Marcus said, irritated: "There was no infection of fungus where I came from, nor in France."

"There may be other plagues, in other lands."

"And yet there may not," Marcus said.

"I will stay."

"And if I order for you to go? If I say to some of the men, Miss Lucy is not wanted here; her father wishes her to go to London, and I have no objection to that destination; tie her up and carry her there in this carriage; and if I see her back at Penderbrook before I call for her, it will go ill for you—they will do it. It is not such a little thing to be heir to Penderbrook; I could have it done."

"You dare not send me away," she said.

"Why not?" he asked. "Why on earth are you determined to be *here*, when all the world knows that you wish nothing better than to live in London, or in Paris, to write sensational tales and become famous?"

She pressed her lips together, and would not answer.

"I am not teasing you now," he said. "Tell me, Lucy. Tell me why I should not plague you, why I should not drive you off, why I should not make you so miserable that you do not simply leave me—leave Penderbrook—and go somewhere—anywhere—other than here?"

Refusing to look at him, she said, "Why do *you* not go? You have no love for this place, or for the Earl, or for anyone else here, now that Barnabas is dead. You have always said this place brings you only misery."

"It does bring me misery, now more than ever," Marcus admitted. "And if you were to go, then I would indeed not regret leaving anyone else behind."

"Do not worry about me!" Lucy said, putting down her pen with a snap. "Do not think that because your brother promised himself to me, that you owe me anything. I have no need of your sympathy."

"Regardless, you have it," Marcus said. "I know your pride. I know, too, that if you were cast up on a shore after a shipwreck with nothing but your wits, that you would soon prosper, no matter how foreign a shore you were cast upon." He asked again: "Why will you not go?"

She half rose, knocking the little desk away from her. "Because you are here!"

Marcus caught the candle and the bottle of ink before it could smash upon the floor, then set the desk upright. What she had said had wounded his pride. "To ask me to allow myself to be defended by a woman—that is injurious to me." She started to say something, but he raised his voice. "I have *fought*. Do you not understand? I have given up everything that made me what I thought I was, so that I might protect others. Do not tell me that I need your protection now. I cannot bear it. I have lived nightmares for women like you."

She stood on the other side of the table from him, fists at her sides, shaking with passion. "I never claimed to be able to save you," she said, her voice thick with strain. "I only said that you were the reason that I would not leave. I will not leave you to...to suddenly think to yourself, 'When was the last time that my father ate? Has he died alone in the nursery, waiting for Barnabas to return?'"

Marcus's mouth opened.

"What if Cook should leave? What if Barton?" she asked. "What if every living soul left this house, but your father refused to go? *You would forget he was here. And when you remembered, you would go mad.*"

They both looked at the door to the nursery. Marcus was ashamed; he *would* forget, caught up on one emergency after another, as he was now. "I do not care for my father."

"I know it."

"I would not suffer unduly, if he were to starve himself to death. Look how much I have suffered at Barnabas's death: very little. I feel nothing. Almost nothing."

She gave him a pitying look.

"I do not need your help, or your presence," he said coldly. "I will care for my father. You may stay or go as you please. I care nothing about it."

Again, she said nothing.

"Open the door for me," he said, picking up the tray. "I will see if he will eat."

"He will eat but little," she predicted.

"He will eat what I give him to eat."

She opened the door; the smell within was that of a sickroom, sweet and foul. Marcus coughed, then retreated from the room. Lucy took the tray from him and set it back upon the spare chair. He went back inside.

The room was dark; Lucy followed him, carrying the candle. He turned to take it from her, but she pulled it close to her chest, illuminating her features from underneath. She stuck out her tongue at him; he rolled his eyes and turned back towards the room.

The flickering candle threw Marcus's shadow over the cot where his father slept. Once again, he heard the sound of his father moving about on the other side of the room; he turned and saw the shadows shift a little in the far corner, the figure of a tall, lean man.

Then a moan came from the bed. Marcus stiffened, and could not move. His skin felt as though it were being stroked with ice.

How could his father be in two places at the same time?

Lucy walked towards the bed, holding the candle aloft. "Lord Penderbrook? Are you well? It is I, Lucy. And Marcus has come."

The Earl moaned: "Barnabas is here, he is here! Catch him before he goes again; tell him that you are not angry at him!"

Lucy turned and the candlelight fell directly upon the figure in the corner. It was nothing: it was the head of a hobby-horse on a wooden pole, leaning against the wall.

"Where is he?" Lucy asked. "I do not see him."

"He has left again," the Earl said, his voice thick with disappointment. "Miss Lucy, do not concern yourself; it is entirely Marcus's fault."

A lump rose in Marcus's throat. He felt such pressure in the room that he was desperate to escape it, yet simultaneously unable to move.

"Marcus is unworthy, but he *was* his mother's favorite, so I could not have him drowned like a sackful of kittens." The Earl chuckled. "I have often wished a child that was more like myself. Barnabas is so strange that I have often wondered if the fairies had taken my true son away and left me a changeling! But with Marcus, I knew that there had been no change. He is the very picture of my older brother William, who died when we were boys. He was loud and brave and gay, the apple of everyone's eye. When we were children, did you know, I was reserved and shy of being around anyone? Can you imagine it?"

"I cannot," said Lucy steadily. "You have always been so open and friendly."

"Oh, you should have known me then! I would not have spoken a word to you, or to anybody. But after William's death, I blossomed. He was a weight that lay upon me, forcing me to be his opposite in everything he did. But when he was gone, I was free."

A horrible smell filled the room, nearly making Marcus gag; the Earl had fouled himself. Marcus said, "Lucy, go out and close the door. I will care for him."

She made a face, but left.

Marcus steeled himself for unpleasantness. "We must take your clothes away for the girls to clean."

His father grumbled but allowed Marcus to begin stripping him. Marcus checked the pitcher of water at the stand, which had been placed behind the cot, near the fire; it was cold but unfrozen. He helped his father wash.

"Your brother has more patience with you than I do," his father said. "I would have had you drowned by now." When Marcus did not rise to the bait, his father added, "You almost drowned in the pond, you know." And then he giggled, showing his teeth. They were in poor condition and needed to be cleaned.

Marcus hunted around the room and found a worn sideboard that had been filled with clean clothing, and dressed his father. He found clean bedding as well, and replaced what lay upon the cot. Then he led his father over to a small table where the tray waited for him: bread, meat, and soup. The soup had gone cold, and his father refused to eat it.

"You're trying to poison me now!"

Marcus placed the meat between two pieces of bread and said, "Taste this, then. I had some earlier."

"You poisoned that as well!"

"No, only the soup," Marcus said. He took a large bite of the bread and meat. "If you don't want it, I'm hungry enough to finish it in two bites."

His father snatched the food from him and wolfed it down. His breath smelled foul.

Through a mouth stuffed with half-chewed bread, his father said, "Drowned. All the way down to the bottom of the pond, yes? Drowned and drowned, into the dark."

"I'm surprised you remember," Marcus said evenly.

His father flicked his fingers in a swooping gesture. "Of course I remember. I remember watching the raft fall to pieces. The knots came loose!" He giggled again. "One moment they were tied, and the next they were not! Barnabas made it to the shore, but you did not. I thought I was rid of you, finally! Down in the deeps, the dark and starry deeps, as deep as the night sky! Just like my brother."

"Oh, I'm harder to get rid of than that," Marcus said.

"You're an encrustation," his father said. "Useless for everything except marching into other men's guns. Too bad you had to get so many other men killed."

Marcus's teeth clicked together as he cut off a rash reply. The Earl was in a mood, and only trying to get under Marcus's skin, the better to abuse him.

"I hated to see Barnabas put himself at hazard to try to save you," his father said. "But there it is: he's a good boy, and *will* try to do good, whether it has any benefit or not. If your positions were reversed, you would have left Barnabas to drown! Oh, you would have tried for a moment or two. And then you would have given up! Because that's what you do! You make the attempt so that you can deny any blame for your failure later! You tried! Oh, how your brother resented you for it! He had lost a medal in the pond once; do you remember it? It was after he had saved your life. He asked you to help him, and you did—for a few moments only. He searched for a full day, and you were there for five minutes! Oh, but you *tried*!" His father chortled.

He had finished eating. Marcus gave him tea to drink—"Why isn't there brandy? Or at least beer?"—and found a tooth-brush in the same sideboard, along with some tooth powder. The Earl refused to touch the bone handle, so Marcus tried to use the brush on him. His father clamped his lips together, shaking his head.

Marcus found himself gripping the brush in his fist, almost snarling: "I should force you to do it."

His father laughed. "You don't have the strength."

But Marcus had been goaded by other men since he had left his father's house, and knew his father's tricks for what they were. Marcus opened his fist and let the brush fall to the floor, then took up the dirty linen and carried it to the door. Let his father's teeth rot, then.

"Wait," his father called to him. "The medal is in your brother's room, if you wish to see it."

"Where did you find it?"

"It was brought to me by a friend."

Marcus saw something move out of the corner of his eye. It was the same part of the room where he had seen movement earlier.

"Who was the friend?" he asked, trying to keep his head unmoving.

"Oh, an old friend. *Quite* old!"

"Have you seen him recently?"

The shadow moved again. Marcus dropped the dirty linens and dove for the shape, attempting to pin it against the wall. For a moment he had it: then it seemed to melt away under his hands. He was left holding nothing, a nightmare only intermittently made of flesh.

His father laughed loudly, the bray of a donkey. "You'll never catch him like that! You'll never catch him at all!"

Marcus picked up the fallen linen and rolled it back into a loose ball.

"Gave him a scare, though," his father admitted. "He'll think twice about coming here while *you're* about. To tell the truth, I've wearied of his company. He lisps when he talks now."

Trying to keep his composure, Marcus said, "Who was it?"

"Didn't you recognize him? I thought not. It was your brother."

Chapter Fourteen

For Fear of Not Being Believed

The rest of the evening was spent in contemplation, which is to say that Marcus shut himself up in his father's study and angrily paced its length for hours, only just restraining himself from smashing everything that could be broken and setting the books and curtains on fire.

Only the thought of what Lucy would say if he burnt the books stopped him.

His father was mad, his brother dead, the countryside soon to commence starving, and all sanity likely to be smashed against the shores of the strange and inexplicable. It would be less trouble if it *were* the end of the world; then, it would simply be a matter of suffering what must be suffered, rather than attempting to salvage life and prosperity from the wreck that his family's fortunes soon would become.

But he must remind himself that tomorrow the secretaries would begin the review of Penderbrook's accounts, so that those, at least, could be put in order. His brother's body would turn up. His father seemed happy enough for now, shut up in the nursery. Either the weather would amend itself the next summer, or it would not; they would make shift as best they could this winter, then regroup in the spring, when it became evident whether the difficulties would continue or no.

The strange events that plagued the world were none of his business, or at least out of his control. If there were some sort of infection upon the face of the sun causing sunspots, well, that was a terrible thing. But he would find *something* to do, and he would do it. And if he died in the attempt, then he had always known that everything that had occurred after the war in France was a sort of dream or false vision, glimpsed in the moment of his true death. Or else he was already in Hell, and this was the Tormenter's idea of the best way to torture Marcus for all eternity, which would not be too far off the mark.

He drank his father's fine brandy and reminded himself not to toss the account-books onto the fire.

Barton looked in on him. "Do you need anything, my lord?"

"Thank you, no. Or rather bring me another bottle, and, if you are not too weary, your company to share it. I am in a melancholy mood."

Barton disappeared, returning a few moments later with a dusty bottle.

"Barnabas didn't happen to put himself back on the corking table in the cellar, did he?" Marcus asked.

Barton shook his head and poured for the both of them, a much smaller portion for himself than for his master.

Marcus seated himself in an armchair in front of the fire. "Barton, what of my brother's inquest? What was said at it?"

"There was no inquest."

Marcus frowned. "Barnabas's death is the most curious thing I ever heard tell of. Of course there was an inquest."

"The Earl discouraged it, saying that Barnabas had passed of a heart palpitation and possibly of typhus, and he did not wish anyone to become infected of it."

Marcus shook his head. "And they believed him?"

"He is the Earl, and if he was satisfied..." Barton shrugged.

"In other words, they let him do what he liked," Marcus said, with disgust. "They always do. They always let us do what we like."

"My lord?"

"I spent some time with my father this evening. His temper was not nice, and his condition seemed worse. I had to clean him."

"I will send—"

Marcus waved him to silence. "Miss Lucy was attending him. She says that so many of the girls have left that attendance on him cannot be kept up, and she worried that he would be forgotten to suffer."

"She has a kind heart."

Marcus pursed his lips. "I have known kinder and more generous ones. I would say that she has a stalwart one instead."

Barton nodded. "She would have made a fine sergeant."

"Just so. Her father has spoken to me, asking me to have her removed to London somehow. I braced her on the subject earlier. She frankly refuses to go."

"Removed to London, my lord?"

"He feels that it isn't safe for her here, and I very nearly agree with him. Too many strange things have occurred here of late. Not to mention Thompkins down in the mill's cellar. It cannot mean anything good."

Barton shifted in his seat, licking his lips.

"Out with it," Marcus said, finishing his brandy in a gulp and pouring himself more.

"You might marry her," Barton said. "And then you would have a husband's right to have her removed."

Marcus screwed up his face. "Even if I did so, and she made my life Hell on earth ever afterwards for it, can you really think that she would obey me? Or that if I had her forcibly removed, she would not find her way back?"

"You could go with her."

"And my father?"

"It would not be the first time that a man of title and property was housed in a sanitarium, my lord."

"You do not think he will recover, then?"

Carefully and slowly, although he had not even finished the small sip of brandy that he had poured himself, Barton said, "I think it would be better to close up the house and move everyone to London, at any cost."

"What about the people who live on the farms? The villages?"

"They will live all the better for not having the Earl in residence."

"You are afraid of what may happen, then?"

Even more carefully, Barton said, "Penderbrook has gone strange, my lord. There is much of which I have not spoken, for fear of not being believed."

"Tell me."

But Barton would not speak of what he had seen, only stared down into the ancient gold of his brandy.

After another half a bottle disappeared, Marcus asked, "What is behind all of this, Barton? Is there some force behind it, or is it simply a collection of ill events, all perfectly timed to have their worst effect at the same moment? Or are we at the end of the world, as some have said?"

"I do not know, my lord."

"What is your guess?"

But Barton would only shake his head. "I do not know, only that it would be better if you went to London."

"Well, then, to return to the subject: You think I should marry Miss Lucy?"

Barton seemed to shrink backwards into his armchair. "If you go to London and put your father in the care of a doctor there, then I do not think you would need to marry her," he said. "She would go and stay with her aunt in Piccadilly, I believe."

"What about *her* father?"

"She would most likely attempt to make him go as well, and if she told him that *she* would not go, if *he* did not, then he would go."

Marcus considered the matter. He had long since spoken strongly to himself about the propriety of having any sort of attraction to Lucy; it was her presence in his life that had prevented he and his brother from having murdered each other a hundred times. She was not pleasant, not in the way a woman could make herself so, but without her, everything seemed to go wrong. To have thought of her as he would have thought of a girl at a tavern or out on the road seemed the height of presumption, once he had learnt to desire such things.

And yet to marry a woman was not to wish to woo her with songs and poetry; it was not to wish to have her on one's arm to gad about at operas. He had known too much of the world to think *that*. Marriage would be a sacred vow to care for Lucy's happiness and health, even if he had to roll his eyes and ignore her half the time to do it.

Without Barnabas to marry her, what would become of her? She would not starve; her father would leave her enough wealth for a modest independence. In fact, she would be happier without a husband at all: he could not imagine that she would, in lieu of Barnabas, marry anyone. She would never bear children. She would shut herself up in some house and write novels, and consider herself satisfied with her lot in life, smugly solitary, while surrounded by attentive secretaries.

He snorted and finished his brandy, handing Barton the glass and pulling himself to his feet.

"I suppose I should ask her," he said. "She will only shout at me and refuse, but at least I should ask."

"Now, my lord?"

Marcus shuddered. "Perhaps tomorrow."

THAT NIGHT HE HAD a series of nightmares which disturbed him. He wandered in the woods around Penderbrook, somehow lost and searching for someone, he knew not whom. He saw other figures, similarly lost, and knew them but did not recognize them, in the way that sometimes happens in dreams.

They searched...they searched.

Marcus found himself in the folly, the Norman ruins. He called out for someone, a name he did not recognize and could not have, awake, pronounced. It seemed to require syllables that strained his throat. Over and over he called out.

Finally, a voice answered him. He had found the one for whom he searched! He called back, stumbling through the false ruins, to discover a doorway in one of the walls, a door which he had not previously noted. The door had no handle, and the crack between door and the stones surrounding it was too small for his fingers to grasp, and he was not carrying a knife with which he might pry the door open. He moaned at the door. To be so close, yet to fail at that final moment!

The door *must* open, but he could not open the door.

He wakened just as the sun had begun to rise. His throat was hoarse, and he thought he might have been calling out in his sleep. In the boundary between waking and sleeping, he knew that he had been searching for his brother, although the name he had been calling had been completely different.

He dressed and walked outside. It was raining, a steady, heavy rain that was really only half-melted snow. It clung to the tops of the trees' bare branches before sliding off and dropping heavily to the ground with a splash: the ground was too waterlogged to absorb it.

Soon he was at the folly. He circled the ruins, looking for the place of his dream.

He saw no new doorways, but felt a presence within the false ruins.

"Hello?" he called out. "Fear not. I only wish to make sure you have food and a warm place to sleep. It is freezing out here."

No-one answered, although once it seemed as though someone had taken in a breath and been just about to do so, then exhaled again.

Shivering, he returned to the house.

Chapter Fifteen

Only but Scratched the Surface

As Marcus returned to the house, he saw several men tending the grounds, huge men with watchful eyes, whose work seemed to cease as he neared, then resumed as he passed them.

Inside, Cook was at work, but the half-dozen assistants that had once helped her were not to be seen. When he asked, they were "down to the village" or "gone to the mill." She would not look him in the eye.

"Surely you have someone to fetch and carry for you," he said.

"I do not, not today, my lord," she sighed.

"I remember when there were sixty people who lived in the quarters in the servants' wing," Marcus said. "And we had more come in for the day, to work the grounds and clear char. People have said the mill sponges everyone up, but are the wages so much better? Why does everyone go? The mill seems no better or worse than any other mill I have seen, and I would think that work at the main house would be more comfortable and pleasant."

"The Earl asked many of us to go," Cook said. "And then other ones followed them. Their families."

"But *all* of the servants? Surely at least some are needed here. How many do you feed each day, now?"

She tilted her head to the side. "A half-dozen men on the grounds, the family makes eight, Barton nine, the girls fourteen, and myself for fifteen. Today there'll be seventeen, with the two secretaries that've just come back."

Marcus blinked.

"I remember when everyone was mad to dine here, when I was younger. I remember looking down from the balcony onto the dances we used to have."

"I remember it, too," Cook said. "But those days are past."

"Are they past for everyone, or only for Penderbrook? Does not everyone else near us entertain each other? Why are we so isolated and alone?"

"You might change that, my lord," Cook said, although her expression did not show any great hope of its being done.

"Did the Earl attend Parliament this year?"

"Yes, my lord."

"Did not anyone return from London with him to shoot grouse?"

"No, my lord. Not this year." She paused, as if hesitant to speak, and he waved her on. "In truth, my lord, there has not been as much hunting this year as in previous. The birds are in bad condition. Even the foxes are low, I have heard the men say. The Earl told Barton not to let the gameskeepers worry overmuch about poaching this year, and you know how wroth he could be at poachers, previous."

"I remember," Marcus said.

"And there have been very few balls," Cook added. "It is thought a great shame by the ladies, both those who like to dance, and those who like to have their daughters married off. A great many families dine with each other, but not as before. Many families, especially those of the lower gentry, do not dine as much as they had done. Or so go the rumors."

"Thank you," Marcus said.

Cook went on: "It is now too late for the grain to sprout and grow, even if the weather turned sunny and fair. There will be many in the district who suffer for it, and not only the poor. Some of the men are saying that it will be impossible to obtain grain at any price, and we do not have enough of it as it is. The seeds are very ill, too, so that next years' crops will also suffer."

"I have heard that said before."

Cook gave him a curtsey. "You had asked, my lord."

"I did. And thank you," he repeated. "But still you should have a girl to help you. I will have the mill send someone."

"What do you mean to do with Penderbrook, my lord?" Cook asked, then curtseyed again quickly.

Marcus put a finger along his chin. "To rewaken it into a great estate? To close it up and flee to London? To sell it off? Everyone seems to wish to know, not the least of whom is myself. But be assured you will always have a place in my service, if you wish it."

Cook curtseyed again, then excused herself and returned to her work. Marcus sat in a corner and watched her, as he had often done as a boy. With the girls coming into and out of the kitchen, it soon became obvious that not only was Cook acting as head housekeeper, too, with Mrs. Symons off to the mill, and only five—five!—girls remaining to keep the entire house. Which would have been impossible, even if one of them hadn't been needed to watch the Earl as well.

Marcus tried to work numbers in his head, adding up what Barton had told him, against what he remembered of the size of Little Millwich. He thought Barton must be right: the mill must hold near five hundred souls.

And yet he had only seen one granary, and it had seemed nearly empty.

Where was the grain being stored? Where the meat, the potatoes, the vegetables and apples for the winter?

Howe had misdirected him, even after all of Marcus's questions and stubbornness. He had thought he had found everything. He suspected now that he had only but scratched the surface.

What did the millworkers *eat*?

He returned to his father's study, all the better to pace its carpets once more. He did not know what to do: it was too much, too much of everything, and there would be no orders from above to help direct him.

In the past he had tried praying, but such activities had never nourished his spirit or given him any sort of peace. He felt a fool, attempting to speak to the Divine. That God existed, he did not doubt. He had heard men say—he had heard *Barnabas* say—that there was no God, no order in the universe other than the laws of Nature itself. Men were fools, or so the argument went, who read meaning into the universe where none existed.

Men *were* fools; with that Marcus could agree.

But he had seen the universe turn too often against mankind to think that there was not some awful power controlling his destiny. If there was an honest man serving under him, that man would be the first to die of typhus. A man with a good wife would find his legs crushed, and have to have them removed. The more hope one felt, the more likely to have one's musket explode, one's supplies turn up missing, and one's women to have the pox.

And yet despair and cynicism were no answer to the world; those who were sure of their demise on a particular day always seemed to find it.

Best of all was to be nothing, to feel nothing, to claim no satisfactions or hurts, to be stoic in thought and deed, to take the best of everything, and to spurn the worst—to be a humble man, but not too humble—to walk a thin line, moving from shadow to shadow, in avoidance of the attentions of the gods.

Marcus might pray, but he knew he would not. He did not like the feeling of attracting attention, doubly so now that he was heir to Penderbrook.

This cursed place! He had no love for it, only a sense of duty.

A knock came at the door. He felt gratitude for its interrupting his bad thoughts, which were sure to lead to worse. "Come in."

The door opened, and Lucy's face appeared. "Marcus? May I speak to you?"

"Please do. Would you like a drink?"

She wrinkled up her nose. "At this hour of the morning?"

"Never mind. What is it?"

"I have been to look in on your father."

"And?"

"He was gone."

Marcus cursed, not least because Lucy had seen this moment coming with all clarity: he had completely forgotten to look in upon the man.

She said, "I sent the men out to search; they found him almost immediately. He was in the folly."

"The folly? But I was there earlier this morning and did not see him. When did they find him?"

"Half an hour ago, I suppose."

"I must have been speaking to Cook then. What was he doing?"

"Scratching at a place along one of the walls."

Marcus felt himself shudder. "Scratching? Where?"

"Just a piece of wall, with no doors or windows or other markings upon it. What were *you* doing at the folly this morning?"

"I had a dream of it, that there was a new door in the wall, and that Barnabas was trapped behind it. I went to look, and to clear my head."

She said, "How curious. But the north window of the nursery looks out over the folly. Perhaps he saw you outdoors and wondered what you were doing."

Marcus exhaled. It was a saner possibility than what he had been thinking. "And now?"

"The men tried to convince him to go to his own room, but he will not. He is back in the nursery."

"Who watches him?"

Lucy sighed. "One of the girls will do it, for now. But the one who would watch him at nights has gone to the mill."

"The mill!" Marcus snapped. "I curse that place. It defies logic. Where is all their food? Their granary was nearly empty."

"This winter will be difficult," Lucy said.

"More than difficult," Marcus said. "With five hundred workers at the mill, they cannot be more than a few weeks away from completely exhausting their supplies. Bread must be baked. And I do not recall at all seeing stores of meat or potatoes or apples or any other things. Where are they? In that cursed cellar? No, for there was coal-dust on the floor. Either Howe did not show them to me, or they have none!"

Lucy blinked at him. "I don't understand, Marcus."

"My brother's body has not been found," Marcus said, turning away from her. "Perhaps they shall eat *that*."

"Marcus!"

He chewed on a knuckle. "The secretaries will begin their work soon. What they shall tell me, I do not know, but I suppose it cannot be pleasant.

News about money rarely is. And Cook! She has no assistant, do you know that? We have no housekeeper, no butler, no one in charge. They have all gone to the mill! I cannot run this place. If I were to try, I would destroy it. And what will come in January when it is time for Parliament? Come to that, what will become of Christmas?"

"You're worried about Christmas?" she asked incredulously.

He ignored her, giving his fears their head. "Father pressured the courts not to hold an inquest for Barnabas. You know that, I suppose, but think of it! He has overturned justice itself, or rather justice has been overturned for his sake. For all we know, Barnabas had been poisoned, and the Earl wished to cover it up!"

"Marcus, you're being ridiculous."

"It is not that I'm worried that we shall all starve. I am the son of an Earl, after all, and I shall manage to ensure that we eat, even if other people must suffer in their turn for it. But there are a thousand and one troubles clouding around me, and I cannot *think!* That is what it is, Lucy, that every moment that I am about to fix my attention on something, something else comes to distract me, to remove my attention from this thing to that one. It feels as though the universe itself conspires to deceive me, like a man with quick hands and a deck of marked cards."

"Sit down," she said. She had already seated herself. The room was chill; the fire had been laid but not lit.

He sat. "Yes? What are your words of wisdom in this matter? What will you tell me, that shall resolve every ill?"

"I can do nothing of the sort," she said. "You are ridiculous."

"Oh, well then! All my troubles are resolved!"

She shook her head. "Listen to me, Marcus.

"There is Penderbrook, and its abandonment and perhaps financial ruination; there is the mill, which contains the mystery of how to feed the workers there without more grain; there is the trouble of the fungus throughout the district and the ill weather everywhere; there is the trouble of your father's madness, and of your brother's missing body; there is the possibility that it is the end of the world. Are those your problems?"

"More or less. There is also the problem of whether I should offer you my hand in marriage."

She gave him a twisted look. "Why should you think to do that?"

"You were my brother's betrothed; he is dead. Someone should at least offer to look after you, although it would probably come to the opposite, with you wasting your time looking after me and preventing me from getting into too much trouble."

"You don't love me," she said.

"That isn't true," he said snappishly. "You are like a sister to me."

"Just so."

He turned towards her and waggled his eyebrows up and down. "There have been some very naughty brothers in British history, you know."

She looked Heavenward. "If you continue in this manner, I shall have to call for some tea. And Cook is too busy for that, and so are the girls, so I should have to go get it myself."

"And leave? Don't do that. I'll behave myself."

They sat companionably together. Strangely, he *did* feel better, which made as little sense as anything else.

After a time, Lucy said, "My advice is as follows: let the secretaries review the accounts before you think of what measures must be taken in order to remedy a tragedy which may not have occurred. Forget the search for your brother's body. It will turn up, sooner or later. Your father's madness, well, I think it must be admitted to. You will be criticized for it, or at least for not keeping silent about it, but think of what might conspire, if your father should take it into his head to set fire to the nursery, or to order the roads closed, or to go to Parliament and make a speech about how your brother will return, so there is no need to amend the Corn Laws."

"And the other things?"

"You can do nothing about the end of the world, it is true; furthermore, I think it unlikely that it is your sole and entire fault that the Savior should judge humanity so ill."

He laughed under his breath.

"Likewise you can do nothing about the weather, and it may be that you will be unable to do anything about starvation, but you can ameliorate neither of these things if you do not get the truth of them. Likewise it seems to me that you cannot know the truth about the mill as it stands. Howe used to work on one of my father's farms, and he was always hiding something. Even when it was not dishonest, he would never say what Father wanted to know."

"I didn't know that Howe had worked for your father."

"He only came after you left. And as soon as the mill opened, he left to work there instead."

"Does he hate hard work?"

"No, I think that he only wishes to be seen as above the run of common men. Power, that is what he craves, or at least the appearance of it."

Marcus shook his head. "It may be the height of arrogance to say so, but I would be a hundred times happier, if I were to exchange my life for his. I would be away from Penderbrook at a moment's notice, and drag you along with me to London."

"Me? Why?"

"To keep you entertained until the money ran out," he said. "And then I would gamble, and get more of it. And then I would put you up in a house—at not *too* good an address—and tell you that I should not allow you to eat, unless you wrote tales of such pity and horror that they made me weep."

She laughed. "Surely you cannot recall the day that I said that!"

"Of course I do," he said. "Or rather not the specific date, because for all I remember of *that,* it might have been snowing, or raining, or sunny, or a day covered in eerie mists. I only remember your seriousness about the matter, and Barnabas and I took it as your given purpose ever since: to write strange and dark tales, as you said, 'like Anne Radcliffe, only stranger.'"

Still laughing, Lucy put a hand over her face. "I cannot believe you remember that."

"I assure you, Barnabas and I mentioned it often enough in our letters to each other. You are to be famous, you know. We have determined it."

"Well, if it is determined—!"

Marcus felt a hard lump in his throat. "Someday, when all of this is over—if it ever is—you will have to write of what terrible and awful thing became of Penderbrook."

"I do not know that I should be able to do it," Lucy said. "My time here has been of too much satisfaction to me. Until recently, that is."

"You must have happiness, in order to appreciate sadness. I think that is what is wrong with the novels I have read—"

"I did not know that you could read," Lucy interrupted.

He made a face at her. "We soldiers are great readers," he said, "although the books that we read are seldom fit for ladies when we have finished bleeding over them."

Lucy snorted.

"At any rate," he continued, "What is wrong with the novels I have read, is that they attempt to wring the most abject sympathies from one, without having first filled up one's heart with joy. If you want to make something pitiable, you must first make it worth being loved."

"I shall take that advice to heart," she declared.

"I did not care for Gregory Lewis's book," he said. "The men were contemptible, the women weak. Do not write your characters like that. Make them more in equal measure."

"So that the women are contemptible and the men weak?"

"Perhaps!"

Lucy lay a finger against her jaw. "You could ask my father, I think."

"Ask him what? For your hand? I should think that I would have to get an assent from you first, and you were quite clear that you would not!"

She ignored him. "To go with you to the mill. He does not know how to run a mill, of course, but he keeps all the accounts of the house and the farms, and he knows Howe's tricks well enough to not let himself be distracted by them. If you were to go to the mill and cause some distraction to keep Howe occupied, Father would be able to discover much of what goes on there, I think."

Chapter Sixteen

All This, and Yet Even More

MARCUS SOON FOUND HIMSELF at Bramble House. Mr. Abbott had to be called in from the fields, where he was overseeing the last of what sad, pitiable straw might be obtained from the fields. The weather had turned from heavy rain to snow, although the transformation from one to the other had not yet been made complete.

The two men faced each other in the parlor. Mr. Abbott said, "You have not convinced my daughter to go with you to London, or to go by herself."

"I have tried, but I have not yet concluded my attempts. I have only discovered more of what makes me agree with you."

"You wish my assistance?"

"I want you to come with me to the mill at Little Millwich and look things over, so that Howe cannot distract me from what must be seen there."

Mr. Abbott lifted an eyebrow. "He is cheating you?"

"He is deceiving me. They do not have the grain they need to last a week, let alone the winter, and yet he spoke as though his main concern was only that beggars did not take away the amount the workers would need for their comfort."

"You think he is stealing food from elsewhere? Or hiding it?"

"I do not think anything. I only know that things are not what they seem, and Lucy advises me that you might be able to help me see past Howe's deceptions."

"Lucy advised it?"

"She did."

Mr. Abbott said, "The last thing I wanted to do was go back out into that damnable weather today, but it seems as though it must be done."

"We shall wait until tomorrow."

Mr. Abbott shook his head. "The weather has turned. We have lost the last of the autumn, and now winter gathers us up. We should go now, lest the snow shut us in and prevent us from going at all."

"It is only October."

Mr. Abbott answered not in words, but in the sweep of an arm across the room, as though to indicate *all this, and yet even more.*

THE SNOW FELL HEAVILY onto the top of the carriage. Although the earth had not yet chilled enough for the snow to remain solid for more than a few moments, Marcus felt the weight of it upon him.

"At least it will stop this damnable fungus from spreading."

"It is in the grain," Mr. Abbott said shortly. "As soon as the grain sprouts in the spring, the fungus will grow with it. And you know that it keeps the main body of its spores underground, as all fungus does."

Marcus gave Mr. Abbott a piercing look. "Did my brother speak of the fungus with you?"

"Yes, a few times."

"What do you think of it?"

"I warn you, he did not like my opinion," Mr. Abbott said, "and you will not like it either."

"Regardless, I wish to hear it."

"The fungus that grows in our district is not natural," Mr. Abbott said. "It comes from a terrible source. It is the touch of the Divine that once changed all the water of Egypt into blood."

"The red fungus is one of the plagues of the Bible?" Marcus asked.

"Nearly, but not exactly, so. Your brother rejected my opinion entirely: to him, there was no possibility of any occurrence but that it should be of natural causes."

"I am of a more open mind on that matter," Marcus said. "Although when Barnabas tried his arguments upon me in letters, I was never able to convince myself of my own opinion. His arguments were very strong."

"They were," Mr. Abbott agreed, although Marcus felt his relief at not having to have the same arguments now. "He said that no supernatural cause was needed; it was only that the same fungus had cycles of death and rebirth, that once was recorded in the Bible at the time that the Jews were under such a weight of injustice from Pharaoh."

"Yes, I can imagine him saying so," Marcus said. "An explanation for everything, and for every explanation, another one behind it, and another, until you were at the first causes of the universe and listening to him ask whether there necessarily *must* be a Creator."

"And you?"

Marcus laughed, and explained his theory that higher powers must exist, or else why would bad luck strike with such unjust precision. He concluded by saying, "But of course Barnabas only laughed, when I told him my theory."

"Yes, it is ridiculous," Mr. Abbott said. "But at least it indicates that you have a more flexible mind."

"I have seen things in France that would freeze your blood," Marcus said. "If you hesitate to speak because you fear that I will not listen, well, I can only assure you that I, too, have known unusual things."

Mr. Abbott took a breath, then put his hands on his knees as though he were about to stand up in the moving carriage. "What I have to say is worse than you can anticipate. The heart of it is what caused the division between your father, and myself. We were once great friends, although I doubt you have ever heard a living soul say so."

"I have not!" Marcus exclaimed. "Not even your daughter."

"It is a sad tale," Mr. Abbott warned. "Not a long one, but one that you cannot forget, and, once heard, will change your opinion of several things."

Marcus shook his head. "My opinions are dark enough as it is. But at least you can be sure that of my believing nearly anything of my father."

"We shall see," Mr. Abbott said. "It begins with your mother, and the woman who was my wife."

Mr. Abbott's Tale

Long before those two excellent women married the two of us, they were the best of friends. They lived near to each other in Sussex, and were of the same age. They were presented at the age of seventeen, and spent nearly the entire Season together at all the dinners and balls. They were the most faithful of friends.

I was the first, between James and myself, to espy the two of them. I went to the Earl and said, "James, there are two of the most beautiful young ladies in London, and we have not yet made their acquaintance."

I had long known James as my neighbor and playmate, for the Abbotts and the Sewells have always been close friends, for hundreds of years. That is why I allowed Lucy to play with you as children, for although it was not quite proper, it would have caused bad luck. For it was clear that you two boys were not made by the Creator in your father's fashion, and no matter how wild *you* were, Marcus, at least you were not *him*.

But I speak forwards of my tale. Your father looked at the two girls and said, "Well, then, let us arrange to have ourselves introduced," and did just that. He had the friendlier manner between us, and was the more pleasing. Quite aside from his future possession of Penderbrook, he was assured of making almost any match that he desired. I, myself, was less assured, both because I could not make myself as pleasing as your father could, and because I had less to offer as recompense for my less amicable self.

We were introduced, and both girls allowed as they might have a place on their cards for us. We joined the dance together—James with Mary, that is, Lucy's mother; and I with Harriet, who was to become your mother. I had somehow claimed the arm of the prettier of the two girls, although of course both were at the height of beauty and fashion. Of the two, Mary was the fairer, with the complexion of the true English Rose. Your mother, Harriet, had a touch of the Irish about her, and your coloration, and a great deal of your temperament, such as might be supported in a young woman at that time.

During the dance, Mary and Harriet changed places, and did not return to them when the next figure called for them to do so, but continued with the partners they liked best, which they never afterwards varied. When I asked Mary about it after we were married, she would only say, "We had only to glance at each other to know that our preferences had been reversed."

I woo'd Mary, and James soon began to woo your mother. Our marriages were both love-matches, although the fondness between James and Harriet did not last for long. Within a year it was clear that they would never suit as friends and helpmeets. Mary said that it was because James showed a second face to Harriet which he never showed to *me*, and that she would prefer not to speak of it further; if she were forced to dwell on the matter overmuch, she would have to do something to remedy the situation, which would see her excommunicated from Penderbrook, and from the presence of her friend, and *that* she could not bear.

I dismissed her sentiments at first; James was my friend, and I was nothing if not loyal. But the truth of the matter began to be revealed to me when James's father, the previous Earl, your grandfather, died of illness when you were very young. Harriet was with child, and, upon catching the same fever as your grandfather, both mother and child died soon after. And thus your father was made the Earl and a widower within the same month. Almost immediately following, he began work on the folly, laying down its design with an unusual haste.

He claimed that the folly was a memorial for father and wife, but it became clear that he neither mourned, nor loved, either of them. He began lingering in the folly at all hours of the day and night, and forbade anyone to come to him there. But he could not keep secret that he would take women there at night, jades from London. His supposed ceremonies of grief were widely spoken of throughout the district.

Finally, at Mary's behest, I went there to see what he did.

The ceremony began at midnight; it was indeed a ceremony, and it did involve a woman. She had been fastened with staples and chains to one of the walls out of view of the house and road. I saw her only because I circled the house, and crept through the woods.

Her eyes were open, but they were languid, nearly insensible; I quickly recognized the signs of some drug having been administered. She was nearly undressed, wearing only a light petticoat. I thought James enslaved by some strange passion; one hears of such things from time to time. But as he knelt before the woman, he did not perform that act which first leaps to the mind of a man who has known the world, but bowed before her several times, laying his forehead upon the stones beneath her feet. He chanted words I did not know. In front of him lay a large, silver dish at arm's length, directly under the woman's figure.

This went on for what felt like hours. From his tone, James must be pleading with the woman for some sign or favor which she declined to give him. She remained distracted, her gaze vacant.

At last, James's invocations reached a fever pitch, and the woman's head rolled about on her shoulders, and she spoke something to him, in that same strange tongue. This seemed to James a cause for celebration. He leapt to his feet and began to dance about giddily, raising his arms overhead in jubilation. He went to the altar and thumped a great book that had been placed upon it, and which I had not previously noted. Then he turned a page, mouthed words without pronouncing them, and turned back to the woman in her chains.

Once again he bowed, striking his head repeatedly on the ground. Again, he was clearly begging some favor of the woman. She listened for a moment, peering at him intently. And then she said, in a loud voice:

"I guard the doorway. Would you have it opened?"

James answered, but I could not hear the response, although I could only assume that he answered in the affirmative.

"I have held the way for overlong," the woman announced, "and whatever purpose I once found in doing so, I can no longer remember. I only wish for release, even though the cost of it be too dearly sold."

Then she nodded her head forwards, and—

Chapter Seventeen

To See What Is to Be Seen

"And?" Marcus asked. They were nearly at Little Millwich now, in the carriage.

Mr. Abbott shook his head.

"I will not describe what happened to the woman, only that when it was done, the dish in front of her was filled with a red fluid that was not blood. The woman was not only dead, but had dissolved into a black stain which lay upon the stones of the wall. James was overjoyed."

"What was it?" Marcus asked. "The red fluid?"

"You know what it was."

"The fungus, or something like it."

"Aye," said Mr. Abbott. "It was only after that night that the fungus began to appear widely throughout the district, amongst the grain and elsewhere. But even then, not for another five years. And, by then, my wife had died in birthing her second child—Lucy's sister, who also died—and all civility had broken between myself and your father."

"What did you do? Nothing?"

"I do not think that what I did could be called nothing," Mr. Abbott said stiffly. "I questioned him; he denied everything as a sort of malicious rumor until finally I admitted that I had seen the events myself. Then he said that I had misunderstood everything. When I asked to see the book, or at least to know its title, he refused to tell it to me, or to let me see it. The name of the woman who had been sacrificed, likewise he denied me, saying only that she was a doxy from London, and of no matter. When I argued that, to a Christian, all souls were worthy, he laughed at me, saying that I spoke truer than I knew, and that he placed more value on that woman's soul than anybody else might do. Around and around we went. I sank into a darker mood, while he rose into a merrier one. I felt myself defeated. I searched the folly, time and time again. While I was still allowed to set foot at Penderbrook, I searched that as well. I came to understand that he had hidden something in the cellars, but I knew not what. I still do not know for certain, but I think that that book is to be reached through the door to the wine cellar, I think within the cave itself. But I was never able to slip alone into that sanctum sanctorum, or to obtain its keys.

"Finally, James reached the end of his patience with me. Our wives were dead and our friendship was at an end. I was tempted to leave with Lucy, to remove her from this place. But already the three of you had become fond of each other, and I told myself that it was a far nobler deed to keep watch over the Earl, to ensure that his foul summoning wreaked as little trouble as could be. I loathed him now; I saw him perhaps as clearly as once Mary had done.

"Marcus, this may pain you, but I suspect James to have murdered his father and his wife; I harbor the darkest suspicions that he somehow caused the death of my wife as well; I believe his work to be the source of the red fungus, which I do not believe to be of a natural type; I suspect that whatever dark ceremony he performed that night, it was only the beginning of what he intended to do.

"What his purpose may be, I do not know. It cannot be to enrich himself, for surely there are easier ways to do so! And it cannot be to acquire more lands, or more power, or more women, or more health, or he would have acquired them by now. I ask myself whether he wishes only to destroy the world, and I cannot suppose that to be it, either. He was never one to smash things: he wanted to *have* them, not to break them."

Mr. Abbott's suppositions ended there; they had arrived before the door of Howe's house, where he waited for them, looking as polite and servile as ever.

He bowed. "My lord. Mr. Abbott. I have received your message, and am ready to answer all questions to your satisfaction."

Marcus gave a glance to Mr. Abbott which said *All shall proceed as we have discussed.* Mr. Abbott gave a little nod.

They began, as Marcus had the previous time, in Howe's study. Although two of the secretaries had been sent to Penderbrook to review its accounts, there were again five men at work in the room, all scribbling furiously at their work, and sitting near the windows, to gain what light might be had. Today the room was also lit by candles and lamps, it being so much darker. The snow had not ceased the entire drive from Penderbrook, and in fact had fallen more thickly, beginning to linger in the fields and the cold, bare branches of the trees.

Mr. Abbott settled himself in amongst the books, eyeing them with all the familiarity of a sergeant overlooking his regiment's boots and weapons. Marcus took Howe by the shoulder and drew him away from the others. Howe's eyes lingered on Mr. Abbott; clearly, he wished to be able to stand over the man's shoulder to ensure that he saw what he ought to, and did not see what he ought not.

"Howe, what of the cellar?" Marcus hissed. "Has the fungus spread? We must look."

Howe shook his head. "It is too dangerous, my lord, although I can assure you that it has not spread."

"I tell you that it gives me nightmares. I must see for myself."

Howe nearly sighed aloud. "We dare not open the door, my lord."

"I know that. And yet I must see that it does not allow any egress of that foul stuff, or the monsters which it hides."

"Yes, my lord." They walked across the snowy street to the closer of the two immense mill buildings, whose machinery ground inexorably onwards, spinning cotton into thread, and thread into cloth. What would the machines make, if they were fed the strands of fungus? Marcus shuddered.

The temperature was falling.

MARCUS LED HOWE AROUND Little Millwich, from this place to that. First they looked over every door within the cellar—although several of them they did not open—and walked the entire floor of both buildings to ensure that the fungus had not escaped. Marcus frequently stopped to question the workers, be they men, women, or children, to determine whether they were healthy or ill, well-fed or starving, troubled or at ease. They all stated, in one way or another, that they were being treated as well as anyone might wish, which was not the answer that Marcus expected. Surely one or another of them would have complained. No matter how well-circumstanced a group of people might be, there was always one to complain—except in Little Millwich.

As they walked, Marcus asked Howe what he, as the manager, intended to do about the monsters underneath the millworks. Howe had no definite answer, hinting that he looked towards Marcus for direction. Marcus, in the finest tradition of superior officers everywhere, told Howe to do whatever he thought best, then asked him what, in his opinion, he thought best.

Howe gave several suggestions that amounted to doing nothing about the matter, except what was necessary to keep the mill running, then began giving Marcus hints that he, Marcus, should leave soon, lest he and Mr. Abbott be trapped overnight or longer by the snow. "Surely you have room for two more men!" exclaimed Marcus heartily, for the pleasure of seeing Howe's face fall. The hints continued: hints that he should stop disturbing the workers, hints that the presence of two extra men for even a single night would place undue strain on supplies, even hints that the mill buildings might not be safe after all.

Marcus ignored the hints, so that Mr. Abbott might continue to review the accounts.

Finally, one of the secretaries arrived, to tell Marcus that Mr. Abbott had finished his work and thought it was fair time for refreshments.

Howe leaped upon the suggestion like a starving dog, and the three of them returned to Howe's house, where Mr. Abbott awaited them in the front parlor.

"How fares it?" Marcus asked him.

"There is," Mr. Abbott noted, "a formidable amount of snow falling. I do not know that I wish to return to Penderbrook this evening. It would surely be dark before we arrived, and quite dangerous."

"As you say," Marcus said comfortably. "Howe? Would you arrange matters? We shall leave first thing in the morning."

"Yes, my lord."

And so it was agreed, whether Howe liked it or not, that they were to be housed in the room left by the two secretaries who had returned to Penderbrook. Then a housekeeper appeared, saying that a luncheon had been laid on for them, and she would have it brought in, if they wished it.

The food was dull, plain, and ordinary: roast beef, potatoes, onions, and sour-tasting, reddish bread.

Mr. Abbott said, as he finished his tea, "I should primarily like to see the grain stores, and after that the stores for the potatoes, and the meat."

Howe said, "We have enough of everything, if only we do not add any additional workers."

Marcus said, "I, too, would like to see what is to be seen of the stores. Your assurances are one thing, but to see them with my eyes would be a great reassurance. I became quite used to calculating men's rations in France, you know."

Howe spluttered and said that it would be unwise to open the doors of the granaries with the snow falling as heavily as it was.

"Then show us the potatoes," Marcus said.

Howe said they were waiting for a new shipment of potatoes, from Ireland, and so it would be of little use to see what few bushels that remained.

"Then show us the meat."

The meat was in an area which was not safe in such weather, down some steps that were in very ill repair.

"And so," Marcus said, allowing his voice to become heavy with threat, "you do not wish us to see the food stores at all. You are hiding something. You say that your people are going hungry, and yet none of them appear so, and none of them speak of it, which, in my experience, anyone who hungers is wont to do. The food you have given us is well enough. You are hoarding, aren't you? Or you have found some other source of food, have you not, from smugglers or poaching or some other illicit source? Come now, man! Do you think that I would punish you for ensuring that your workers, who look to me to see them fed, eat well? If you have done that which you ought not, well, let us discuss it, and discover what must be done."

Howe had gone pale during Marcus's speech, and his hands were shaking. He did not have the look of an angry man, but rather a man suffering under the full force of terror. His jaw was clenched, as if to keep his teeth from chattering.

"If—if you must see what we eat, then you must see," he said. "I beg you to wait until tomorrow, when the snows are lessened, and then we can see the grain."

"And if the snows do not lessen?" Mr. Abbott said, deadly calm in his voice. "Will you send the Marquis back to Penderbrook without having his questions answered? Come, man: where do you obtain the food that your workers eat?"

Howe looked to Marcus with eyes pleading for mercy, but Marcus pretended not to see.

"You shall see!" Howe said with a wail. "Then you shall see what you see!"

It was as though they had taken a mechanical doll and broken its spring; Howe muttered to himself, "See what they shall see! They shall see!" over and over to himself as they dressed themselves for the outdoors and followed him from the house.

The granary that Marcus had previously seen, they avoided entirely. Howe pointed out another one: "See, that is the granary!" He waved his hand again: "And there are the potatoes!"

"And the meat?" Marcus asked.

"Oh! Soon, we shall see it!"

The further he proceeded the more agitated he became. Likewise, the snow seemed to sense that they were at their most vulnerable, and thickened so that it was nearly impossible to see, although it was only just after noon.

"Is there no church?" Marcus asked. "In all this snow, I cannot see the steeple, and I have not heard the ring of the bells. I seem to remember having gone to the little church here once, when I was younger."

Howe cackled with laughter, the sound of which the snow muffled before it could echo. "Soon! Soon! You will see the church soon!"

Chapter Eighteen

Under the Church

AND INDEED THEY SOON arrived at the church, which Marcus recalled seeing during his previous visit. It was small and built of old stone. They had not come to the church alone, for Howe had deemed it necessary to have strong men with them to open the door to the cellar where the meat was kept. He collected two men from a nearby tavern, which was nearly empty despite the hour. The five of them stopped outside of the front doors of the church, with flakes of snow alighting gently, but heavily, about their shoulders.

"Is that a Norman church?" Marcus asked. "It looks ancient."

"I have never been told so," Howe said. The men shrugged.

They hesitated as the snow fell ever more thickly about them.

Mr. Abbott added, "In fact, it reminds me of the folly that the Earl had built next to Penderbrook."

Marcus grimaced, then said, "Are we here to pray? Or is the meat kept in the cellar of the church?"

"There are too many workers for services to be held in such a small building," said Howe. "Our worship is held on the floor of the mill."

"The vicar can hardly be in favor of such an arrangement."

"He understands that it will be some time before we are able to build a new church. In the meantime, we use the church for storage."

Mr. Abbott said, "That is hardly respectful of the sanctity of the church."

Howe tugged on Marcus's sleeve. "Come, we shall see the stores! As you wished! We will see them!"

He directed them through the church, which still seemed to await celebrants at any moment, to a small door along the back wall. When Howe opened the door, a set of stairs led downwards into darkness. One of the men was sent down the stairs, lantern in hand. Then Howe waved Marcus and Mr. Abbott forwards.

"Once you are in the cellar, you will see what you have come to see!"

The man who had gone down the stairs before them said, "My lord, walk slowly. The stairs are in no good repair, and there is a trickle of water from the snow running over a few of them."

"Do you see the fungus down there?"

"Down here? No, my lord. It is only in the mill buildings next to the water."

Howe said, "My lord, you hesitate! Is it not your most fervent wish to see what is in the cellar? Our food stores?"

"What are these stores, Howe, and where did you get them?" Marcus demanded.

Howe giggled. "Are you afraid?"

Mr. Abbott said, "I warn you, that if you intend to cause us harm, we shall pay you back in kind." And he reached inside his coat, as if to touch the butt of a pistol.

Howe giggled. "I do not intend to harm you, Mr. Abbott. I swear it. And the men, neither."

"It is safe?" Marcus asked.

At this, Howe threw up his hands. "If you do not wish to go into the cellar...!"

Marcus shook his head. If they did not go now, then he would have forever yielded to Howe, and that he could not abide. Surely Howe would be able to prepare for any further encroachments, now that he was aware of their attentions upon the stores.

"I will go," Marcus announced.

Then came from below a gasp, and the sound of something being dragged across stones, sounding damnably like the heels of a man's boots.

Howe stiffened. "Smith!" he called. "Smith!"

There was no answer, and Howe and the other big man looked at each other. The unnatural giddiness drained from Howe's face.

"Smith!" he called once more.

There was no answer.

Marcus said, "Howe, this man and I shall go downstairs and attempt to find Smith. Stay here, Mr. Abbott, and call for help if we should not return."

Mr. Abbott withdrew a calvary pistol from within his coat and handed it to Marcus, then reached in again and withdrew another, also giving it to him. Both pistols were loaded, but the flint had not yet been pulled back to ready it for fire. "I loaded these but a short while ago," Mr. Abbott said. "Early this morning."

Marcus looked at Mr. Abbott with a new eye; he had suspected more than Marcus had, and been prepared.

"I accept them gladly," said he, and waved at Howe. "Hold the lantern. This man and I shall descend first, with you holding the lantern overhead."

Marcus carefully descended the dark stairs. He was prevented from seeing what lay beneath the church by a turn in the staircase.

Behind him, the big man said in a low and secretive voice, "Smith is a dead man, my lord."

Marcus felt implacable. "And yet we shall go, in case that he is not. I shall not leave him in cowardice to a terrible fate."

"My name is Westin, my lord, and I would shake your hand, if it were allowed that I might do so."

"If we live, Westin, then it shall be so."

The lantern cast shadows before them, swaying as Howe held the lantern high.

Marcus reached the landing and turned, and found more stairs before him. He smelled the thick scent of the butcher's trade. Down here was certainly hung a great deal of aging meat.

"Have you been down here before, Westin?"

"I? Not I, my lord."

"Who tends the meat?"

"One or another of Howe's men does, my lord, depending on who draws the duty for the day."

"Where does the meat come from?"

"I know not, my lord. I am one of the workers who generally maintains the machinery."

"A machinist, then."

"Yes, my lord."

They reached another landing, another turn in the stairs; it was then that the stairs showed a much greater age, and crumbled at the edges.

From above, Howe said, "We are nearly there, my lord." His voice sounded utterly without tone, as though he considered himself a man already dead.

Marcus slowed, lifting the pistols and drawing back the firing pin on the one in his right. He peered into the darkness, straining his ears to hear past the sound of his own heart. What he looked for was one of those white creatures which had attacked in the other cellar: a twisted figure, pale, emerging stealthily out of the darkness to snatch at them. But he neither heard nor saw anything, and did not smell any trace of the fungus—only hanged meat.

"Smith!" he called. "If you live, make some sound!"

Smith made no response. Marcus cursed under his breath, a favorite curse that had seen him through more battles than ever a prayer had done. He stepped onto a floor of rough, squarish stones, made sure of his footing, then stepped to the side.

"Come forwards, Westin, then step to the other side and let Howe stand between us. In a place such as this, the most important weapon we have is light."

"Yes, my lord."

Westin reached the floor and stepped the other way, leaving room for Howe to stand between them.

From above, Mr. Abbott called, "How goes it?"

Marcus called back, "We have reached the floor below."

"What do you see?"

Howe stepped between them, shuddering to such an extent that the lantern's light shivered with him. He had lowered the lantern to his waist as he descended the last few stairs. Now he raised it again, and in a low voice began to speak, in a language which Marcus did not understand.

Slowly, Howe dropped to his knees, still holding the lantern before him. Marcus peered into the church's cellar.

Whatever it was he had expected, it was not what he now saw.

Before him in the cellar carcasses were hung, split and gutted, but not skinned. They were the carcasses of men, of women, of children. Their hair had been cut and singed from every surface, and the excess of ash brushed away, so that the skins were colored in patches, gray and pink, as though they were slaughtered hogs.

Howe continued to speak in that strange language, his voice desperate, as though he pleaded and begged.

Before them the flesh hung so thickly that it was impossible to see for any extent. The limbs of the hung bodies dangled over the floor by a foot's width or more, depending on the height of the upended victim. Marcus attempted to estimate the number of bodies which hung there, but it was impossible: they were so closely packed that he could not see the walls beyond them.

The walls on either side of them were lined with endless canvas bags, filled to bursting.

Westin breathed a half-heard prayer. Marcus took the lantern from Howe's hand and bent down, tucking one of the pistols into a pocket of his coat.

"Did you know about this?" he asked Westin.

"Oh God," Westin whispered, which Marcus took for a denial.

"Damn you, Marcus Sewell!" shouted Mr. Abbott from above. "What do you *see*?"

"Evil," called Marcus over his shoulder. "Ware the door. We may be interrupted."

"You have my only weapons."

"Don't be absurd, man! Have you never learnt to lie?"

Bitter laughter echoed downwards at him. Marcus bent his head down to peer between the strange forest of dangling arms. Where was Smith? What had taken him?

Deeper within the shadows, he espied several of the thick-crowded hands swaying slightly.

"Something moves," he said in a low voice to Westin. As he spoke, the forest of dangling hands shivered as though something moved between them, coming closer.

Westin said, "I swear, my lord, that I did not know about this."

"Hush," Marcus said, rising to his feet. Leaving the lantern on the floor, he raised one of the pistols, then the other, drawing back the firing pins on both.

Howe's uncanny chanting ceased, and now Marcus could hear the sound of something moving among the bodies. By the hushed, intimate sounds of its passage, it was not more than a dozen feet from them.

Marcus moved one pistol to follow the sound, the other still covering his flank.

Howe hissed through his teeth.

"Do you see it?" Marcus asked.

Howe did not answer, but continued hissing. In a moment he dropped his hands forwards on the floor, then stretched them in front of him, so that he lay prone—but still hissing.

"Be quiet, man!" Marcus said, trying to peer between the swaying bodies.

Westin said, "My lord...Howe..."

Howe's form had become impossibly twisted, halfway between that of a wooden marionette and a dead snake's.

A creaking sound came from before them, and their attention snapped back to that thicket of dangling flesh. One of the bodies in the front row had begun to turn and swing, as though it had been pushed from behind.

The figure, which had been facing away from them a moment ago, was now turned so that it faced them.

Although its hair was shorn and its skin charred, Marcus recognized the face of his brother.

"Go," he said to Westin in a low voice. "*Go.*"

He heard Westin scramble up the steps. Marcus kicked over the lantern, and, just as he wished, the oil spread out on the floor in front of it, quickly coming alight from the flame of the wick.

Marcus kicked Howe's clothes into the flame. In the short time that they had been distracted by the motion of Barnabas's body, Howe's misshapen form had disappeared, leaving his clothes abandoned.

Marcus grabbed one of the bags alongside the wall and threw it into the flames, then backed up the stairs.

Already the heavy scent of aging meat was joined by the reek of burning hair.

Chapter Nineteen

This Cursed Place

MARCUS ASCENDED THE STAIRS of the church cellar, backing carefully away, and holding both pistols at the ready. As he reached the last of the stairs and backed into the church, Westin slammed the door.

Marcus felt gorge rise in his throat. "We must leave this cursed place."

"Where is Howe?" Abbott asked.

"Dead or worse."

Mr. Abbott was a wiser man than even Marcus could have anticipated, and asked no more, but accepted one of the pistols from Marcus and checked that it was still fit to fire. Then the three of them fled the church.

Once outside, the three of them paused with dismay at the view before them. Although the sun had not yet set, the air was so thick with snow as to be generally blinding.

Marcus pulled up the collar of his coat, de-cocked the pistol, and tucked it into his pocket. 'Twere better not to allow the firing powder to become damp.

"What now?" Mr. Abbott asked.

"We must flee!" Westin shouted. "We must warn the mill, we must flee!"

Marcus quickly drew a small knife from his coat, and used it to nick a finger. What oozed from the wound was red blood. Mr. Abbott grimly accepted the knife and did the same. Blood also flowed.

The two men turned to Westin. Mr. Abbott commanded, "You must nick yourself with this knife and show us what comes of it."

"Why?"

"It must be done."

Westin accepted the knife and held it to his finger, but did not cut.

Mr. Abbott raised his pistol. "If you will not, I will shoot you where you stand."

Westin groaned. "I know that I must. And yet I fear to. For I have eaten of that meat. God! My soul is already forfeit!"

Marcus and Mr. Abbott looked at each other: they, also, had eaten.

Then, swiftly, as if to deceive himself of his own intentions, Westin cut himself, then turned away his face. A red drop of blood flowed from his finger and dripped to the snow, a bright flash of red against the white.

"That is blood," Mr. Abbott said. "If you were not a man, you would have no need to eat."

Westin groaned again. "Then why did you make me...?"

"There is no idea that should not be overturned upon evidence to the contrary," Mr. Abbott said sternly. "Sewell, it is as this man has said. We must reach the millworks and warn the others."

Westin coughed. Smoke was beginning to add its haze to the air. The fire in the cellar had spread with surprising quickness for a windowless room underground, whose only door they thought tightly closed.

Marcus turned in a slow circle, searching the heavily falling snow for signs of movement. He wished to have the pistol in his hand, but knew that drawing it out of his coat before it was needed might lead to his being unable to use it at all.

"You set fire to the church?" Mr. Abbott inquired approvingly.

"Yes, but I thought it would smother itself, in that closed cellar," Marcus said. "This is an ill circumstance."

"It should burn," said Mr. Abbott, who did not know the half of it yet.

Marcus said, "Little Millwich can burn to ashes for all I care, and take my fortune with it. But that the smoke escapes so freely means that there was another exit from the church cellar."

Mr. Abbott frowned.

Marcus said, "In short, gentlemen, we must assume that they are warned."

"What is to be done?" Mr. Abbott asked.

"To Howe's," Marcus decided.

They began their journey, Westin leading them through the heavy blizzard. In places the snow had already fallen to such a depth that they must trod with care, lest they fall. Marcus watched Mr. Abbott closely, fearing that the older man strained himself to move so quickly.

Mr. Abbott, too, had pocketed his pistol for the moment. "What will we do when we reach Howe's house?"

"First we will test the secretaries. And then we shall destroy the building with an eye to doing the same to the mill-works," Marcus said. "Westin, do you know where the horses might be kept?"

He did; Marcus gave instruction to him to leave the two of them at Howe's residence while he saddled and bridled the horses. Westin admitted that he did know how, but that he was unsure of whether the stablemen had been "turned." He feared to go alone.

"That raises an excellent point," Mr. Abbott said. "What if they turn one of us, unbeknownst to the others?"

"I do not think they can work so quickly," Marcus said.

"How do you know it?"

"If they might turn us so quickly, then we are lost," said Marcus. "Therefore, it cannot be so. This was a lesson that I learned in France, to ward against despair."

Mr. Abbott wheezed out a laugh. He was beginning to tire from struggling through the thickening snow; fortunately, they had almost reached the manager's residence.

The windows were dark and the building silent.

"Shall I go to the stables?" Westin asked.

"No," Marcus said. "You and Mr. Abbott are right in that we must fear being taken by those we suppose our allies. Perhaps they might even believe themselves as such, until their true nature is awakened."

They approached Howe's door, which was unlatched, and went inside. Closing the door after them, they hesitated on the threshold to listen for movement. Hearing nothing, they proceeded forwards, Marcus and Mr. Abbott now drawing the pistols and pulling back the firing pins.

The ground floor they found empty. Climbing the stairs to the study, they found the room abandoned and disarranged. More than a few books and ledgers had been removed, leaving behind empty shelves. Paper lay strewn across the floor. The monk-like desks near the windows had been cleared as well.

Mr. Abbott bent to the papers and began to take what he could from the floor.

"What are you doing?"

"Collecting their less valuable papers in the hopes that they might give us some clue to the more valuable ones that have been taken," Mr. Abbott said. "The question arises: why were they required to write so many letters, and to keep so many records? Answer: this is a millwork, and one presumes that the cloth manufactured here might go to any place, perhaps to spread whatever disease rages here."

"Whatever has occurred is more than a disease," Marcus said.

"And yet I do not know what else to call it," Mr. Abbott said wearily. Westin found him a leather satchel which had been overlooked, and the two men proceeded to fill it to the brim with loose paper and account books. Marcus picked up a sheet of paper from the floor: it was written in a language which he could not read, but that it chilled him to recognize. It was the same characters—which Lucy had presumed to be some sort of invented shorthand—that had been in his brother's journals.

He dropped the paper.

"We must abandon this place," Marcus said. "There is only one thing of any importance now. We must return to Penderbrook immediately and make Lucy flee to London, or to America, or to the North Pole."

"I agree with you," Mr. Abbott said.

Marcus said, "My brother's corpse hung down there like a pig on a hook, down in that cellar. There were a hundred bodies hung down there, if not four hundred, all of them as though they were waiting to be smoked for hams. My brother did not die at Penderbrook. He had long since been replaced by one of these monsters. What lay in the cellar at Penderbrook was one of these *things*. And now it is running loose."

Mr. Abbott shuddered. "And she has been keeping watch over the Earl at night, easily within arm's reach," he said. "Good God, Sewell. You are right."

Chapter Twenty

To Flee or Not to Flee

Mr. Abbott could not resist gathering a few more papers as they left the study. Quickly the two men dashed out of the house and to the stables, following Westin closely. Mr. Abbott's feet were sure and steady; there was no question of his falling now.

Westin reached the outside of the stables and pressed his head against the wall. "I hear nothing."

"We can only hope by Providence that it is abandoned and the horses are safe," Marcus said. "Otherwise, we are doomed."

"You have a curious notion about Providence," Mr. Abbott said. "In that you assume it will provide you exactly what you wish."

"We will discuss the matter later, when we are on the road," Marcus said. "In our carriage, being drawn by our horses."

Mr. Abbott barked a laugh.

Marcus slipped through a gap between the stable doors, pistol at the ready. He found himself unsurprised, yet shocked by what he saw: nearly a dozen horses lay in the center of the stable floor, where they had been butchered. And yet the smell of blood and death was not as thick as it should have been.

He turned and slid part of the door open, to allow the others to follow him more easily.

"'Ware the horses." He took up a pitchfork and prodded the side of one of the horses; the mass encountered by the tines was not mere flesh, but solid and wooden.

Where, then, did the smell of blood come from?

He soon found the body of his coachman in the back of one of the stalls. The man still lived, but only just. He whispered between his teeth, and Marcus bent forwards to hear what must prove his final words: "They are monsters...no cross, no silver..." The man relaxed, his hand revealing a silver crucifix. The man had been a secret Catholic, and had tried to defend himself with an article of his faith. Now he was dead.

In their hurry, the monsters had butchered the man and forgotten to replace him with one of their own—forgotten, or found themselves unprepared. After the man drew his final breath, Marcus lay him flat on the ground to investigate his wounds. His abdomen had been torn asunder. It was no clean-edged blade which had done the damage; neither was there sign of shot or powder. The damage seemed to have been caused by a claw or tooth of some kind. The man's cavities were filled with blood and other mortal material. Marcus then pressed down on the man's chest; the lungs compressed as they normally would.

Neither of the other men asked what he was doing.

"They replaced the horses," Marcus said, "But did not yet have time to replace the man."

"Without the horses we are trapped!" Westin cried.

Marcus stood from the coachman's corpse, wiping his hands on some clean straw. Then he exited the stall to review the center of the barn. In a moment he saw that which he sought: hoofmarks, which led to the back doors of the stable.

"To me!" he said, throwing open one of the doors and plunging out into the snow.

The coachman had only just been killed; therefore, the horses had only just been replaced, and there was some chance of their still living.

They followed hoofmarks through the alley behind the stables, passing the tavern where they had found Westin and Smith earlier. The tavern's back door lay open onto darkness.

The trail led into a square with a small stone war memorial, a raised stone platform with a carved stone urn in the center, the hoofmarks disappearing in the deep snow near it.

Marcus swore, loud and long, kicking clumps of snow to break them.

Mr. Abbott stared at the hoof-marks. Westin strode through the snow, saying that the marks would resume on the other side of the square. They did not.

Marcus finally regained control of himself. He and Mr. Abbott watched Westin desperately searching the other end of the square.

"And now that the horses are gone?" Mr. Abbott asked in a low voice, lest the snow carry it.

"I was hoping you might advise me," said Marcus.

Mr. Abbott shook his head. "Soon it will become dark, and if we do not go to a place of safety, we will die. If we *do* go to a place of safety, we will still likely die."

"And Lucy?"

"Is likely already dead."

"Then we will find a place of safety, and we will fight," Marcus declared. "Or else we will spend our lives in a foolish attempt to destroy the mill-works, this entire town if possible. Well? I am up for it, although I do not like you leave you alone without me."

"And Westin?"

"I do not think he will survive without us. We should use his strength with ours as long as we can," Marcus said.

Mr. Abbott said, "It has come time to tell you another thing, one I hoped to never speak of to another living soul."

"What is it?"

"I have learnt the language," said Mr. Abbott, in tones of utter regret. "It came to me in dreams, after once I had heard it spoken. I fear that it has twisted my mind."

"That is no light matter," Marcus said.

Mr. Abbott watched Westin turn about in the snow, his eyes bulging as he realized that the horses had not traveled through the square, that they were truly lost. "But there is more. I have looked into your brother's laboratory after his death, in the hopes of discovering something that might be of aid in this dark time."

"And did you?"

"I may have done. It will destroy this town. It may take the entire district with us. It may take all of England...it may destroy the universe, for all I know. But your brother made note of a...he called it a 'theory,' but what it was, was a dark ritual."

"Of what sort? Of the butchery that my father performed those long years ago?"

"No, worse. If I read it correctly, which I may not have done, your brother being the genius that he was, even in his final madness, it would cause an irritation to the nature of time itself."

Marcus tried to keep a reasonable expression upon his face. "I do not understand you, sir."

"This red fungus that your brother studied. You will agree that he knew as much regarding it as anyone alive."

"I will."

"Then you might also agree, conditionally, that when he said it came from outside Creation itself, that he might be correct?"

"Conditionally," Marcus said, puzzled. Whatever conclusion Mr. Abbott might be leading towards, he could not anticipate.

"Creation is that which was created by the Divine," Mr. Abbott said. "Unlike the Divine, Creation is not infinite; it has beginning and end. And when something such as the red fungus—this was your brother's theory—comes from outside Creation, it must necessarily come from outside the time in which Creation exists."

"I suppose it may be so," Marcus said. "Really, though, I cannot comprehend such things. Let us say that the red fungus comes from outside Creation and leave it at that."

"But it is an important point," Mr. Abbott said. Over by the memorial, Westin was beginning to calm himself; Mr. Abbott began to speak more rapidly. "For if this ritual is performed correctly, then time itself will become irritated, and close up around this irritation, sealing it away like an oyster with a grain of sand, as a sort of pearl."

"And what of us?" Marcus asked.

"Dead—destroyed," Mr. Abbott said. "Sealed up with the rest of this madness, for all eternity."

Marcus laughed, then brushed the snow out of his hair. "As though I have not felt that everything that has happened since my return from France to be an illusion! Why not? Will it save Lucy? What is the ritual?"

"It is unpleasant," Mr. Abbott said, "and I think I am the only one who can do it. I shall have to summon more of the red fungus here, enough to upset the balance of the universe, so Creation will seal up around it. Or it will not. Your brother never had the opportunity to test his theory."

Now Marcus paused. "That sounds ill, to bring more of the red fungus here."

"It may be," Mr. Abbott said. "Although—" He shook his head. "I fear that I am already lost. The whispering in my head...that language...I fear that I am not entirely myself."

"And yet I cut you, and you bled."

"And yet," Mr. Abbott said, "at times when I wake in the morning, I dream that I am not where I am, but elsewhere, in a darkened, airless place. To my right and my left are other still, pale forms, which, to my horror seem just on the verge of being able to move. Then I feel something tearing, and I wake in my own bed. I think my end approaches, no matter what I do. I have eaten the fungus in my bread for months now, and heard the language, and read the journals."

Marcus felt a chill. "And Lucy? Is it too late for her as well?"

"I cannot say. I hope it is not."

They both turned towards Westin, who now walked towards them, dragging his feet dejectedly through the snow. They only had another moment's uninterrupted conversation, before the man would hear their low voices.

Mr. Abbott grimaced. "I fear that he is a spy amongst us, unwitting though he may be."

"He bled," said Marcus.

"And yet," Mr. Abbott said. "We whisper as he approaches."

"We do," Marcus agreed grimly.

Westin finally arrived beside them, asking what they were to do now that they were trapped in Little Millwich for the night: fight or hide?

"We must bring Mr. Abbott to the millworks," Marcus said, "for he has discovered a way that we might yet be saved."

"How?" Westin asked.

"By the power of prayer," Marcus said. "Mr. Abbott is very devout."

"You cannot go in there!" cried Westin, eyes wide. "We know that they have been alerted against us! We will all be killed!"

Marcus drew the man aside. Mr. Abbott threw his arms up towards the heavens and began to pray loudly.

Marcus said, "He is a secret Catholic. He believes he can perform an exorcism against the evils in the mill."

Westin shook his head. "Whatever horrors have come here, they do not belong to the Devil. It is something worse than that."

"There can be nothing worse than the Devil," said Marcus sternly, although he did not himself believe it.

Westin only gave him such a look as would have chilled a man not already in flight from monsters, or standing in the snow.

Marcus added, "You and I will discover the stores of lamp oil or some other flammable material, and use Mr. Abbott's devotions as a distraction. We may not live, but I do not intend to die in vain. As for yourself, you may flee from this place, once you have told me where I may find the oil."

Westin only shook his head. "I do not like this, my lord. The three of us should flee to the road as we may...take from Howe's house as many blankets and as much food as we wish, and make our way to the next village or farmhouse."

"You may do so," Marcus said. "As long as you tell me where I might find the oil stores."

Westin rubbed the back of his neck. "My lord, I do not know where they might be. I know where the coal is, but it is guarded by the monsters, as you discovered when you were here previously." At Marcus's sharp glance, Westin added, "We millworkers have spoken of little else, my lord."

"And the oil?"

"I do not know, my lord, I swear it."

"What is in the cellar of the second millworks?"

"Only old equipment, my lord. But we do not descend there, either. It is not safe."

Westin continued to rub the back of his neck.

Marcus said, "What will you do, then?"

"Do?"

"While Mr. Abbott and I attempt to destroy the mill. Will you help us, or will you flee?"

The two of them looked out into the blizzard that had was now sweeping through the square.

"I cannot flee," Westin said bitterly. "I cannot. I cannot flee. Not into that snowstorm."

"Will you hide, then?"

"I..."

It had come down to *that* moment, one that Marcus was intimately familiar with. When faced with the choice of how to proceed in the face of death, some men turned coward. Marcus put a hand on the big man's shoulder. Westin had faced the cellar easily enough, but *that* moment did not always come when mortal danger was first encountered. Often it came the second time, or the third, when one knew more of fear.

Marcus knew full well what sort of grandiose statement worked best in circumstances such as these. "If we must die, we will die like men. We will find the oil and burn this place to the ground."

The fact that the two of them were to provide a distraction for Mr. Abbott and his work, rather than the reverse, was not a fact that Marcus chose, at that time, to mention.

Chapter Twenty-One
Something Is Coming

Marcus and Mr. Abbott walked together, Mr. Abbott struggling with his footing, but refusing any assistance. Westin was behind them, dragging his feet.

The lane leading back to the millworks was thick with snow, but not yet impassable. The snow was broken by markings that seemed at one moment to come from snakes or lizards, and the next to come from birds making large hops. Here and there were traces of red fungus, smudged against the snow.

Marcus shivered. What mad army would they see at the mill?

"How long do you need us to distract them?" Marcus asked Mr. Abbott.

"As long as you can give me."

Marcus had asked as much of his men before, knowing that he was sending them to their deaths. Rather than dreading what lay before him, he found himself walking even faster, outpacing both Westin and Mr. Abbott. Mr. Abbott required of Marcus only that he cause as much trouble as possible; trouble was Marcus's especial talent. His company of men had always been the one to be sent in, if some commander needed a supply line fouled, or reports confused, or a supply of cannon shot to disappear, or a thousand men suddenly all become quite ill. It was the sort of thing Marcus loved. He did not love the Army, but he did love the work he had sometimes been able to do for it, and he found himself resisting the urge to whistle as he approached the mill.

The snow had made the last of the day bright with whiteness, yet too dim to make anything out. None of either of the mill buildings' windows were lit, although it must be dark indeed within. The ground showed a tangled pattern of odd and inhuman tracks, most of which led to one of the doors. The door must have been opened quite recently, for a half-moon had been dragged across the surface of the snow, and was still visible. But now it was tightly shut.

He strode towards the door and tested it: it was locked and bolted. He pounded on it with his fist. "Open up!"

There was no response, which pleased him. Now he dug down under the snow and found a stone from the lane, and threw it at the nearest window, one he might easily climb through. In London or some larger town, one might expect the windows to be barred or otherwise protected, but not in Little Millwich. It was a more innocent place—in some ways, at least.

The stone was large, the window fragile, the sound muffled by the falling snow, but nonetheless startling.

Westin arrived at Marcus's side and quickly began searching through the snow for another stone. Mr. Abbott did not appear. Marcus hoped the man was sneaking around to another entrance, but he did not allow himself to look. Instead he used the butt of Mr. Abbott's pistol to smash the glass from the window before him. Westin walked to the window he had broken and kicked out the glass with the bottom of one boot.

Marcus shouted through the window, "I'll not be denied my property!"

He could see no movement. He swung one leg over the sill and stepped inside. Beside him, Westin did the same.

The room was nearly lightless. He could see the hulking forms of machines before him in the darkness, although they were eerily silent.

"Westin!"

"My lord!"

He could see a silhouette at the window beside him as Westin stepped inside. The silhouette of the man looked familiar enough.

"Where is the lamp oil kept?"

"I do not know, my lord!"

"Then we shall search for it!" Marcus strode into the room. In his pocket he had a flint and steel, which he fingered. Besides the oil, he wished for a supply of gunpowder and shot, both to reload the pistol and to use for setting a fire. Even loose cotton might do, in a pinch.

Before him lay a row of what he thought might be looms. He was no expert, but the machines appeared to take in a comb of threads on one side and put out a heavy roll of cloth on the other. Overhead were the rods and gears that carried the motion of the millwheel to each of the machines. In turning, each rod drove large wooden cogs the size of a whisky barrel, to which the heavy belt of each machine was attached. He remembered the room from his tour now. If the rods had been turning, it would have been the easiest game in the world to foul the works from one end of the room to the other.

He heard the slightest whisper of movement in the darkness, and pretended he had not. Instead, he drew his knife from inside his coat and, still holding the pistol at the ready, slashed across the roll of fabric which the loom had produced, cutting it lose.

"Lift that bolt out," he ordered Westin.

Westin pulled a pin that released the bolt from the machine, and slid it off a long rod. "What will we do, my lord?"

"Whatever we like. What do you think, Westin? If we were upstairs where the spinning machines were, we would surely be able to set the building afire using the bales of cotton which are stacked there, awaiting their transformation into thread. Here, we have fewer options, the fabric being much less unruly than the unprocessed cotton. What do you suggest?"

"I...I do not know, my lord."

Marcus took the bolt of cotton fabric that Westin carried, raveled the edge nearest him, and sparked at it with flint and tinder. It soon began to smolder.

"Do not let that go out."

"No, my lord," Westin said nervously.

They walked deeper into the shadows. Behind them the light flickered: their attackers had crossed between them and the windows. If some sort of trouble did not occur to him soon, they would be killed.

Marcus had the sense of being closed in upon; overhead, one of the rods pinged as some thing shifted its weight upon it.

Westin blew harder upon the smoldering cloth, and a flame briefly brightened their visages.

"For God's sake!" called a voice on the far side of the room. "It is the son of the Earl! Hold your fire!"

The room came to light, as the front panels of several lanterns were removed: about a dozen men had surrounded them on every side, each man holding an improvised weapon. On the opposite end of the room were a group of huddled women and children.

Marcus looked the men over admiringly. "You defend yourselves well."

"Are you still human?"

"I am."

"Where is your proof?"

Marcus lowered the firing pin on the pistol and pocketed it, then drew his dagger and cut himself on the back of his left hand, holding up his hand and letting the blood run down into his sleeve. Westin did the same, although with a greater hesitation.

Marcus asked, "And what about all of you?"

"We have all been watching each other," said one.

"Then you have all been turned!" Westin exclaimed. "And are lying!"

"Don't be a fool," Marcus said.

One of the men lifted his arm and cut a thin, dripping line along it, holding it close to one of the lanterns so that Westin could see. Westin touched his fingers to the blood, then nodded.

A sigh of relief was exhaled by all. But they were no nearer to salvation.

Marcus said, "Now we must plot to destroy this place." And he explained what he wished to do. The men and women exclaimed against this: to burn the mill was to put them all in danger, if not of being burnt alive, then of starvation.

Finally, Westin cried, "I do not like it myself, but every second we delay is an opportunity for the situation to become worse than it already is. We are already in danger of more than mere death!"

Marcus put a hand on his arm, and Westin refrained from saying anything further to the small crowd before them. Instead, Marcus drew several of the foremen aside and told them what they had found in the cellar. Most of the men were less than surprised.

Marcus concluded, "Whatever good might be found in Little Millwich, it has been perverted and rendered unclean. If we are to prevent whatever horror occurs here from spreading, it must be destroyed."

The workers' lives had already been put up as stakes in a game that none of them could play, or benefit from playing—win or lose.

But Marcus was their lord's only living son, and his heir. If Marcus wished Little Millwich burnt to cinders, burnt it would be.

After receiving a promise that their families would be brought to Penderbrook and housed there if need be, they began to prepare. The lamp oil was found, and likewise several loads of cotton bales which had only just arrived at the mill, and not yet brought upstairs for the spinners. It was the matter of moments for an enormous bonfire to be readied. In a moment, they would start the blaze, then flee to the nearby tavern, which could be closed up tightly, and which held food stores that did not resemble those found in the cellar of the church.

From the windows, one of the men called, "Something is coming."

"What is it?"

"A man? I think it is a man."

"Douse the lights."

The room became utterly dark.

Marcus walked towards the windows. The snow was descending as hard as ever. A man was indeed running towards them, wearing a heavy coat and holding a pistol. The man paused in front of the millworks, looking this way, then that. He peered towards the windows but did not look at any of his watchers particularly; it was obvious that he did not see them.

The man before them strode towards the locked, bolted door and tested it, ignoring the two broken windows. "Open up!"

Then the man bent down into the snow, then straightened up, holding a stone in his hand, which he threw at one of the already-broken windows.

It was as if the stone struck the glazing of the window, shattering it—but the glass that fell from the window did not land on the floor below it.

Westin, standing next to Marcus now, gave a start. He cried, "Watch out!"

Behind the man who had just thrown the stone was a blur of darkness. Marcus squinted, but could not make out what was behind him. Whatever it was, it was immense.

Then two red shadows curled around the man in a half-circle, and he bellowed in surprise. Then he vanished into the snow, leaving two trails from his boots behind him. The red half-circle drew back, and the shadow shot upwards with a sound like a sail snapping in a high breeze.

Man and monster, both gone.

From overhead came a roar—the sound of something more than human giving voice—something as immense as the millworks itself. The unbroken windows shivered, then burst, as a force struck them all, knocking men and machines and glass all astray.

A chime of shattering glass rang throughout the building. Shards of it fell in front of Marcus, slashing downwards into the snow like icicles falling from the roof. Next to him, Westin began to lean out of the already-broken window, thinking himself safe.

Marcus pulled him back just as a large shard of glass sliced into the snow in front of them. "'Ware the glazing upstairs," he said.

More glass continued to fall.

Then the darkness was broken by the first sign of hope that Marcus had seen that day: the snow outside turned orange and began to flicker.

Marcus took a deep breath and smelled smoke.

The millworks were on fire.

Westin swore. "So that's where Mr. Abbott went, not to pray! He must've found something good, to make such an explosion!"

"We must evacuate," Marcus said calmly, turning towards the millworkers behind him. "Bring the women and children together, with the men around them. Bring what weapons you have, and come quickly. All of you, walk towards the taverns together, and do not look back until you are inside."

In the few short moments before the group was ready to exit, the ceiling of the room filled with smoke, and the heat increased in a way which caused the workers to press towards the door. The men shoved themselves into place, bristling with knives and iron rods.

"Open the door!" Marcus shouted. The door opened, and the millworkers began to stream out. "Stay together!"

"They're moving too far to the right, my lord!" cried Westin, from the window.

"Stop them!"

Westin jumped out the window and disappeared into the snow.

Marcus looked behind him as one of the doors within the mill burst open, and a spill of red monsters burst out, surrounded by smoke.

Time to go.

Marcus turned back to the window, stepping—

Chapter Twenty-Two

The Opportunity Which Has Been Afforded

—OUT INTO A PATCH of unbroken snow in the center of the square holding the memorial.

Marcus blinked. His eyes stung from fine flakes of snow, which was so white, and which so completely surrounded him, that he could not see more than the edges of the square. And yet he was certain of where he found himself, for the small memorial and its stone urn were not to be mistaken.

He turned in a slow circle. The mill buildings, which rose above the other buildings nearby, were not afire. He could only just see the stable; likewise, the church had not been disturbed, and there was no smell of smoke in the air from its burning.

In a muffled tone, the church bells rang twice. It was two o'clock in the afternoon.

It could not be only two o'clock in the afternoon, not when a moment ago, it had been past sunset.

What had Mr. Abbott done?

Something sped through the snow of the lane behind him; he turned to see it, but he was too slow, and the snow too thick, for him to get a sense of it. It was white, that was all he knew, and, other than the whisper as it moved through the snow, deadly silent.

There was a bang. The back door of the stable, a dim shape in the whiteness, opened with a rattle and scrape. Marcus stood where he was, mouth agape, and watched eight horses—their own four, and four others—running towards him.

He put out a hand and whistled, and one of the horses turned towards him and came to a stop. Marcus put a boot onto the dais of the memorial and leapt onto the back of the horse that had stopped for him. The other horses all pressed in close, whickering and nodding at him, stamping at the ground.

Save us, they seemed to say.

Movement approached the square from all sides. He could see the movement but not that which made it, for the creatures were as white as their surroundings, other than a few red smears which were soon brushed off by the snow.

He knew where he was now: the past.

The three of them—he, Mr. Abbott, and Westin—would soon be approaching. But what would happen when they arrived?

He could not save them, he knew: it was Mr. Abbott's ritual which had afforded him this opportunity, and he dared not overturn it.

He gripped the horse with his thighs, leaned forwards, and urged it to run out of the square in the direction of the road to Penderbrook. The horse was glad to obey, and the other horses followed it speedily.

He had to get to Lucy, and find some way to save her, and himself with her, if he could manage it.

A white shape reached for him, and his horse kicked out, striking something that was flung away. Another of the horses screamed.

Marcus pressed tighter and lower against the horse's neck, refusing to look back.

A curtain of snowflakes hit him in the face as he and the horse removed themselves from the square, blinding him. He wiped his face against his shoulder to try to clear his eyes. It did no good. He released one hand from the horse's mane to wipe at his eyes—

—AND THE NEXT THING he knew, he was straightening up from one of the stools in Barnabas's workshop. His back was weary and his eyes strained against the dim light. He knew, somehow, that he had been reading there for hours, although he had no sense of coldness, thirst, or hunger, only a certain stiffness. He stretched and found himself less sore than he feared.

He had been reading his brother's journals, the last of which ended two weeks before his brother's death. Therefore, a final journal there must be, leading up to his brother's final days, if not hours: but where was it?

Marcus turned around in a slow circle. Lucy had told him that he was reading the last of the journals; therefore, she must not have found another. And she *would* have looked.

She would have patiently searched the room and its hundreds of drawers and shelves. She was the patient sort who would tell herself that she was putting Barnabas's things back in order, but her tidying-up would be driven by curiosity, not a desire for order.

Marcus therefore eyed the room for a hiding place that would not occur to her: not with the other ledgers and journals; not with the samples; not with the instruments. It would not be placed along one of the top shelves, which were easy enough to see from the top of one of the stools.

Calmly, Marcus walked downstairs to the lower part of the boathouse.

Lucy was curiosity itself, but she was also short.

Marcus walked to one of the small rowboats still hung on a set of hooks along the wall above the water, and brushed a hand along its upper surface. A shape hidden from view brushed against his fingers, a wire leading behind the rowboat.

He fumbled around until he was able to pull up that which had been hidden out of Lucy's reach: the last journal.

He returned to the laboratory, where his lantern still burnt, and opened the journal. The strange, unworldly shorthand that his brother had begun to use were mixed together, more shorthand than English.

And yet Marcus found himself able to read the full text. In fact, he had been reading it for some time, as he had read the other journals: but he would not consider that now.

The first page of the journal read:

The fungus known as ergot has long been a plague running through the English countryside, but it is only with the red fungus that it has reached the pinnacle of its design. Or is it proper to call the work of Nature a design? I find it increasingly difficult to put faith in a Creator, when it Is easily to be seen that that Being's so-called Works are filled with error, false starts, abortions, and other mistakes of a thousand different sorts. If there is a Creator, then that Creator is a being more of opportunity and trial than ever It was of Perfection.

Marcus thought that it was no wonder Barnabas had taken to writing almost exclusively in his odd form of shorthand, for he wrote such blas-phemies!

He continued:

The red fungus has the ability to cloud men's minds. This is true of any ergot, and many other substances besides. But the level of perfection the red fungus reaches has not previously been seen. It does not cause mania and derangement in Man or Beast, but only a sense of worry, of urgency; that urgency becomes applied to activities which help spread the fungus and help it to reproduce.

Where before ergot-infested grain would be destroyed, now it is hoarded, lest some famine strike and leave the infected starving.

Where common ergot causes seizures, diarrhoea, nausea, and vomiting as the flesh attempts to rid itself of the poisonous alkaloids and other toxins that are absorbed from the ergot kernels, the red fungus causes none of these symptoms, but rather a sense of brief well-being and security. Bread which is made with the red fungus feels more filling. Walking through a field infected with red fungus likewise leads to a feeling of contentment and calm.

However, if one over-eats, the effects of the red fungus's toxins become more familiar, but can be passed off as simple greed. Eat too much, linger too long in the fields—and one is "punished," as it were.

Grain which is infected with red fungus does not produce noticeably less grain yield than uninfected grain; in fact, the fungus seems to increase the yields, swelling the individual grains. This increase is a false one. However, to separate the fungus from the grain is impossible, even if one mills it.

In other words, the fungus has perfectly adapted itself, not only to prevent its destruction, but to make itself desirable. It appears to be well along a path to becoming a partner of the human and the grains which support it, in a kind of circular system.

In fact, the red fungus appears to adapt itself to whatever it infects, becoming, on the whole, more beneficial than otherwise. It has come to infect many of the trees in the woods surrounding Penderbrook. The red fungus works itself into the soil at the roots of the trees and forms a mass there which attracts ants, beetles, earthworms, and other insects. The insects carry the red fungus all over the tree; the fungus forms a thin film on the leaves and along the branches, and protects the trees from cutting insects (having increased the amount of alkaloids that it excretes while found on leaves—but not while in the soil), and in turn is allowed to sprout microscopic fruits: as the wind plays in the leaves, the spores of the red fungus are spread. The tree receives an increase in the life-giving elements which sustain it at the root, as the insects and worms frequent them; in turn, it provides support for the fungus, so that it might spread its spores further than it would otherwise do. But, again, there is a point at which the red fungus overwhelms the natural cycle: birds disappear from the area, or sicken and become weak, especially their nestlings. I have seen a number of nestlings push their weakened counterparts from the nest to die on the ground below. I have examined many birds I believe have been killed in this fashion. The survivors seem all the stronger, however, for having ejected their weaker brothers from the nest, and come to dominate their territories. But once the red fungus has spread too much, all the birds leave, often in a great, swooping mass that seems ordinary enough if one is watching a flock of starlings at dusk, but can seem rather shocking when viewing owls in daylight. I suspect the local bats of being similarly affected.

—A note, I should investigate the possibility that the red fungus can prevent the spread of rabies. In woods infected by the red fungus, I seem to think—although I may be imagining things—that the incidence of that fell disease is lessened, if not eradicated entirely.

Another curiosity which I have noted is the fact that, upon afternoons in which I have lost myself within Nature, attempting to coax from it a few precious, if humble, secrets, I have suffered the strangest sort of vision upon several occasions.

In short, I have seen myself!

It happens when I am in the woods and straighten up to ease the strain on my back, from bending over to search among the roots, and discover another man wandering among the trees. I will give him a halloo only to see him straighten up, stretch to ease the pain in his back, then glance towards me and start. If I am wearing a hat, he will wear a hat as well, and his will be in form and color most similar to mine. If I tie a red scarf upon one arm, he will be wearing one also. But as soon as I attempt to approach him, he will vanish.

When this happens, I often find myself in a different location than I last remembered, or discover that I have (according to the angle of the sun) gained a second hour in which to lose myself. I do so most contentedly—what man of science does not wish he had additional time in which to conduct his studies?

But I wonder, too, whether I am wise to do so. I suspect that my sense of well-being is merely the effect of the red fungus upon my nerves, and that if it not for its presence, I should be entirely terrified!

The journal entry ended; after the slash of a pen across the center of the page, another one began:

After finishing my previous entry, it occurred to me that the several items which have puzzled me lately might be due to the presence of the red fungus and its effect upon my nerves. I began to investigate them, and discovered that which I should have feared, but did not. The matter involves the red fungus only indirectly.

What I have learned is in regards to the Earl, my father.

Down in the wine cellar, there is a sort of natural cave to which a wrought-iron gate has been added, to protect those vintages which are most dear. Among the Sewell family, that is counted as all of them! While the beer and whisky are not worried over (and can be obtained if only one might have the use of the cellar key for a few moments, as my brother has so often discovered), the wines and brandies are considered to be of a more precious nature, and are put into the cave. This cave goes back two dozen feet into the bedrock of Penderbrook, and no further—or so, at least, I had previously believed.

Now I know better. The cave runs not only the extent of the house, but beyond it to the northwest. In fact, the cave vents to the folly which the Earl had built in that direction, and can be reached through a disguised entrance.

The cave—I know not how far it travels altogether—holds something more precious to the Penderbrooks than wine or brandy. It holds secrets.

I discovered the further extent of the cave by accident, after seeing red footprints on the floor of the wine cave, and, after much searching and tapping, discovered the secret of opening its door.

I crept inside, carrying only a candle, with the strongest trepidation.

Within the cave were several tunnels. Following a soft sound, I soon discovered a most singular creature in one of the tunnels.

The creature was the size of a man, and formed generally in its shape, possessing a head, torso, and limbs. It even had a face of sorts: eyes, nose, mouth. But the face could not form itself into that language which most men speak without sound, and had no expression. The skin was unbroken, and completely smooth.

It was blind, hairless, and white, so white that I could not think of it as having been formed from the same flesh that I was. It tried to hide from me, behind a narrow curve in one of the tunnels. I was so startled upon discovering the creature that I stumbled, and my candle, which I had brought with me to search the cellar, nearly went out. I was lucky it did not; I wonder what would have become of me, if the thing in the caves was able to sense my location, and I could not see it. I have no doubt that it could see in the dark, for even though its eyes were not able to be opened, it seemed to find the light of the lantern almost blinding. As I looked at it to where it had fled, it pulled a dark cloth from some hidden cache and tied it about its head, covering itself from forehead to the tip of its nose.

Then it moaned, an eerie sound, and straightened up, holding its hands out in front of it, and stumbling towards me.

I took several steps backwards, and it moaned louder, as if to cry, "Please, do not go!"

I struck the opposite wall of the tunnel and came to a halt. The creature continued to stumble closer to me, and I was able to see that the creature, despite its general outline, was not, could not, have been human, although I shall not describe the monstrous differences here. It was clear to me in a flash—as unworldly as I am, I am not precisely ignorant—that the creature before me had its use rooted in the needs of men, and not in the necessities of Nature. It obviously had been designed or crafted.

Blushing in shame, I took off my coat and handed it to the creature, who took it and clutched it to itself. It did not know what to do with the coat! I took the coat back, and guided its limbs into the sleeves. When I was done, it held out its hands to me and cooed at me in an enquiring fashion.

I felt revulsion towards the creature, which surely did not deserve it. It reached for me, and I shook my head, waving both hands in front of myself, hoping that the creature could comprehend my denial.

It stopped, tilted its head, and enquired again: "Ooo?"

"No," said I.

"Ooo?" it repeated, waving at itself, offering its flesh.

"I thank you, but no. I have come here for another matter."

In a slightly different tone, it cooed again, then pointed further into the cave. I nodded, and the thing seemed pleased. It began to walk further down the tunnel, towards what I knew not.

Soon it had led me to another alcove, this one blocked by a wooden door with a heavy lock on its outside, to which I did not have the key.

The creature cooed at me. I shook my head again to indicate that this was not what I wanted. From behind the door I heard the rustle of movement, but it was clear that whatever that door was locked against, had not the force to come through.

The creature's shoulders dropped, and it lowered its head. I think that it rather dreaded whatever it was about to show me, and had hoped that I wished something—anything—other than that which it must now offer me.

We followed another offshoot of the cavern. This one was longer, and we traveled at least twenty feet before the creature squatted down and scraped some handfuls of pebbles back from the floor. Then it scuttled backwards, to the edge of the light.

I could not quite see what it was the creature presented to me. I crouched low, and brought the candle close to bear.

Below us was a fruiting body of what appeared to be the red fungus. I brushed more of the loose pebbles away to discover that the fruiting body extended for nearly six feet.

The fruiting body was in the form of a man, if a man were to lie before me as an anatomical sketch, skinless and exposed. Here was "flesh"; there was "bone." The bone had a different texture than the flesh, and the flesh from the deep purple "organs."

I wondered if it was a man who had been infested by the fungus, the way the wheat could be so infested? Or was this "man" a creature designed, much the way the one before me had been designed? And if so, for what purpose?

I took out my knife and scraped a small sample, which I put into an empty jar. I am always carrying small specimen jars with me, a useful habit indeed to have adopted in this case. As I took the scraping, at first the creature who had shown the "man" to me whimpered, as if in fear and terror, but as it proved that I only wished to take a sample, the creature seemed to realize what I was doing. (I, however, did not!) When I had finished taking the sample, the creature began to cover the "man" with pebbles again, and I helped it to do so. When the figure had been hidden to the creature's satisfaction, it pointed back towards the entrance to the cave, then away from it, again cooing a question: Which way did I wish to go?

I pointed away from the entrance I knew, and was led to the opposite exit. At that point, the creature disappeared back into the shadows, cooing pleasantly and still wearing my coat. The exit was small, a tight squeeze indeed. I crawled upwards, muddy and slipping, through the narrow stone hole, and exclaimed out loud to find myself in the most unexpected part of the folly. I remained until I had discovered the secret of unlocking this door as well, then climbed out into the gray haze of fog which now passes for daylight.

The Earl knows of the secret cavern. He knows of the creature (of this I have no doubt). He knows of the doors, and of the secrets to opening them. He knows of the figure buried beneath the pebbles.

That which is hidden by the wine cave might have existed for generations—but the folly is relatively new.

I will speak to him about these things. I am trying to recall who built the folly itself; I should ask Barton, who has been at Penderbrook long enough to know.

If I do not continue this journal—and I suspect it will be either Lucy or (if he should ever return in sober enough state to investigate) Marcus who will read this—then you have my permission to suspect that I have been struck down in violence for the offense of my inquiry.

Or, well, something worse may always have occurred.

Chapter Twenty-Three

The Footprints

THE JOURNAL ENTRY ENDED with a slash of ink; the rest of the page was empty. With a trembling hand, Marcus reached to turn the page. That which followed was blank.

He had not forgotten that his brother had died—or, rather, that some sort of fleshy body had appeared to die, and had been brought down to the wine cave in the cellar. He had not forgotten what he had seen in the cellar of the church. But that he should here meet with proof that his brother had written no more, shocked him.

A sudden grief finally came upon him, in its fullest form. His brother was truly dead. Marcus wept.

Uselessly, with blurred vision, he continued turning the blank pages. The remaining leaves in the journal were all the same: blank. His brother had hidden the journal atop the boat, gone to confront the Earl, their father, and—had perished. The meat of his body had been taken to the mill and hung there, to feed the workers who remained human. A substitution had been awakened and sent to take his place, returning to Penderbrook, and appearing as Barnabas, fooling everyone until it, too, had been killed.

Or had it been killed? *Was it dead?* Or had it only seemed so, waiting until Marcus had returned and had seen it, then sat up in the darkness, stumbled as it climbed off the corking table, and gone into the secret tunnel and out again, via the folly?

Now Marcus's grief turned to rage, and he began to smash everything in the laboratory, which did nothing to soothe his emotions and even less to reduce the madness of the situation.

When he had finally regained control of himself and repaired as much of the damage of his distress as he could, it was dark and his lantern had gone out. He returned the journal to its hiding place atop the boat, not because he wished to hide it from Lucy, but because he did not wish it to be known that he had found it.

Finally, the chill reached him, and thirst, and hunger.

He emerged from the boathouse and turned his feet towards Penderbrook: but he could not force himself to take a single step in that direction.

His father, the Earl, was there, and today he could not endure the thought of having to confront the man, to see him, or even to sense his presence.

Why had his father done as he had done?

Marcus did not wish to know.

But was Lucy there, keeping guard over the man, feeding him, *cleaning* the foul beast, inside the grandest of all country houses? The thought was repugnant. If he was to save her from Penderbrook and his father, he must first rescue her from the house itself.

Yet he could not, at that moment, force himself even to begin to do it.

"Lucy," he said. "I cannot take another step forwards, even to save you. I *cannot.*"

In the last dim shreds of twilight, he saw a few of the windows lit by candlelight. The nursery itself was dark. The outer door at the kitchen opened, throwing an orange glow across the snow, then closed. The light in the kitchen lingered for a few moments, then passed out of the room, the dull glow moving to another window, then fading out entirely.

Had someone just entered?

The snow had ceased falling, and the wind had likewise died down. The clouds had begun to clear, revealing a few stars here and there, but it was not yet dark enough to see them *all*.

How had he come to be here? The last thing he remembered before he had straightened up in the laboratory had been taking the horses and riding from Little Millwich. He remembered crossing out of the square; he remembered the scream of one of the horses behind him, as it likely had been pulled down by one of the pale monsters.

And then?

He had supposed that Mr. Abbott's ritual had taken effect. He little understood what was to happen, if all went well, only that it was to have afforded them the opportunity to get Lucy away from Penderbrook.

A blink, and it had given him the horses. And then, with another blink, it had returned him through a blizzard to Penderbrook.

But *when*?

The blizzard had indeed occurred, which was a timepiece of sorts: the deep, unbroken snow, which glittered as the moon revealed itself, proved that snow had fallen. The snow had blown into drifts that clung to the side of the boathouse and along the lee-sides of the trees. In places the ground had even been blown nearly bare.

The icy lake itself had been swept clean, all but for a line of white footprints across the center. The footprints were of a man wearing boots. With a start, Marcus realized that the footprints had come *from* the center of the lake.

Marcus walked through the snow towards the edge of the pond, squinting into the dimness.

The footprints disappeared under the snow when they reached the shore. Marcus bent over and began scraping away the thin layer of snow, to see whether any trace of them remained.

Behind him, he heard the crunch of footsteps on snow. He straightened and turned: he expected, almost certainly, to see a ghost.

But it was the opposite of a ghost, a man of such flesh and blood that the possibility of his being merely a spirit was out of the question. It was Barton.

"My lord? I thought you at Little Millwich to-day."

"I have only just returned," Marcus said.

Barton gave him a glance that said *And how that might have been accomplished, in absence of a carriage, I certainly would not know—unless you did not leave at all, but sent Mr. Abbott in your place.* It was an eloquent sort of look, full at first of disbelief; then, Barton's expression smoothed itself: *Whatever you say, my lord, shall henceforth be treated as true.*

Barton bowed. "Cook has prepared a supper for the house, and I will warm you some wine." He turned towards the house.

Marcus said, "One moment, Barton. Take a look out at the lake."

Barton turned to look, then visibly started. "It appears as though someone has walked out of—my lord, excuse me. But it seems as though someone has walked out of the lake itself, during a blizzard and with wet boots, no less, or the snow would not have clung to them like that."

Marcus held one foot next to the nearest of the footprints. "The size of them indicates a full-grown man, even a tall one. It is only October, and it has only just begun to freeze properly. Can the ice be so thick?"

"I have been warning the men away from it; there is always one or two of the younger men who wants to try his hand too early at ice-fishing and ends up freezing nigh unto death. If it had been the pond, perhaps it would have frozen enough. But here?"

Together they stared at the lake, squinting through the darkness to see if the ice at the center had been cracked and refrozen. But the dusk was too dim for either man's eyes to be sure.

Barton stood next to the nearest footprint, turned, and placed his foot against the other, being careful not to step upon it. "It is a larger boot than mine," he said, then took a step backwards. The ice at the edge of the lake was thick enough, and held him, but his stride was much shorter than whoever had made the prints. "And a taller man than I."

Marcus took his place beside Barton and copied his experiment. The boot was about the same size as Marcus's—he had always had large feet for his moderate height—but the stride was much longer.

He and Barton looked at each other. The tallest man that either of them knew in the district had been Barnabas, but he was dead.

Barton said, "It seems as though the footsteps, at least in the beginning, aimed themselves towards the north end of the house, in the direction of the folly."

"It does," Marcus said, then added, as though it were a comment of little moment, "I found Barnabas's final journal."

Barton said, "Aye?"

"It told of caves under the house, in particular one leading from the wine cellar to the folly, or perhaps in the other direction."

Barton made no answer.

Marcus said, "Did you know that that thing that lay upon the corking table was not my brother?"

Barton said, "I suspected it, but I did not know; if you say it was not he, then I shall take it as true, my lord."

"Then I say surely that that figure was not Barnabas. I have seen Barnabas's true corpse, Barton. He never returned here after his last journey to Little Millwich."

Barton gave Marcus a hard look: *and how would you know that, if you did not go there today? And if you did go there today, how is it that you are here now?*

Then he began to shiver. "My lord..."

Marcus said, "I shall go to the house, Barton. You must hide me for a while—bring me some supper—and when I have gathered my wits, I will go down to the cellar, and look for the entrance to the cave, and try to find my brother, or that which passes itself off as my brother." Marcus licked his lips. "We will know each other by our actions, Barton. Take up one of my father's pistols, and ready it. Shoot anyone who attacks Miss Lucy."

"Anyone, my lord?"

"Even myself, Barton. Especially myself."

Together, they began the short walk back to the house.

This time, Marcus's feet did not hesitate.

Chapter Twenty-Four

The Missing Volume

Lucy slept.

Almost immediately after she had spoken with Marcus, advising him to take her father with him to Little Millwich, she found an unused guest room—none of them had been used in recent memory—and pulled the covers atop her, sinking so quickly, and so deeply into sleep, that she was startled when Cook came to wake her.

"Ach, girl. You look as though you needed that," said Cook.

Lucy's mouth tasted of ashes. She had dreamed of only just being saved from a house fire, in her dreams.

Cook had a mug of tea awaiting her, not a dainty china cup such as a lady might use, but one of the plain, chipped servants' mugs, which was entirely to Lucy's preference: it held more tea and kept it hotter. "Thank you, Cook." It was strong tea, only a little diluted with cream. She looked towards the window and found it dark. "How fares the Earl this evening?"

"The girls say he has been restless," Cook said. "Back and forth to the window, making the floors creak."

"Did he eat?"

Cook only sighed.

Lucy let the tea scald her throat, which forced out of her the last few dregs of her dreams, although the taste of ashes remained.

"Will you take something to eat before you see him?" Cook asked.

Lucy shook her head, trying not to make a face. Of late, it was better to face the Earl on an empty stomach. "Whenever you are finished eating, bring something up to me."

Cook gave her a sympathetic smile, one that meant well but that, like Lucy's dream, provided little actual warmth. Lucy stood, patting her hair. She had pulled it back and braided it earlier. "Am I presentable?"

Cook brushed her fingers against Lucy's temples. "You seem to be setting on a few gray hairs, my dear. You must be careful not to worry too much, or you shall look old before your time."

"If my appearance were to be of a centenarian crone, it should look only half as old as I feel," Lucy said, hoping to make Cook laugh, but succeeding in eliciting only another fleeting smile. She took a deep breath, looking up towards the nursery. Ever since the Earl had taken up residence there, one could sense the location of the room, as a magnet might feel the orientation of the Poles. "I shall look in upon him and see if he needs anything before I send the girl away for the night," she announced. "And then, I should like to sit outside his door and read a book. Which means I should go to the study and select a new one, since I have finished the one I had been reading."

Lucy had been so distracted that she could hardly remember what it was that she had been reading; she had only asked of it that it help her pass the time.

Cook didn't respond; she was looking over Lucy's shoulder at the dark hallway behind her. She turned back and gave a sudden curtsey. "I'll bring something hot up in about an hour, miss."

"Thank you, Cook."

The woman practically fled, leaving a candle on the table beside the bed for her. Had something startled her? Lucy hadn't heard anything, but the atmosphere of the house was such that it could unsettle one at the best of times.

She let herself into the study, where she saw signs that the two secretaries had been at work: the untidy piles of paperwork that Lucy hadn't dared to touch had all disappeared, replaced by neat piles of papers on either side of the table on the far side of the room, away from the fire. She yawned, putting the back of her hand to her mouth. The clock in the study needed winding; it reported the unlikely hour of two o'clock. She put her ear to it; it had gone completely unwound.

There was no point in winding it, if she did not have the right time. She took the candle with her to the bookshelves, thankful that, even though her tasks seemed onerous, there were sufficient books and candles to be had that she might read all the night long, if she chose—although often it was too chill for her to do so, and she was forced to walk about, lest her feet go numb in this unseasonable weather.

Most of the books that the Earl kept in his study showed little taste or discernment, their only virtue, in his eyes, being that they had matching, gilded spines. With the removal of most of the housekeeping staff to Little Millwich, standards had become lax, and a layer of dust had begun to build up on the shelves in front of the books.

Lucy passed over *Les liaisons dangereuses* and nearly selected a volume from *Die Leiden des jungen Werthers*, but stopped on a volume of poetry by von Goethe. The volume had not been settled properly into its place, and it seemed almost to leap out to her fingertips. In addition, the second volume of "Young Werther" was missing. The dust on the shelf below those books had been disturbed, but not recently, for a thinner layer of dust had already begun to accumulate. She removed the volume and saw that several of the pages did not sit properly against the spine. Something had been inserted into the book.

She turned the pages, coming to rest at the poem "Prometheus." A piece of paper, which might have been torn from one of Barnabas's journals, had been folded up and inserted there. In addition, a few lines of the poem had been discreetly marked with a pencil:

Wer half mir/Wider der Titanen Übermut?

Lucy was not as skilled at German as she was at French, and it took a moment, hunched over in the candlelight, to muddle out the marked passage:

Who helped me/Against the Titans' arrogance?

She had read the poem many times before, and had copied it into her commonplace-book, but in translation. It was a poem describing how Prometheus felt abandoned and betrayed by Zeus, after a childhood of admiration, and stating—with hubris, perhaps—that Prometheus had worshipped Zeus, worshipped and scorned him both. Prometheus was a Titan himself; in some versions of the Greek myths, he was the creator of humanity, molding them out of mud with his hands in his own image. It was a poem very nearly declaring von Goethe in rebellion to God the Divine Creator, but thinly veiled so as to prevent the author's being burnt at the stake.

Had the Earl put the paper into the volume? Of course not. The Earl read no poetry, and he certainly did not mark passages such as that one. She set the paper aside and put the volume back into place, making sure that it now aligned with the others near it.

She unfolded the large sheet of paper and nearly cried out: it had been written in Barnabas's hand. It was almost completely written in the strange shorthand symbols which she had taught herself to read, and which meant that the note could only have been written shortly before his death.

She seated herself on the edge of a chair and began to read the note, which was undated and unsigned. The miniscule shorthand read:

I will have left word with Lucy as to the whereabouts of this letter, asking her not to read it, but to instead give it to you without reading it—but I know she will read it. Nevertheless (my dear Lucy), these words are not meant for you, but for Marcus. I would have written this in my final journal, which I have hidden for Marcus to find—only Marcus would find it, so do not bother to look—but I have run out of time and I suspect that the laboratory is being watched. Thus I have chosen the current location, which I should be able to remember to tell you, but which should attract little attention from anyone who ought not to read what I am about to write.

Know that I love you, my little crow.

Marcus—

I have spoken with the Earl, our father. I have asked Barton about the builders of the folly as well. I find myself constrained, even in writing, with the knowledge that to commit the answers I received to paper is to commit the severest folly: in this case, the knowledge itself is a thing of error deeper than ignorance.

But I shall write regardless, because it is what honor, decency, and self-regard all demand that I do. Strangely, I feel the choice to write this note will be shown to be the supreme test of my character, the final answer to the question of my being, of my having been born: Did I deserve to ever have existed? Or should I have been replaced with someone more worthy? You, Marcus, have always looked up to me, and will find the question absurd: I am the finest of men, you will insist, finer by far than you yourself. And yet I know myself better than you do.

I find myself longing to have been someone other than who I am. Someone braver, with more compassion, with more understanding of his fellow men, with a sense of proportion that might allow me to fit seamlessly into the fabric of humanity, instead of the cowardly, solitary, even cold *man that I sense that I have instead become.*

But it is too late to change my nature, if such a thing were even possible.

So, to wit:

Our father knows of that which lies underneath Penderbrook. More to the point: he knows now that I know, for I have confronted him about the tunnels that lead from the wine-cave in the cellar.

Our father is unabashed. I would say that he is even delighted by my knowledge. He paced the floor of his study, near to crowing in victory. You know his moods as well as I; I immediately determined that it would be useless to accuse, to rail, to plead.

Instead, I became a spy.

Father told me that he intends to give entrance into our world some sort of creature from beyond it, and that he only wants my assistance to finish some small matters before the final steps can be taken.

I asked him what I could do to assist him. He told me that it would be most beneficial if I should test the fungus scrapings from the creature in its shallow grave (of which I have written in my final journal) upon some innocent member of the village or the mill—but, he cautioned me, I should be wary of testing the scraping on one who had already been infected, for my results would be without additional benefit! I said that I should of course perform a test, and I began to outline a procedure of taking up a sample of blood, smearing it onto a glass slide, and examining it under a microscope. He laughed at me. I must not have encountered one of the infected, said he, if I thought such a test was necessary. It was only needful, he confessed, to give the man a scratch. Honest blood would flow from an honest man, he said, winking at me, but if I encountered the other, there would only be spongy flesh without emission.

I apologized for my misapprehension, which he accepted with a wave and a conspiratorial laugh. "I am glad that you have found me out," said he, somewhat repeating himself, "for it has become necessary to request someone's assistance. I am glad that it is you, for you have the intellect for the task, and it would have been damned annoying to have to hide this from you for much longer."

He proceeded to tell me the following: the fungus had failed time and again, for the last twenty years, to co-exist with animal life in the same way that it existed with grain or even with the trees (as I noted in my final journal), although it had made great strides with insects, most especially ants. But that was of no moment: if the fungus was to spread properly, it would have to come to some sort of agreement with that species of creature most likely to carry it across the globe.

"Mice?" I asked, in all ignorance.

He only laughed again: "No, men! Mice do not have the intellect of men, and although they were well-known to be great carriers of disease from this place to that, it is the ambition of the fungus to achieve more than a mere plague, but, as you know, Barnabas, to conquer a planet."

I nodded as though I really did know, and refrained from deeper inquiry on the matter.

"However," the Earl cautioned me, "you must not tell Lucy, for she will never embrace the truth as we have. You must marry her; it cannot be avoided; but deceive her. She is clever, but I think that where you tell her she is not allowed to enquire, she will not; for although she seems independent-minded, I believe her to be so proud as not to prod about where she is told not to."

I said, "She has always behaved as such, from childhood on."

He said, "And, of course, you may make use of the creature in the tunnel, if that is what you desire—I am not jealous of it."

I thanked him, hoping that my disgust did not show upon my features.

He responded by saying, "My hope is that soon it will be time to travel to the place where the fungus finds its roots, as it were, and that you will travel as my emissary. It will require returning to Little Millwich, for it is there that the barriers are thinnest."

I told him that I should do whatever he liked, as soon as it might be done. I am to leave in the morning. He shook my hand then, and we drank a brandy to our "partnership." I hesitated, then asked what was behind the locked door in the cave: he told me that it was filled with various experiments of his, failures that had mainly been taken from rats, or cats, or loose dogs—several men, too, who had never been missed, "Not that you can tell them from the dogs, now!" He laughed and told me what a great relief it was that I was open to joining him in his great project, that I had immediately seen what benefits I might obtain from it. I was to be allowed the use of the experiments behind the locked door howsoever I should wish, although I was not to release them, at least, "Not yet," he said.

I bit my tongue nearly until the blood ran. It was difficult to endure my father's presence until the end of the interview, but at last his exuberance had run its course, and I was able to excuse myself. Afterwards, I questioned Barton about the builders of the folly. He named their names as prominent men of fashion, and noted that afterwards, they had gone to the Continent to study architecture in Rome, but had not yet returned.

"Those were the men who designed the work," I said, "I am interested in the men who built it, who put stone upon stone."

Barton hesitated, and I began to think that he, too, had knowledge of my father's secret. "I believe they have all gone to work at the mill," he said, and provided a few names, saying that he might have forgot one or two. He noted that the manager of the mill, Howe, had been the foreman while building the folly—although it was my understanding that Howe had only recently come to the area.

"And you, Barton? Were you of assistance?" I tried to keep my tone light, but I think he saw some of what I was feeling.

He would not answer, but only shook his head and excused himself, saying that he had matters to attend to. I am left with the question of whether Barton is a willing participant in our father's endeavors. He knows—he does not seem to approve—and yet he does nothing to overturn the order of things as they stand. Does Father have some hold over him? It seems incredible, and yet it must be so.

I returned to my room to write down what I have seen, and to consider what I must do. For, in the writing, I have both calmed myself and become resolute that I must do something regarding the matter. I am the son of an evil man, a man who would casually destroy the world that we know, for what reason I know not, and can scarcely imagine. But as I write these words, I imagine you reading them, Marcus, or you, Lucy, and think that I could scarce live with myself if I did not take some step to prevent or to lessen the effects of our father's plans.

He means it to be the end of the world of men, Marcus, this red fungus. I have considered his words, and I think that he means for men to be replaced by this fungus—this "spongy flesh without emission." The fungus will take on the forms of men, and travel about the world, spreading itself this way and that. For what reason? And for what reason has our father agreed to this thing? I should very much like to find out, but I fear I never shall.

My plan is this: I shall go to Little Millwich, find this place where the "barriers" are thinnest, and travel as a diplomat to communicate with those creatures. I shall study them and learn of their weaknesses, so that, when I return, I might find some way to defeat them, or otherwise cut off their access to our world.

There is much I do not know, which I must know in order to formulate such a plan. And there is even more that I must know and plan for, in order to ensure that such a plan, if one can be made at all, is preserved against the event of my death. How will I tell you, Marcus, where I will leave any message, if I am able to leave one, if I return from across the "barriers" at all?

If I survive the trip, and if I am able to write, I shall ask to be taken to Howe's study, the place where those strange secretaries sit at their desks by the windows and scratch at their letters all the day long without pause. They seemed as automatons, when I saw them there, and would not converse with me. I shall tell them that I need to pen a letter to my father—or rather that I should like to make notes of the meeting? No matter. I shall tell them anything that will make them allow me time, paper, privacy, and ink.

I cannot trust that they will deliver any letter which I write, either to our father or to anyone else. I cannot trust that the study will not be searched—it will be, and thoroughly.

Very well. I shall bring a book with me, which I shall prepare for this endeavor. It will be a book of von Goethe's. There, I have taken the second volume of Young Werther: it is tucked under my vest, and I have already prepared a slit in the end-papers so that if the book is shaken, it will still fail to reveal its secrets. I will leave the book in Howe's study on one of the shelves, wherever it seems best to disappear amongst others of its kind.

Marcus—I bid you adieu, I think—I have the terrible premonition that it shall go ill in Little Millwich, and that I should be fortunate indeed to retain enough of self and sanity to write you a letter outlining any plan at all, if, by some miracle, I can invent one.

I wish to know. I wish to understand. I will plunge into this madness with a semblance of eagerness, in order to do that which I most dread—all from curiosity. That is my true sin, I think, not cowardice or coldness, although those are mighty weights as well. I will damn myself to Hell or worse: all in the name of curiosity.

I am sorry that I wasn't paying attention that day at the pond, when you almost drowned. I can't remember whether I ever mentioned it—I don't think I have. But the memory has lingered. You almost died, but even more, afterwards you were never the same. When you slept, you muttered to yourself, saying things so strange that I dismissed them as mere dreams. I did not listen, then.

You spoke of drowning, but not of yourself being drowned—you spoke of the house itself, Penderbrook, drowning.

It is true. Penderbrook is drowning. I shall dive deep and see if I can disentangle it from you and Lucy, and, if not, at least tell you what weeds are tangled about your feet.

With all my love to you both,

Barnabas.

Chapter Twenty-Five

The Double

LUCY EXHALED; THE ROOM, its fireplace unlit, was chill enough that her breath released itself in a puff of white mist. Marcus needed to see the page that Barnabas had written, and sooner rather than later, for there would be very little delay between his deciding what must be done, and carrying it out: he would soon be off to Little Millwich, no doubt in the company of her father.

She stood, tucked the paper into a small pocket cut invisibly into her skirts, and straightened her dress. The book of poetry she carried in her hand. It would look odd for her to leave a room with books in it, and not carry off one or two of them with her: it would seem positively ominous.

She hurried up to Marcus's room, hoping that he was still present, and knocked. "Marcus, are you there?"

But there was no answer. She tried the handle of Marcus's door; it was unlocked. She let herself in. The room seemed to have been overturned by burglars; however, this was nothing unusual. She resumed her way upstairs, to the nursery.

The girl at the door was shivering, although she had a thick quilt thrown around her shoulders, as she sat at the little desk. Her candle had burnt down to a bare nub; Lucy was later than she thought.

"Are you all right?" Lucy asked.

The girl shook her head.

"Is it the Earl? Or are you cold?"

"I can't seem to stop the shivers, miss," the girl said. Lucy felt as though she should recognize her, but didn't. She had a plain face and hair pulled back into a bun underneath her cap. "As soon as the sun set, I could feel them coming on."

"It's been so gray today, I don't know how you could tell *when* the sun set," Lucy said.

"Oh, I can feel it, miss. It's like when a young man breaks your heart, that's how sad it is. And then I gets the shivers."

"Have you checked the Earl lately?"

"About an hour gone, and he was in good spirits then, walking to and fro on the floor, swinging his arms and singing to himself. The fire was all right. I peeked in a little bit ago, and heard him snoring, but he might have been pretending. I took it as him being well enough to play games, begging your pardon, miss."

Lucy told her to take herself down to the kitchen to get something hot to eat. "You aren't planning to leave for the mill, are you?"

"No, miss," the girl said, still shivering. "If it's a choice between the shivers and the mill, I'll take the shivers. I'd rather get off to London, though, if I could."

"Oh? What would you do there?"

The girl shook her head. "It's only a idle thought, miss. The city would eat me up, the way it always seems to do with us poor folk. Your best friend goes to London, you get a letter or two, and then they're gone. You might hear about them later, although it's never anything pleasant. They're either working in a factory or floating down the river. I ought to have found a man and married him quick, is what I ought to have done. But the boy I was seeing, he went off to the mill, and I never got a single letter from him. So between the mill and London, I take it that the mill is worse, and I'll keep myself away from *there*, thank you kindly."

Lucy commended her for her wisdom. The girl seemed reluctant to give up the quilt, so Lucy sent her off with it, with orders to come back after she had eaten, and bring her another. The girl's form, with the quilt pulled up over her head, shrank away down the hallway, looking like a ghost.

The wooden chair was just giving up its last bit of warmth. Lucy huddled into it, but it was not the sort of chair into which one could comfortably huddle. She put the candle and the book down on the desk, then steeled herself: she must look in at the Earl, and handle whatever must, for decency's sake, be handled.

She opened the door.

The smell was ghastly, overpowering. It was the smell of death, of a slaughterhouse.

Lucy's breath caught in her chest. She backed out of the room and closed the door, shuddering. What was the girl's name? Was she near enough that Lucy might call her back? Had she not heard *anything*? Lucy turned towards the desk and took up the fresh candle she had brought with her. The girl had left the little nubbin of her candle behind, and it was very nearly out, guttering in the last bare half-inch of wax. As she watched, it did go out, turning from yellow to orange to scarlet, and then the flame was gone, and only a wisp of smoke remained.

Her heart still in her throat, Lucy took her fresh candle with her into the nursery. "My lord?" she asked, almost before she had opened the door.

There was no answer—but there *was* a sound.

She stepped inside the room and turned towards the cot, lifting the candle.

Before her was a figure which could not be called human. It was at least eight feet tall, and the top of its head brushed the slanted ceiling of the nursery. It crouched on impossible, long limbs, so that it appeared the figure would be at least twice as tall, if it had been able to stretch out to its full length.

It was lifting the Earl from his cot—or, rather, part of the Earl. His upper torso had come apart from the rest of him, which rather explained the smell.

The torso dangled from a pair of stubby claws. As Lucy watched, the monster drew the upper half of the Earl's body to it, clutching it to its chest. It turned its face away sharply, as if the candlelight hurt its eyes—only, as far as Lucy had been able to catch at a glance, it had none, and only a blank sort of place where a face ought to have been.

An ugly thought tore its way across her chest like the cough of a consumptive.

"Barnabas?"

The monster before her shivered, then, in a single movement, spun and charged towards her. She hadn't the time to do so much as lower the candle.

At the last moment, it leapt past her.

She turned a moment too late. The monster, and more than half of the Earl, had vanished. She stepped out of the door of the nursery, but saw no trail of blood or any other sign that the monster had gone in that direction.

She returned to the nursery. Shaking, she walked along the walls of the room, searching for any sign of the monster having hidden somehow.

When she reached the corner of the room opposite the windows and the fire, the corner that always seemed to collect shadows the way the floor underneath a bed collected dust, nausea struck her so strongly that she nearly doubled over. She tried to back away, but it felt as though each footstep she made, was made while wading through a syrup.

The corner of the room had gone wrong. Instead of the walls being at right angles—which it should have done—a sort of angled, false wall had been erected. She put a hand on it, but it was solid. She knocked on it, but heard no echo. It was as if the old wall had been bent to accommodate something, or to conceal it. And yet the wood of the wainscoting showed no sign of having been changed—it turned at an angle, but had not been cut. It was only bent.

The trail of blood, quite voluminous, led directly to the wall. The floor immediately before it was splattered.

The wall itself—was not.

Lucy resisted the urge to panic. It was obvious that something beyond the ordinary run of things was occurring. It was quite useless to pretend that this offense against Nature was of any different character, simply because she happened to have seen it.

Calmly, she walked to the bucket which served as the receptacle for the Earl's refuse, put the candle onto a table nearby, and vomited into the bucket. Black marks swam before her eyes; she felt as though she were nearly turning herself inside out; she was coldly disturbed to note the black marks were the marks of Barnabas's strange shorthand. But after she was finished, she felt better.

She heard footsteps coming up the stairs. *The girl mustn't see this. At least I might save her that.*

Lucy picked up the candle and walked swiftly across the room, closing the door behind her just as the girl approached, carrying three or four quilts in a high stack in front of her.

"I brought you something warm to wrap yourself in, miss," she said cheerfully.

Lucy took a breath. Her mouth tasted foul; her lips were stinging. She asked, "Did you hear anything from the nursery after the last time you checked the Earl?"

The girl said, "Why, no, miss. After I closed the door, he snored for a few moments longer, then stopped." She looked up and down Lucy's dress suddenly. "What is that shining on your dress, miss? He hasn't given you any trouble, has he?" She sniffed. "It smells."

It did indeed, even with the door closed. The creature must have splashed something fowl on Lucy's dress as it passed.

"The Earl has hurt himself," Lucy said. "Please find Barton. Tell him that the Earl needs a doctor, and quickly."

The girl dropped the quilts on the floor, gave Lucy a curtsey, turned, and ran.

Chapter Twenty-Six

We Have Not Gone Mad

AFTER THE GIRL FLED from the hallway outside the nursery to call for a doctor—she would have to run all the way to the village—Lucy swayed on her feet. All the ills of the last few days seemed to pull at her, in every direction.

Lucy licked her lips, then wiped them carefully on the sleeve of her black-dyed gown. At least she was still dressed in mourning. Something heavy and wet dragged down the front of her dress and made her eyes water; she refused to look down at herself and see what it was. She turned back towards the nursery door, breathing shallowly through her mouth.

She opened the door, an act that required far more bravery than it had to stand and watch as the monster fled, earlier. *Then* she had been too numb to conceive of what danger she was in. *Now* she prickled with terror.

The door opened silently, and she stepped inside the room. It was dark: she had left her candle outside the room, on the desk. The curtain over the farthest window had been pulled back, and faint moonlight drew her eyes to that side of the room. She whispered something under her breath—she hardly knew what—and the moonlight seemed to rise off the floor in the corner, and spread itself about the room more evenly, so that the entire room was lit with a faint gray light.

One of the black marks appeared before Lucy's vision, then faded. A spear of pain pierced one temple, leaving the taste of blood along with the other foulness in her mouth.

Lucy hesitated, then stepped into the room, her jaw locked.

The floor was splattered with blood and other material, in a line leading from the cot to the corner. The corner seemed to have resumed its normal dimensions. The trail of blood led to it, then stopped.

Lucy investigated the state of the rest of the room. The furnishings did not seem to have been disturbed. Only the cot, which had fallen over on its side, showed any sign of having been moved. The Earl was generally tidy in his ways, and had spent most of his waking hours either pacing the floor in the room, or reading military histories. A small writing desk sat near one of the windows, papers spread out on top of it. Most of the books in the room had been jammed only a small set of shelves, in every direction; only one of the books was out of place, in a basket near to the cot; the book had been ruined by gore and blood.

The rest of the Earl's corpse still lay upon the floor.

Lucy walked swiftly to the remains and knelt. She must look, in order to determine what had happened to the Earl. She must know.

The moonlight flowed towards him, brightening him, as if it, too, were curious.

Had that monster killed the Earl? Had it ripped him in half, or had it only tried to carry the Earl away? Had he been cut with a sword or blade? Had he been shot? She could smell no gunpowder, which she should have done, if a gun had been fired in so close a room, even despite the stench.

The lower half of the Earl's torso was still dressed in trousers and under-things, although they were now sodden with blood and other material.

The place where the Earl had been parted did not show evidence of having been clawed and attacked, or cut with a sword, or even shot with a cannon or other projectile, but—dissolved. The musculature appeared almost rotted, although the coloration of it was fresh; the softer organs had puddled upon the floor. The spine appeared to have melted like candle wax, but was hard and firm when Lucy steeled herself to prod at it with a sleeve-covered finger. The flesh did not seem to be "cooked," which struck Lucy as strange. She had seen men and animals injured by acid burns before; their muscles would discolor themselves. What had done this? She could smell no tang in the air that had not come from the body itself: no chemicals, no foreign substances.

She lifted herself to her feet, careful not to touch the floor. She had already trod in the blood when she had run to the door to stop the girl from coming in, but there was no reason to dirty her hands worse than they already were. She crossed the room to the writing desk near the window.

Obligingly, the light followed her. She bent down to the pages, which were soon illuminated. The pages were, as far as Lucy could tell, merely notes about what the Earl had been reading, a volume of Tacitus covering the reign of the Roman emperor Nero.

Lucy shuddered. If the Earl believed himself to be Nero reborn, that *would* explain all.

She straightened up and stared at the closed drapes, out into the great valleys of her imagination. The Earl had never touched her, never abused her flesh, but he had had a way of saying this or that to her, that would leave her shuddering in horror. What was it that he had said a few days ago? *You must get yourself another husband, Miss Abbott.* It was exactly the sort of thing that would sound innocuous, except that she had been caring for his bodily needs at the time, and the Earl had leered at her as he said it. She had finished cleaning him, then bid him good morning and fled, shuddering.

He had always been thus. The sly comment, the suggestive look, the impeccably filthy implication.

She took the papers—she was a great believer in keeping scraps of paper—and straightened just as Barton came to the door.

He retched at the door of the room. "Miss Lucy!"

"Oh, Barton," she said, then stopped.

She had known him since she was a child, and yet—had he done this? She could not believe it. To suspect that he was part and parcel of whatever the Earl had done, was to suspect the heartwood of an oak she had climbed as a child: had it always been rotten?

"What happened?" he asked.

She shook her head. "You would hardly credit what I have to say, Barton, except that we both saw that creature attack Barnabas in the woods that day."

Barton stiffened. "Did it…?"

"It was here, or something very like it." It would take wild horses to drag out of her the way the monster had paused to turn its head away from her, as if out of shame, and the way it had reacted when she had called it by the name of her betrothed.

"And it did this," Barton said, his voice taut.

"I do not know, but I suspect it did not," Lucy said. "If you will…" Her throat clenched. "If you will examine the spinal column, it seems to have been…to have…to have *melted*. Or dissolved."

"You didn't touch it, did you?"

"Only with a bit of my sleeve, which appears undamaged. I have been around Barnabas's chemicals enough to be wary."

Barton nodded, then crouched down to study the Earl's body. "Open those drapes, would you? I can't make it out, even with this candle."

Lucy wiped her hands on the backside of her skirt, then opened the curtains and drapes. The moonlight, which seemed to have gone shy in Barton's presence, brightened the floor at her feet.

She said, while Barton was bent over the remainder of the corpse and thus not watching the expression on her face, "When I first arrived, I sent the girl who was watching the Earl off for the night, telling her to come back with a blanket, then stepped inside the room to check on the Earl. I opened the door, and the monster was there, lifting his body from the cot. In the surprise of my entering, the top half of the Earl's body came away from the bottom, and the monster fled with it."

"Where?" Barton asked.

"Into the dark corner of the room."

Barton turned towards the corner in question. "But there is no place for it to go in that direction. On the other side of the left-hand wall is the corridor; on the other side of the far wall is a store-room."

"And yet," Lucy said, "you see where the trail of blood leads."

"I see it," Barton agreed. "I do not doubt what you have said, but, pardon, Miss Lucy, I can't believe it."

"I understand." She stepped carefully again over the trail of gore, then scuffed her shoes on the rug by the door. All the furnishings in the nursery were of the sort only fit to give over to a pair of boys; still, it galled her to stain the floor further. But she did not want to track blood all throughout the house. God knew it would be difficult enough to clean the nursery as it was, with as low-staffed as Penderbrook was. "If you give me a moment, I will check the other side of the wall."

Barton grunted a "Yes, miss," and went back to his investigation of the Earl.

Lucy found Cook standing in the hallway, holding a candle and trembling. Lucy took the candle away from her and set it down on the writing-desk next to her own.

"Is it true?" Cook said. "The Earl is dead?"

"Yes."

"And it's devils what done it to him?"

"It may be," Lucy admitted. To Barton, she could describe her suspicion that the situation was more complex than that, but not to Cook.

"We ought to get a priest in," Cook said defiantly. "A Romish one." She crossed herself.

"It couldn't hurt," Lucy said. "Excuse me, Barton has asked me to look into the storeroom next door."

Cook breathed out a horrified sigh. "What *happened*?"

Lucy needed a moment to sort herself out before she attempted to tell Cook what had happened—or, rather, something other than what had happened. Cook wasn't the worst sort of gossip, but with the house as barren as it was, she was all Lucy had to rely upon to spread news. "Would you make me some tea? And warm some water?"

"Warm some water?" Cook looked over Lucy's dress, taking in the wetness, which had turned gummy and thick. "Oh, Lord."

"And keep the girls away from the room until Barton tells you it's safe enough to clean it."

Cook shivered. "We're all going to die in our beds."

Lucy shook her head. She had suddenly realized the way the story must be presented. "We are perfectly safe now. *We* have not gone mad."

"Miss Lucy!" Cook said, shocked.

Lucy stopped and put her fists on her hips. "If you had seen what the Earl had done to himself..." She cut herself off, pressing her lips together, then pushed past Cook to open the storeroom door. But it was locked. "Do you have the keys for this?"

Cook jingled a ring of keys. "No, but Barton will."

Lucy looked towards the nursery door. "I hate to disturb him."

Cook sighed. "I'll put on water for tea. Mind you, it'll be from an iron pot from my fire because the stoves are out, but it'll be hot. The water to wash with might take a little longer."

"I'll take a damp rag as long as it's not covered in ice," Lucy said. "I've gooseflesh enough already. I'll have to burn this dress."

Cook retreated, and Lucy interrupted Barton's investigations in order to obtain his heavy, jingling keys.

After fumbling with the ring for a few minutes, she cursed under her breath—another black mark seemed to pierce her through the temple—and the door unlocked.

She shivered. There was no sign of blood or anything else out of place in the storeroom.

Chapter Twenty-Seven

The Real Story

BARTON WAITED TO GO back to his room until the women were downstairs in the kitchen, Lucy telling Cook the lie that she had come up with, told to Barton, and asked for his approval: that the Earl had harmed himself. Barton didn't like it, but it would keep people's tongues from wagging in public, and get bruited about in whispers behind their hands. It would keep anyone from digging any deeper. The King might even give a speech about how the Earl had been a right good 'un, everyone knowing that he had never been any such thing, but telling each other that the decent thing was to keep the Earl's true nature—such as they knew of it—a secret.

The Earl was a complicated subject for Barton. He found himself wishing he had known better, all those years ago, when he had had a chance to leave the man's service. But his father had said the Earl was a good man, and if good men had a few failings, why, it was not *their* place to let those failings come to light outside the family.

The family had been everything, to his father. Not their own family but the Sewells. Barton's father thought of himself as a sort of horse-breeder of nobility. Care for the line, and everyone would profit. That was how his father might have put it. But his father had not grown up in the shadow of the current Earl. His father took the position that Earls come and go. But Barton had known no other. It seemed the current Earl would always be the head of the family. It seemed there was no escape. Barton thought of himself as a faceless, nameless valet, a piece of furniture even, while in the Earl's presence. It was only when he was away from that presence that he dared to think otherwise—and those thoughts had only become the more difficult, the older he grew.

He had never married, never had children, never cursed them with the burden of growing up in the Earl's shadow. *He* knew that, underneath the fashionable powder that the Earl had still used on his face when he had still been keeping up appearances, that the Earl, once Barnabas had been born, had stopped growing older. He had seemed to, but it was only powder and paint: a womanish art, turned to the appearance of giving him mortality.

Barton did not know what had happened in the nursery. But in his heart of hearts—or maybe in his waters—he knew that the Earl was not dead, not truly.

The Earl had been up to something. What it was he was up to, Barton didn't know. A deal with the Devil, it may have been. Witch-craft...dark magic...abominations...Barton had never exactly been vouch-safed the truth. But it was *something*, and it was outside the natural. That much he was sure of.

The Earl wanted to live forever. Sometimes Barton even thought that he intended to become a god.

Whatever he had done, whatever had happened to him, it had not *killed* him. Barton was sure of it.

Cook had put on a kettle for tea, then started to reheat their supper, which was a good, thick beef stew, strongly spiced, with potatoes that had suffered from the year's lost sunshine and heavy rains, but would be no less the welcome for all that. It had been strange, this year, to come to think of meat as the thing that would stretch a potato a little further, but there it was: a very strange year. A haunted year. A dark night as well. Just after sunset, Barton had gone outside to see what had been making noise down by the old boathouse by the lake. He had thought one of the shutters on the boathouse might have come loose and been thumping against a wall, but it was such a dark night that he could not see to tell.

When he returned, he grunted an assent that it had been the shutter to blame, and strode off to his room, muttering something about a hammer. Barton had to be everything to everyone now, not just valet to the Earl. But then they were all stretched thin. Two more of the men had left for the mill the day before.

What would they do when the meat ran out?

Cook had pushed the thought aside. They were one of the largest houses in Britain, the Earl was a wealthy man with a great deal of influence, and they would not starve. But they may want for potatoes now and again.

The Earl had always been an odd one. She had been with the house since she was a little slip of a thing, under the old cook, who had been a Frenchman of great standing, and whose cooking had pleased the old Earl that was. The boy James, who had become the Earl after him, had been by fits and starts the sweetest little boy—and the worst scamp she had ever seen. One moment he would be throwing rocks into the glazing, promising that it had been an accident; the next he would be telling her that she made the best bread in the whole house, and that if she would give him a slice of it, he would make her cook when *he* was the Earl. And then there were the times he would cross himself out of the corner of her eye, then wink at her when she turned to look. Was he reminding her that he knew about her Catholic faith, which she must keep hidden away, lest she be removed from the house? Was he teasing her? Mocking her?

She had grown into reticence in this house. Better to only say "aye" and "nay" and "yes, my lord" than to have a song in her throat, lest James catch one unawares and spend the week teasing her for singing Irish drinking songs. Penderbrook had already trained her for service; it was James who had trained her to subservience. If she did not make him his favorite dishes, to be served behind the back of the old Earl often enough, her hair would be pulled and there would be found dirt in the bread and weevils in the flour. It was not just her, either. The entire house had danced to his childhood whims.

When James became the Earl and his loved ones lay buried in the churchyard at the back of the house, she had stayed. She was the gray-haired Cook now, who had once been little Sally O'Reilly with the red hair and the fine voice, and if she had not done as well for herself as she thought she might have done, well, she had only herself to blame for not having left when she ought. She had turned a blind eye on a thousand transgressions. She was not above the happenings that went on in the house. The Earl kept rein on her by giving her what she wanted, but only so long as she danced to his whims. He had molded her and cultivated her, so that she was like a trained tomato vine in a hothouse, unable to live anywhere else. Now she was almost all he had left. The others had all gone to the millworks.

What puzzled the woman who had once been Sally O'Reilly the most, was the way the house—it was one of the largest houses in Britain, she told herself again, which should have been something she never needed to remind herself of—had become isolated in upon itself. Penderbrook, when it had been under the old Earl that was, had been a beehive of people and supplies and messages going in and out. It was a place where paths crossed, and some of those paths ran very far indeed, with all sorts of men from other continents come to do business with the old Earl, or to discuss matters of government. Where were those visitors now? Where were the carriages from all around the countryside, asking to tour the house, to walk through some of the public rooms, or to sketch the folly? Where was everyone?

But Cook asked no questions. The ones spinning around in Sally's head stayed locked up with all the songs she had ever learned as a child, and all her prayers.

She caught herself staring into the fire just as the girl had come down, a quilt pulled up over her head, saying as how it should be a quiet night (the young not being cursed with premonitions), and begging for her supper.

"It's almost ready," Cook had said.

"I'll sit in front of the fire, then, and warm myself."

"I would think you'd be warm enough, wrapped up in a quilt like that. What will Miss Lucy do, with no quilt? Shiver?"

The girl exclaimed, "Oh! I promised to bring her another one. Shall I go into one of the spare bedrooms and take the bedding off one of the beds?"

"You'll do no such thing! Go to the linen closet. There should be a stack of quilts in the back."

"They have mothballs."

"So they do. Give Miss Lucy the one that's been aired, and keep one of the mothballed ones for yourself. She's the one as must sit up with the Earl all night, not you."

The girl gave her a short recrimination, but folded up her quilt as she talked. "I'll bring her the one *with* mothballs and two *without*. One quilt

was not enough, and it's colder now at night than it was during the day."
And off she went.

Barton appeared, as if by magic: "What supper is to be had?"

"Beef stew, from yesterday. But there's a lot of it."

"Where is it?"

"Before the fire."

He scowled at her. "Why is the kitchen all gone dark?"

"It's warm enough where it is."

Barton grunted. But Cook understood him. The kitchen being so cold made the house feel as though the heart had gone out of it, although he didn't like to say it. But that was the way of it, in this house, under this Earl: the things which ought not be said crept up on you, so that what was a perfectly innocent comment yesterday became unforgivable today.

The Earl must not question himself in any regard; they were paid to make him happy; for him to lack happiness was to give him an excuse to repay them misery.

They were all trained, like dogs.

Barton said, "Give me some of that stew. A lot of it."

"Hungry?"

"Famished."

She gave him a double portion, along with some bread she had baked that morning. He disappeared again.

A few moments later, the girl had come shrieking down the stairs. "The Earl has hurt himself! Miss Lucy says the Earl has hurt himself! We must call for a doctor! Where is Barton!"

BARTON HAD KNOCKED ON the door of his own humble room with one hand, bracing the tray with stew with the other. "My lord?" he asked softly.

"Enter. Damn it, I've bolted the door, haven't I? A moment."

The bolt was thrust back and the door opened. Lord Marcus inhaled deeply of the covered bowl of warm stew that Barton had brought, then shuddered, then shrugged and accepted it.

A few moments later, Barton had gone to see what the girl was shrieking about, cautioning Lord Marcus to remain in the room. "What the women know, everyone knows," he said. "I'll return as soon as possible."

His return was somewhat delayed.

COOK WENT DOWN TO the men's quarters in the lower part of the house and roused one of the men to run the errand for her: "Find the doctor. The Earl has had an accident."

Then she climbed to the nursery—all those stairs—but had been forbidden to enter the room. Miss Lucy, shaking and upset, asked for hot water to wash in and tea, but nothing to eat. Soon enough Lucy had come down to the fire and was seated in front of it, holding a mug of hot tea, wearing a different dress. She told Cook in a cold, superior tone that the Earl had had an accident, that what he had done could not have been intentional.

Cook heard the lie, clear as day. The Earl must have done himself in. But why?

When had the Earl ever felt any sort of remorse for what he did in this life, or blamed himself for anything, or ever despaired when he could instead find someone to punish? If he had, *she* had never heard of it.

Maybe it *had* been an accident.

Then Miss Lucy met her eyes directly. In them was fear—blunt fear, the ugly kind that will make you push a friend in front of your own self in a moment of danger.

Cook looked away. Whatever had caused Miss Lucy's eyes to appear as frightened as they were, she wanted none of it. She could keep the real story to herself, and welcome.

Miss Lucy left; the doctor came and was shown up to the nursery.

Cook knew she ought to have felt pity for Lord Marcus, who was out at Little Millwich for the day and had likely got snowed in and had no idea of what was going on, and for Miss Lucy, who was the sort of girl who would try to put all the pieces back together again for him.

She remembered the three of them as children. Master Barnabas always too long for his trousers and solemn as a sexton, Master Marcus always running wild—but reminding her no less of her younger brother, long dead now, for all that—and Miss Lucy staring off into the distance, appearing not to have heard a word that anyone said to her, then tilting her head to the side and asking the most impertinent, but hardly ill-minded, questions. "Do you have a brother in Killarney?" she had asked once, watching Cook watch Master Marcus at play. "Is he dead?"

Miss Lucy and Master Barnabas, well, that had been the expected thing, hadn't it?

But Cook still had eyes in her head, it was Lord Marcus who had pulled Miss Lucy's gaze this way and that way, and it always had been.

THE CREATURE UNDER THE house—the female figure that had so engendered a sense of pity and horror from Barnabas—rose to its feet from where it had been waiting, unmoving, since the man of the blood of the summoner had been there. It trembled, feeling something moving within it.

It scrambled through the tunnel until it reached the figured buried in the ground, in repose. From under the layer of soil were erupting sporocarps, the fruiting bodies of their kind, which in this case were a pale bloom of flesh, something like the bloom of a flower or a slowly creeping stain on fabric.

The creature examined itself. The orifices which it bore had dampened, beading up with clear red liquid. Its "skin" had begun to sprout a lacy structure as well. It touched its face—what the man had called its face—and found, with relief, that the horrible features had somewhat subsided. The bulging black beads had sealed themselves shut, the nostrils closed, the mouth spread wide and thin, with filaments stretching from lip to lip, to seal it shut.

It was a sign that this horrific nightmare would soon be over.

Chapter Twenty-Eight

Through the Killing Jar

THE DOOR OPENED, AND Barton entered.

Marcus, who had eaten most of the bowl of stew and left off the cover to let it get cold again besides, said, "What were the women worried about, Barton? A mouse?"

Barton said, in an uninflected tone, "Hardly a mouse, my lord. Something has happened to the Earl."

It was as if a cold winter breeze drew itself along the back of Marcus's neck. "What?"

"I hardly know what to say, my lord, but that the Earl is dead, and that you must take his place."

Marcus shook his head. The man's words could hardly be true. "He has run away again, hasn't he? Let us go to the folly, and see if—"

Barton snapped, "He is dead! Part of his body is missing! I have seen his lower torso, and his legs, left bloody upon the cot! Miss Lucy says that she saw a pale, long-limbed creature stealing the rest of him away, into the dark corner of the room, where both disappeared! I saw the trail of blood, and I saw it stop abruptly at the wall and go no further! He is dead! You are the Earl!"

The man stood in front of him, panting, eyes wild.

Marcus had not heard him use that tone of voice upon him since he had been a child. He supposed he deserved it now. "I—I hardly know what to say, Barton."

Barton subsided. "I apologize, my lord. If you wish me to resign my post, I shall do so."

Marcus waved a hand. "Sometimes the sergeant must bawl out the lieutenant for being a fool and a coward. It wasn't the first time I've needed to hear it, and I'm sure it won't be the last. There is nothing to forgive."

The weight of the house seemed to be settling upon him, in a very nearly literal fashion. Abruptly, Marcus found himself sitting upon the single chair in Barton's small room. He was stunned. He put a hand in front of his face.

"Barton, would it be beyond the pale if I simply ordered everyone out of the house and burnt it to the ground?"

"How would you do it, my lord?" Barton asked.

"I would be able to take it apart easily if we had a half-dozen cannon," Marcus said. "But I suppose that if I attempted to set fire to the curtains, it would only burn down the contents of a room or two before it smothered itself. Please disregard that statement. I have known this day was coming since I received Lucy's letter saying that my brother was dead. How should it be a surprise now?"

Barton didn't respond.

Marcus struggled to his feet. The house dragged at him, as if it were hanging from his ankles. "We must hunt the thing that killed my father. It cannot be allowed to run rampant. Is Miss Lucy safe?"

"She had to change her clothing; it had become excessively soiled."

Marcus looked at Barton, and only then noticed that the man's knees were covered in stains, in blood. "And now?"

"She is with Cook."

"That is well. I shall make some excuse of having just returned with the horses."

Barton's mouth parted a moment. He licked his lips. "Without Mr. Abbott?"

As Barton and Marcus had returned to the house, the whole business had come out, in bits and pieces. Barton had plied him with whisky, and Marcus had held forth. Barton, in turn, had claimed to have known none of it, but had had suspicions that the Earl practiced witchcraft or some other dark sorcery, and admitted his shame at not having been able to stop it.

Marcus did not castigate the man for his failure in somehow holding an Earl to account, or at least leaving Penderbrook: Marcus knew his father, and how difficult it was to escape the man's orbit. One always had some string which might be tugged or held at tension, to lead one around by the nose. It would have been easy to decry Barton's behavior, but to do so was simply another snare set by the Earl. He trapped decent men by playing upon their decency, much the same way as a seducer trapped a girl in the corner, then told her that her charms had overwhelmed him.

Marcus considered the situation.

He could not believe that his father was dead.

"I should shoot myself and let this all go to the American cousins," Marcus said. "No orders, no strategies, not even a clear idea of who plays the rôle of the Enemy. No idea of what resources I might be able to muster. I am more the captain of a sinking ship than the Brigadier-General of an armada."

"My lord?"

"We must evacuate, Barton. Women and children first. Everyone must leave the house. Send them to Bramble House. The first step: find Lucy and send her here. I shall tell her what I know. She deserves to know that her father is dead, or worse, and that I abandoned him at his request. Then, if she does not simply beat me to death with her fists, we will leave this place."

"Leave this all behind?" Barton sounded incredulous.

Marcus clasped Barton's arm. "Something I learned in France. One moment you hold one position; then, like a chess piece, you and your men are moved somewhere else. The value is not in the place itself, but in that you are in the right place at the right time. Sometimes you and your men are made a sacrifice of—that's how the game is played—but you always hope it is by a player who knows your worth, rather than leaving you exposed out of ignorance, arrogance, or sheer idiocy. Penderbrook, in itself, is nothing. It cannot even move. Let us not be cornered here, and waste our play, eh?"

Barton nodded reluctantly.

Marcus said, "Bring me Lucy. Then begin the move to the Abbott's."

Barton left.

MARCUS PACED THE ROOM until Barton knocked again.

"My lord? I have brought her."

Marcus swallowed, then unbolted the door. Barton was already striding away, which was likely a wise assessment of how the conversation with Lucy was likely to go. She wore yet another black-dyed dress, this one smelling slightly of mothballs. Her expression was distant and unfocused, a soldier's mien.

He stood aside from the doorway to let her in. "Thank you, Barton," he called, although the man had rounded a corner of the hallway and disappeared. "Lucy."

"You're back," she said. "Where is my father?"

"He is dead. I pray that he is dead."

She nodded calmly and walked into the room. He closed the door behind her. In a glance she took in Barton's humble furnishings: the narrow bed, single chair, humble writing desk, and a shelf along one wall, lined from one side to the other with books.

She peered up at them. "I can't see the titles."

"Now is hardly the time."

She sat on the side of the bed.

He took the chair, turning it to face her. "Lucy..."

They looked at each other. He should have told her what had happened to her father, although he hardly understood it himself; she, for her part, should have told him what had happened to his.

"I no longer know anything," he said. "I no longer even know whether I am human or otherwise."

She mumbled something almost under her breath, and abruptly the room brightened.

"You did that?" he asked.

She nodded. "It is the...that is, I seem to see the characters of Barnabas's shorthand appearing before my eyes, and then wonderous things occur."

Marcus said, "It is not shorthand, I think, but the language of the creatures who plague us. I heard your father speak it, in Little Millwich, and it was as if the hearing of it changed something within me, so that now I can read it."

"Oh!" Lucy reached into a pocket to present him with a piece of paper that had been torn from a journal. "I had nearly forgotten. Your brother—I found a letter from him, hidden within a book of poetry."

"You found it?" Marcus said. "How?"

"The dust around it had been disturbed."

Marcus read the letter. Barnabas was to attempt to create a plan to defeat the monsters, and he would hide it in a book in Howe's study in Little Millwich, which Marcus had only left a few hours previously.

"I must go back," he said.

Lucy bit her lips.

A knock came at the door; Barton had returned, looking perplexed. "My lord, a messenger has come. He says that the road to Little Millwich has gone."

"Gone? A flood?" Marcus asked.

"No, my lord. I assumed the same, but he said that it was not: that the road to little Millwich stopped at the bridge crossing. The bridge was gone, and on the other side of the river, were the houses of Northampton."

It was six miles to Northampton.

Marcus said, "I see. Thank you, Barton."

"My lord?"

"It means that Mr. Abbott succeeded in whatever he was attempting to do, as I described before."

"I did not understand your explanation."

"I did not understand it either. But Mr. Abbott did, and that he accomplished his purpose we can only take as a sacrifice chosen by a man better and wiser than I."

Barton retreated, closing the door behind him, and Marcus bolted it.

Lucy said, "Then the book with Barnabas's plan in it is gone, and we are on our own again. And, I fear, my father's sacrifice did not end this madness, since your father was taken after that, if *after* is a word that contains any sense any longer. What will we do now?"

The momentary relief of thinking that Barnabas might have come up with a plan dissipated, and the weight of the house dragged at him once again. "We will leave Penderbrook, abandon it."

"But the fungus will spread."

"It will, but only in the spring. After you and anyone else who will go to London have gone, then I will return here, with cannon if necessary, to destroy this place."

"It may be too late by then," Lucy said.

"You must go, Lucy. I will not have you die here."

"I am already too tainted by this place to be able to leave it. I would only carry the infection with me."

"Lucy!" Marcus said. "Do you think I would, for one second, lift a finger against this place, if I thought it would hurt you in doing so? To hell with the rest of the world! You will *go*. I promised your father. He died that I might give you this chance. Surely there are other men of such knowledge, who would be able to lift whatever curse this place has laid upon you, or to clean you of whatever infection you carry with you. If you will not go, I will end it here. Damn you, woman!"

Lucy closed her eyes. Slowly, her mouth turned from a pressed line into a terrible grimace. Her shoulders hitched. She was crying.

She put a hand over her mouth, as if that could cover her weeping. Tears began to roll down her cheeks. "My father is dead." Her head tipped forwards, hiding her face from view. Her shoulders pulled in, as did her legs, drawing her feet up onto the bed. "Barnabas is dead. Oh, Marcus. I cannot lose *you*, too. You are all I have left."

"You will *live*," he said. He sat beside her, and she leaned against him. "Likely, I will, too."

"Even if this were so, it would still remain that we carry within ourselves this horrible thing." She pressed a hand against her chest. "Does it not lie within us, like a sickness? Does it not lie in all of us who have been here at Penderbrook for too long?"

"If so, then it has been carried all over, for no one stays at Penderbrook always. People come and go."

"They *used* to come and go," Lucy murmured. "Now it seems as though anyone who comes here finds themselves fastened here like a moth pinned to paper after it has been through the killing jar."

Marcus said, "*I* left."

"Yes." She did not say that he had returned, or that he was now fastened here more firmly than ever.

"You think, then, that we ought to remain here, to destroy this place?"

"I think," Lucy said slowly, "that whatever my father did to Little Millwich ought to be done here as well, and as soon as possible. But I do not know that it can be done. I feel...I *feel* as though I should be able to do it, if I knew how to do it. But I do not know."

Marcus shook his head. He could offer her no assistance in the matter. "We could search Bramble House. Perhaps your father kept notes."

Lucy's shoulders hitched once. "You are not trying to drive me away?"

He shook his head. "I want you to go. If it damns the world, I want you to go. But if it is only you who might erase what my father has made of Penderbrook, then I must at least give you the opportunity." He grasped her shoulders and turned her, so that he could be sure of her expression. "But if the words are not there—you must promise me that you will go, and you will not look back."

She had closed her eyes again. He touched her cheek, to make sure that it remained flesh.

Lucy burst into tears. "I promise," she sobbed. "I promise that I will not look back."

He pulled her to him, touching the sweetness of her hair, pulling it free of its pins, tasting her tears.

"Do not look back," he whispered to her, as she struggled with the fastenings of his clothing. Nothing could surprise him now: she could have him if she wanted him, as unworthy as he was; he would give her that. "Do not look back."

Chapter Twenty-Nine

Flight to Bramble House

A LONG WHILE LATER—ALTHOUGH it felt too soon—Barton came for them, and said that the servants had all been told, and were taking up what few possessions they could, to carry with them to Bramble House, and now the two of them must, finally, go.

Marcus considered: should he take anything from Penderbrook? The ledgers, the deeds and titles to his father's property, some keepsake?

No. He would be free.

They exited quickly, before Marcus could change his mind, and fled towards Bramble House.

Bramble House, from which Mr. Abbott had maintained his watch upon Penderbrook for all the long years—at first in admiration, and then in horror—lay across the pond, favorably enclosed by the slope of a low hill to its north. It was a much humbler house than Penderbrook, which stood proudly exposed to view, displaying its glazing and marble. Bramble House was more turned inwards, its southern face half-concealed by a line of old oak trees which, in summer, provided shade, and, in the winter, let play light upon the south-facing rooms. The aspects of the other sides of the house were more restrained in glazing; enough to let in what light they could, but not so large as to seem arrogant or proud—or to let in the greater part of the chill which seemed to continually haunt the cold, gray rooms of Penderbrook.

Lucy carried herself proudly along the path: to Marcus's eye, she seemed the same as ever. Perhaps it was the dark that deceived him, or it may have been that, to her, there *was* no change. She had always loved him; he had not felt himself her equal; they had both fervently wished his escape from Penderbrook, like a starling released from a boy's cage—although his reasoning in the matter had been more selfish than hers; she had offered herself to Barnabas, and he, not being a fool, had accepted; she had loved them both, although she had assumed herself long ago to have been promised to Barnabas, who needed a helpmeet far more than did Marcus.

What else could it have been, among the three of them?

No, *she* had not changed at all.

Barton had sent the rest of the household ahead of them: their footprints lay in the snow along the trail leading along the pond and through the woods that lay between Penderbrook and Bramble House.

Lucy said, sharply, "Marcus."

She had stopped along the path where it was about to cross the stream, and was pointing back to Penderbrook.

Marcus half-expected the house to be aflame, but only shadows lingered there—shadows which seemed to move. Barton had fallen behind them, his lone figure gray against the glittering drifts of snow.

Towards it loped a pale figure from the right. A monster, it was the size of an elephant in a menagerie, but slighter, built something like a spider, and something like the swiftest deer that ever sprang through forest.

"Barton!" Marcus bellowed. "Run!"

They saw Barton startle, then turn, then freeze into place.

Within a heartbeat, the monster was upon him, then continued in an arc towards the far end of Penderbrook, taking Barton with it. Then it circled around the house, and was gone.

Marcus turned, grabbed Lucy's hand, and swung her up onto his back. She clung to him: he ran.

He had been away from the war for some time, but his body remembered its paces. After the first sprint of energy, he settled into a dull, aching rhythm.

The monster which had taken Barton had moved far more swiftly than he could run. He knew he could not escape.

Well, he would run, that was all.

He crossed the stream and continued among the trees, still following the path. The trees where they had played as children were near—they were past. His heart had no energy to do anything but beat. Lucy's head lay against his back. He hitched her up as he ran, and her arms tightened, but not enough to choke.

His feet punched through the snow where it had not already been trod by the servants. He wondered if Barton had wakened the secretaries from Little Millwich, or if they were still asleep in their beds. He wondered if the secretaries had shaken off their seeming humanity and were even now pursuing him through the snow. If they were, he did not hear them.

Soon they were very near to Bramble House. The path climbed upwards and curved. Marcus had traveled it a thousand times. Soon they would have arrived. They would search Mr. Abbott's study, and find nothing of any help whatsoever.

And then he would be able to send Lucy away.

If only they could reach Bramble House. They had almost crossed the boundary that delineated the furthest bound of Penderbrook; a few more steps would see them across.

He felt, more than heard, Lucy gasp. Then she was snatched away from him. He was falling, falling—

Chapter Thirty

Summer

THE SUN LAY WARM upon Marcus's face, the grass cool under his cheek. He was on a great, grassy lawn. It was summer, the sort of summer that one imagines exists, or that one remembers as having existed, deep within the labyrinthine memories of childhood, which understand only happiness or unhappiness, and shade the skies accordingly. In other words, it was perfect.

Was it Heaven? Was he dead?

He sat up. He lay upon the lawn of Penderbrook. The house lay behind him, overlooking the pond. The pond! He turned towards it. It sparkled in the sun.

He stood. Where was Lucy? What had happened to him?

He turned around in a slow circle. Everything was as he remembered it, tinted in golden sunlight.

"Marcus!" He turned; someone was calling him from the house. A figure waved at him, one hand overhead. He recognized it as Barnabas. "Come here, Marcus!"

He began walking up the hill towards the house, his heart near to over-flowing. Barnabas stood just outside the door to the kitchen. Behind him stood someone else.

Lucy.

Marcus started jogging. His limbs felt freer than they ever had before, even as a boy. He ran faster—he could not seem to tire.

He laughed.

Barnabas began to run towards him. In a moment the two brothers had embraced, laughing and thumping each other on the back. "What happened to you?" "Where are we?" "How did you get here?" "I woke up here! And you?"

It was a joy to see his brother. He looked well, better than he had upon the corking table in the wine cellar, at any rate. No, more than well. He looked perfect. The lines that Marcus had recognized around his own eyes in the mirror had not yet formed at Barnabas's brow.

Marcus looked at Lucy; she was similarly perfected, every loveliness brought out rather than hidden under her natural frumpishness and modesty. She wore a pale lavender dress with gold embroidery over the deep bosom, and her hair had been pulled up in ringlets.

He felt not the slightest self-consciousness at having made love to his brother's once-intended bride, not even with his brother standing there, and there was no moment of shame or even embarrassment as the three of them exchanged a glance. Marcus smiled.

Lucy said, "We have lost."

THEY WALKED THROUGHOUT THE park around the house, discussing what they remembered.

Barnabas had gone to Little Millwich as he had planned. While investigating one of the rooms in the cellar—which they soon established to be the one haunted by the red fungus and the white creatures—Barnabas had been struck down, and lost consciousness.

"I had not been able to formulate a plan to disrupt whatever my father planned," he admitted. "I had only begun to suspect a smidgeon of an idea."

"What was it?" Marcus asked.

"The tongue that is spoken by the white creatures contains mysteries which I had not suspected," Barnabas began to say, in his ponderously deep, slow voice, but was interrupted by Marcus, who told him what Mr. Abbott had done.

Barnabas shook his head. "Mr. Abbott had twice the intellect that I have."

Impatiently, Lucy exclaimed, "We are lazing about in the grass instead of attempting to leave this place. Are the two of you mad?"

It seemed mad to wish to leave; they were in what must be the most blissful of all existences. But she *would* insist. Barnabas and Marcus walked with her along the path, the same one which had seen Barnabas (or his replacement, rather) cut down, and which had earlier seen their attempted flight.

At the little bridge which crossed the stream, Lucy hesitated, but discovered nothing untoward about the experience. They proceeded forwards along the path.

Soon they had reached the trees where Barnabas had encountered the first of the pale monsters, as it had emerged from underneath its nest of red fungus strands.

Barnabas stopped. "I had not considered...but..."

"What is it?" Marcus asked.

"The sunspots that Lucy brought to my attention. We are...that is, I suppose I know what this place is, what it must be."

Lucy shook her head.

"*You* knew what it was, the moment you first saw it," Barnabas said. "But I did not wish to know, and therefore did not, until this moment."

"Where *are* we?" Marcus exclaimed.

"We are in a false place, a place which should not exist. We are in Summer."

"It *is* summer," Marcus said.

"Not merely summer, but..." Barnabas looked towards Lucy, as if to ensure that he did not misspeak himself. "...the essence of it? The idealization of it?"

"Summer," Lucy said, "with a capital *S*."

Marcus snorted. "What, then? Is that why there was no summer anywhere else? Is that why it has rained continuously, the skies have been overcast, the air chill, the world faded? Because our father has stolen all the goodness of summer, all the world over, and tucked it away, the way he might put coin in his coffers?"

"Well," Barnabas said, "yes."

"He has stolen summer."

"Yes."

"All of summer. Everywhere."

"Yes."

They continued walking.

"Why?" Marcus asked. "He must have been planning this since before he had the folly built. Decades of waiting, of destroying everyone around him, of damning us all. For what? Nice weather?"

Ahead of them, the trail seemed to lead to Bramble House, leading upwards, and curving.

Marcus hesitated; so did Lucy. Barnabas strode forwards, then stopped abruptly and stumbled back a step. He put a hand to his face, then in front of him, seeming to trace a flat surface.

"What is it?" Marcus walked forwards until he met with whatever his brother had struck. It was a hard, invisible surface of some type. He could not make it out.

Barnabas said, "Ah."

He was shifting from foot to foot, tilting his head this way, then that. "The rest of the hill is only an image, an illusion. There is a barrier here." He stretched out his arms and began walking sideways, moving at right angles to the path. "It seems to be flat."

From behind them, Lucy murmured, "I suspect it will prove to be slightly curved."

"Indeed," Barnabas said.

Marcus asked, "What are the two of you talking about?"

Barnabas cleared his throat. "We seem to be…within a sort of solid bubble that contains Penderbrook, or rather a moment of perfect summer which must necessarily contain Penderbrook."

Marcus bent down to pick up a rock with which to test his brother's theory.

Lucy put her hand on his. "Wisdom suggests that it remain intact for now."

"You were the one who was only just insisting that we must escape."

She shrugged.

Marcus leaned forwards until his forehead was touching the surface before him, unseen but certainly felt. He breathed upon it, fogging it. The image seemed to soften. He breathed upon it again, then, like a boy who has made a windowpane frost over with his breath, raised and arm and used the back of his sleeve to wipe the spot.

What he glimpsed there told him that Barnabas was not wrong; what lay on the other side of the "glass" did not resemble that which lay within it.

"What do you see?" Barnabas asked.

Without a word, Marcus stepped away from the spot, and Barnabas peered through it. The two brothers looked at each other.

"What is it?" Lucy asked.

Barnabas stepped in front of her; Marcus took her arm and turned her aside. "It is nothing that you wish to see," Barnabas said. "It is that which is outside the bubble."

Marcus stumbled on the path, and Lucy kept him from falling.

"Are you all right?"

"I'll be fine in a moment."

He knew that he would not; neither would Barnabas. What he had seen was so strange, that it seemed to linger before his eyes. He wished that he had not looked.

Moreover, it was clear to him—so very clear—that there would be no escape from this place.

They retreated towards the pond, and the house. As they approached it, it seemed to loom above them, rising far higher than it had, growing so that it occupied most of the low hill upon which it stood.

As it grew, it pulled at Marcus, and he found himself walking more quickly, as if he were walking down a hill, rather than up one. He released his arm from Lucy's; his eyes seemed to have adjusted to their new sort of vision, and his footing was sure. He tried to keep his eyes upon the house, the ground, the trees: anything which did not require him to allow his gaze to rise skywards.

Lucy said, "What will become of our..." She did not know how to say what it was that she meant, and yet Marcus understood her perfectly. "...our home?"

She did not mean Penderbrook, but rather the entire world from which they had come.

"Terrible things," Marcus said, with assurance.

Barnabas cleared his throat. "Due to that which has been removed from it, I suspect it will close in upon itself. The universe will seal around it a bubble of area and duration, so that nothing may enter it, and nothing leave."

"Penderbrook? Penderbrook will vanish?" Lucy asked, almost hopefully.

Barnabas shook his head. "As it seems the entirety of our world has been afflicted by this curse, at least in its weather, I would think at the very least the Earth must be set aside, lest the rest of existence fall."

They stared at the house, continuing to walk ever closer to it, almost without willing to do so. They reached the kitchen door: it swung open before them. They stepped within.

The interior of the house was as it had ever been. Entering the house did not ease the pull, but rather drew them forwards more strongly than before. They *must* go forwards.

They exited the kitchen, traversed the entryway—whether it was a perfect replica or Penderbrook itself, it was impossible for Marcus to ascertain—reached the curving balustrade of the marble stairs with their red velvet runners, and ascended them, past the first storey, to the second, then the third: along the long hallway, then, towards the nursery, where all three of them knew they must go.

They approached the nursery door. It had been changed. It was no longer made of oak and brass, but of some other material, dark and filled with distant stars.

They looked at each other. Then, before Lucy could reach out and touch a hand to the strange material, Barnabas stretched forth his, and opened the door.

Chapter Thirty-One

Apotheosis

THE NURSERY HAD BEEN transformed. Its shabby nature and dilapidated furnishings had been overcome, or rather transcended. The room of a thousand days' afternoon entertainments had become a celestial throne room.

In front of them, just past the doorway, was the stub end of the original room, a scuffed wood floor covered with threadbare rugs. It ended abruptly, only a few feet into the original room. It seemed as though the rest of the nursery—or perhaps Creation itself—had been snapped off, leaving splintered wood, broken plaster, and twisted lathe along the edges.

Beyond that was open space, stretching into infinity.

And the throne.

Joining with the end of the original room was a ramp of green marble, leading upwards to a sweeping, immense, distant dais comprised of several successive platforms, the topmost of which contained the golden throne.

And such a throne!

It was no mere gilded chair, but a work of art. The seat itself was immense, the size of a cathedral pipe organ, and surrounded by spans of gold, as elegant as ripples in a field of wheat, and as warmly beautiful. Near the throne itself, the spans spread into a delicate web of gold wire. Two torches blazed at either side of the throne, each of them at least fifty feet high. The light in the room seemed to come from elsewhere, however—nowhere and everywhere at once.

Lucy murmured, "The pattern in the gold filaments is very like the sunspots," and Barnabas agreed with her.

The throne was—for the moment, at least—empty.

In every other direction, the throne room stretched as far as the eye should like to see. Above them was an overarching roof or sky, the top of the "bubble" that they had discovered earlier.

Marcus shuddered, to think of that which lay outside it.

On the level below the throne itself stood three figures, so distant that it was impossible to make out who they were, or even whether they were human.

KNEEL.

The command was driven into their minds directly, and all three of them dropped immediately to their knees. Then, without further command, they each found themselves lying prostrate on the floor, covering their faces and trembling.

After a moment, it was given to them that they were allowed to rise. Without command, the three of them removed their footwear and set it to the side. Then their feet began to draw them forwards again, inevitably, towards the throne. They walked three abreast; the ramp before them was wide enough to accommodate them all at once, as if by design.

Marcus studied the three figures, which, as they approached, were seen to be female—and unclothed.

The face of the one on the left came into focus, bonny and red-haired. It was a face which he had often seen in portrait, but could not remember ever having seen in the flesh: his mother. He could not look away, not even to see whether Barnabas, who might still have some memory of his mother's true image, recognized her.

But who were the others?

Lucy made a faint mewling sound. "Mother," she whispered, and Marcus knew the identity of the other woman, the one on the right, the English Rose.

They approached closer.

The third figure, standing between them, was not a woman; it was not in the least bit human at all, but one of the monsters which had come to populate Penderbrook and Little Millwich. Marcus recognized it all the same: it was—could be no other than—the female figure described by Barnabas. It was covered in orifices, which opened and closed as Marcus watched, not in the way of a woman's breathing, but in the way of a fish, lazily gaping at the water which surrounded it.

It was gravid to the point of bursting.

As Marcus and the others approached, the two women—who could not be who they seemed to be—on either side of the central, monstrous figure lowered it down to the dais. It had the features of a woman, but not the face: the features on what ought to have been its head seemed melted, mere bulges under the flesh. Not the least opening pierced the monster's head. And yet it was heard to hiss as it was lowered, through which orifices Marcus did not care to contemplate.

The monster began to give birth. It was not the birth of a woman, or that of an animal; the monster's flesh split along lines which had been heretofore invisible, and strips of flesh—or whatever material made up its corporeal body—shriveled back, so that they did not impede the birth.

Within the figure lay a child, seemingly made of pure gold. It climbed to its feet.

The two women on either side helped it step free of its parent, its fruiting body. The child was male, about eight or ten years of age, hairless, and perfect. The two women brought forth overlarge white robes from the air, clothed it, then knelt. The monster which had given birth to the figure had disintegrated entirely, leaving only a black smear on the dais.

Meanwhile, the golden boy ascended to the uppermost platform, and seated himself upon the throne. The two women remained where they were, at either hand, on the next circle down: only the god-king was allowed upon the highest of heights.

Marcus, Barnabas, and Lucy had come to a stop as they watched the events which occurred upon the dais. Now they continued moving forwards: once again, their actions seemed to occur outside of their own wills. All thought, all memory, all identity had silenced itself within them, as they watched the golden god-king apotheosis.

About halfway from the dais's furthest edge, they once again knelt.

It was the Earl before them, James Sewell that was. He had come into maturity as they approached, and now he was a beautiful young man, of such grace and wisdom as could not but overcome their hearts.

"Love me," the god-king commanded, looking more regal than ever did any portrait of Napoleon. And they did: they loved him; they adored him. All other ability was removed from them; there was only love, only admiration.

The golden man before them studied their faces.

At first, his expression reflected their amazement, their devotion. But, even as their faces continued in adoration, his own expression began to falter.

"Love me!" he commanded.

They loved; they had not ceased in their love.

The god-king stood up on his throne, his face contorted into a grimace of rage: "Love me!"

They continued to venerate, to admire, to tremble in awe.

With a slash of his arm, the god-king gestured towards them. "You are nothing. Go."

The three of them rose trembling to their feet. As the god-king had spoken, so had they become. Their faces registered shock, dismay, and shame, even horror. They had failed.

The world which had been created to their benefit, they did not deserve. They had been invited within that most sacred of sanctums. They had knelt before the god-king of a new-born universe.

He had reflected upon their worship, and found it less than he deserved. They bowed their heads and began to retreat, never turning their backs on the god-king, for even in his disappointment in them, they could not force themselves to fail him further.

Further and further they retreated, not daring to look behind them, only to stumble, lost to all divinity, until they emerged from that glorious throne room, from the presence of the god-king, from that single, perfect summer day, and—

Chapter Thirty-Two

A Return to Winter

—INTO A BLIZZARD WHICH seemed to have nothing of Nature to it: the flakes which were hard driven before them were not of snow, but of a thick, whitish, powdery substance. The winds were just as sharp, and the cold just as bitter, but the powder that surrounded them did not form droplets on their eyelids, or dampen their faces. It felt more as though they were being bombarded with frozen, dry sand.

"It is the fungus," Barnabas shouted, pulling his shirt over the lower part of his face. "Cover your mouths against the spores!"

The three of them stumbled blindly through the white darkness, which made their heads throb and their lungs ache.

Marcus bumped against something hard, and immense, and pressed his face to it: they had been sent to the edge of the bubble somehow. A few more steps led him to the path back to Penderbrook, which they followed by the main trick of feeling along the stone-paved path with their bare feet. Lucy shivered: Marcus carried her.

When they had crossed the bridge over the stream, the storm eased somewhat, leaving the air clearer, although it was still necessary both to squint and to keep one's mouth covered.

"What happened?" Marcus asked.

Barnabas said, with a dry humor: "We discovered what Father has been up to. Stealing summer out of our reality, to put into his."

Marcus cursed. "As long as he should not bother us about it again, let him have it."

"He will have it, and more," Barnabas said. "Look."

He pointed above them. Through the swirling, fine spores, as sly as particles of smoke, the two brothers saw that which they least wished to see. As if a dusty glass were being cleared, the illusion of blue sky above them was disappearing, revealing a truer aspect.

Lucy said, "What is it?"

Barnabas covered her face with his hand, and said, "The world which was created for our father was of a limited nature, being entirely bounded by some terrible substance, which may either be the substrate of the universe, or something which attempts to consume it. Marcus saw it when he looked through the wall at the end of the trail leading towards Bramble House; when he showed it to me, I saw it, too. You do not wish to see it."

Lucy readily agreed, and had already closed her eyes tight against the sight of it.

Marcus said, "What went wrong at the end? I do not remember what occurred clearly, only that we were given some test and failed it."

Lucy said, "I found it most distressing as well, although I find anything having to do with your father to be so."

Barnabas said, "I...I suppose that I have never felt his disapproval to such an extent."

"You're the eldest," Marcus said drily. "And you've never acted in such a matter as to attract his wrath. Father imagined himself a man of science; *you* are a man of science, and you did not bother to gainsay any statement of his. You pleased him; therefore, he had no need to chastise or humiliate you. He imagined himself to be much as you were: calm, cool, rational, and altogether admirable. And you allowed him to do so, because it meant that he would not interfere with your work."

Flushing, Barnabas said, "You may be correct. But, regardless, his disapproval was a disconcerting experience."

Marcus found himself tempted to shake his brother: it was a disconcerting experience that his brother had allowed Marcus to have in his stead, year after year, as children, then as young men. It had suited the Earl that Marcus had gone to fight in France; it had suited him admirably. And Barnabas had done little or nothing to defend his younger brother, saying only that he should "not allow the Earl to irritate him so."

Lucy said, "What shall we do, then? I had hoped that the removal of the Earl to his own private ground would ensure that our world remained intact, or at least in such a state that we might hope to remove his taint from it."

Barnabas shook his head.

Marcus said, "If we cannot reach Bramble House and Mr. Abbott's notes from here, then I do not know."

"The Earl might have his own notes," Lucy said.

Barnabas turned suddenly, and dashed along the side of the pond, towards his laboratory, the old boat-house. Marcus sprinted after him, leaving Lucy far behind.

Barnabas, with his long legs, disappeared inside the door with a bang as it struck the wall inside. Swirls of frozen spores drifted across the near side of the lake, but became a wall who could not be penetrated by sight along the far shore. Before he followed his brother within, Marcus looked back, and saw that the far side of Penderbrook had been similarly engulfed: their little world had become even smaller.

Barnabas was standing next to the hung boat where he had hidden his final journal, reading under his breath. When Marcus came upon him, there was a flicker in the dim light, and for a moment his brother was not there, but instead there was a Barnabas-shaped hole in the world, that was filled by whatever was outside it.

Barnabas flickered again, and returned. He raised his eyes to his brother's and said, "I know what must be done to destroy all of this."

"We have to save her," Marcus said.

"We cannot," Barnabas said coldly. "We must reconcile ourselves to that. There are no miracles; there is only this strange and corrupt science which lies before us, and which we must invoke in order to preserve Creation itself."

"You can weigh Lucy against Creation? And find *Lucy* wanting?" Marcus considered the existence of that small, dark figure, that irritated gaze of hers, the delightful sighs with which he had consigned himself to this Hell. He abruptly found himself alienated from his elder brother: "You're a fool. And she pledged herself to *you*."

"What of it? You left."

"You let me go." Marcus found his heart breaking as he said it, words that had never before crossed his thoughts, but seemed immediately to consume him now. "You let Father drive me off. You let Father take his strange whims out on me, so that it would leave you undisturbed in your researches."

"You brought Father's attention upon yourself. What could I do to stop you?"

"You could have stood between us!"

"Why?" Barnabas said. "You would have learnt nothing."

"I would have learnt that you loved me," Marcus said. "I would have learnt that you loved me more than you loved ease and lack of conflict. You allowed Father to lash out at me, at anyone or anything, as long as you were allowed to be undisturbed. You were given the boathouse, you—"

"*I was watched*," Barnabas snapped. "You were free to be whatever it was that your disgusting little fancies drew you to be. Women, guns, hunting—you could do anything. But I had to be perfection itself. *Father* wished to see himself as cool and rational; therefore, I must have no emotions. *Father* wished to see himself as well-respected among his peers; therefore, I must have no vanities, no foibles, no flaws. I was trapped, and what did you do in your freedom? Lay women, arouse trouble, and disregard the health and happiness of everyone about you! You speak well enough of Lucy, but you did not hear her weeping over you, telling herself that you *would* go, you *must* go, that you would never find happiness except elsewhere, far away from us! You abandoned *us*! What right do you have to speak to me, to either of us, about how unjustly we treated you? And what right do you have now, to stamp your foot and exclaim that we must save Lucy, above all else?"

Behind them, Lucy said, "Stop it. I won't have it."

They both turned towards her guiltily.

"It doesn't matter what was done, or not done, between the two of you, and less still to me," she said. Her face was wet with tears. "I love you both. I know what has been done to you by the Earl, and in his name. I know the weight on you both. Do not—*do not*—attack each other at this moment, in which if you must hate, then it is clear who must be hated. You lived. Can you understand that? Both of you lived. My father used to speak of the two of you with pity, saying that he would not wager a penny that either of you would live long enough to have children. He swore that Marcus would find himself in an accident, and perish; and that Barnabas would finally succumb to the darkness within himself and hang himself in the boathouse one day." She wiped her face, but it did not seem to stem the tide. She tried to speak again, but found herself unable to, wordlessly sobbing.

Finally, still brushing at her tears, she turned away from them, placing her head against the doorframe through which she had entered.

Marcus and Barnabas exchanged a glance.

Barnabas looked down at his journal, and began to read.

Marcus went to Lucy.

Upon taking her in his arms, Marcus found himself shivering. Outside, the wind had risen; the edge of the storm was closing in on them. He glanced through the doorway: the end, regardless, would occur soon. He took Lucy from the doorway and closed it behind her, so that she might, at least, be spared the sight of their world's dissolution.

The three of them, together, in this tiny boathouse, waiting for death.

Chapter Thirty-Three
Transformation

BARNABAS DID NOT SPEAK any more loudly than a boy reading a primer to his schoolmaster in the nursery. And yet Lucy hid her face in Marcus's coat and shuddered, wincing at his words. It was as though she must sustain herself in the face of physical blows.

Marcus watched his brother. As Barnabas read, obscenities occurred to his person. He vanished, then reappeared in quick succession; his face lost its features, or erupted far too many of them; his limbs twisted, reformed, and twisted again. The mystery of his reappearance and whether his nature was human or otherwise was resolved: whatever he had been, he was human no longer.

Lucy sobbed: "Father—Father—!" For added to her present horror, was the knowledge was that *this* was the way in which her father had died, and no other. It was no mere cold and calculating sacrifice of a chess piece, but the perversion of the soul, that her father, and now Barnabas, had done.

Marcus knew he ought not to find his brother's efforts insufficient. And yet, there remained the simple fact that Lucy would die with them.

Barnabas vanished, and, for a moment of time, the horrible vision of that which lay outside the bounds of their little world did not quite occur.

What Marcus saw were flashes of other places, other worlds. Things that, unlike whatever it was that lay in wait for them outside of the universe, *existed*.

He saw places without men, but with other beings of intelligence and grace. He saw cities which could not have existed in the world that he knew. He saw gardens...farms...parks... He saw children, unmistakably so, although they were in forms he did not know.

He saw other worlds. Why he saw them, he did not know. They did not quite give him hope.

Barnabas continued to read, his voice cracking and changing in tone, both from that which happened to him, and from the emotions which gripped him. One moment his face would be twisted with rage; the next, a mask of regret. He would laugh in horror...he would weep from joy.

A lifetime of emotions, sealed in the bottle necessitated of him by the Earl, were being released.

Thunder cracked. Then the air went still. Barnabas finally ceased.

The storm had stopped.

"Did it work?" Marcus asked.

Barnabas did not answer, perhaps no longer trusting his voice to human speech. He clutched the journal to his chest and looked at Marcus beseechingly with his dark eyes. Little else remained of him that was recognizable.

Marcus could not find it within himself to feel revulsion or disgust, only love. "I will take Lucy," he said firmly, "and we will see."

Lucy had not yet lifted her head from Marcus's coat. With care, Marcus opened the door and led her outdoors, closing the door behind him.

He heard Barnabas's voice begin to murmur the dark words again.

Outside, the world had been transformed.

Penderbrook had become a sort of fairy-palace, with tall towers and graceful archways. The bricks of its building had been torn down and cast aside, and lay scattered as ruins. From them a new palace had grown, as a mushroom would grow in the forest.

The main part of the growth was of smooth, white and pale lavender columns which stretched, elegant and capless, towards the sky, golden threads of filigree grown like vines along the sides. Clusters of smaller growths, in red and ivory, sprouted here and there along the columns, and were decorated with jeweled drops of liquid. Lacy mesh spread overhead to provide shade; underfoot were spread fine, varicolored strands that waved in the air like undersea growths.

Above them flew monsters; around them strode, slithered, and galloped more. Humanity had been replaced. Marcus looked back over his shoulder, and saw that the boathouse was in its final stages of collapse. The lake shimmered just past it, while under the surface lay growths of incredible beauty.

Was this a world to be dreaded? To be destroyed?

Marcus said, "Lucy, look."

She turned to see the world around her with a small inhalation of surprise. "But...it is beautiful."

It was more beautiful, in truth, than Penderbrook had ever been; far more beautiful than the cold and golden throne that the Earl had placed himself upon.

They stood and watched, as the glory of a new nature took root upon that which had previously been stately marble, stretches of well-cut grass, and trimmed hedges. Instead there was wilderness and civilization mixed in equal measure, with great harmony and loveliness contributed by both.

It was to prove but a brief glimpse.

Within Marcus came a sound something like the chime of a bell, but which had no sound at all. Marcus and Lucy both turned at the same moment back towards the boat house.

It collapsed inwards upon itself, the wood splintering as it was torn to pieces. A howl went up: the sound of roaring wind. The boathouse was falling in upon itself. Glass shattered; nails rang as they twisted, stretched, and snapped.

Barnabas had succeeded.

Marcus reminded himself that his brother was dead; that he had been dead since before he had returned to Penderbrook, since before his supposed death, his corpse hung under the church in Little Millwich. What he had spoken to, only moments ago, could not ever have been human—although it had clearly been possessed of his brother's spirit.

The destruction of the boat-house spread: the light itself around it grew dim, and the water from the lake rushed towards it. The ground in front of the boathouse stretched, and the boathouse itself seemed to retreat from them—or rather to shrink—taking the shore with it.

Penderbrook, and its unnatural, stolen summer, was ending.

Sadly, Lucy said, "This is victory, then. Goodbye, Barnabas."

The monsters had noticed what had happened; how could they not? But they did not scream, did not panic. Quickly, they snatched up bits of fungus here and there, then fled towards a single tower that grew in the heart of Penderbrook that was. Surely it would become crowded: but the monsters only brought that which they carried to the tower, where one of their kind collected what had been brought. Then they lay themselves on the ground in so orderly a fashion as to keep themselves, for the main part, out of each other's way.

"Should we run?" Marcus asked.

"This is what we wanted," Lucy replied numbly. "Where would we go?"

The boathouse had completely vanished; in its place was the sort of blankness that might occur if one stared too long into the sun: both brightly illuminated and completely impenetrable to view. Marcus raised an arm to shade his eyes. The blank place was spreading.

"The pond," Lucy said, pointing.

Out in the center of the pond, a figure had appeared, golden, with flowing white robes.

It was the Earl.

The god-king of Penderbrook strode towards them from the center of the pond, his footsteps remaining in place on the surface, as though frozen in ice. He walked towards the place where the boathouse had been, and suddenly, without word or gesture, the boathouse reappeared.

"*How dare you*," said the Earl. "How *dare* you interfere! You cannot do anything but that you ruin every joy in life!"

Next to Marcus, Lucy shuddered; Marcus, however, had heard these words, or their cousins, many times before.

Suddenly he felt as though everything he had done in life was in preparation for this moment: every woman woo'd, every battle fought, every dead man grieved.

All so he might discover within himself that which could resist his father.

"Good," Marcus said. "I am glad of it. I am glad that everything that you wished for, is ruined."

The Earl's rage was dreadful to behold.

"How *dare* you!" he cried once more, unable to state the violation that he had suffered at the hands of his son in any severer fashion.

The Earl's golden skin began to crack, to split, and to flake away. Underneath lay that which was not smooth, not fair, and not golden.

The white flesh bulged from beneath the flaking gold. Parts of it had already begun to blacken and to rot. The pure white robes fell away. The form which had been so finely drawn, so appealing, and so elegant, had become deformed, repulsive, and vile to look upon. Even to compare it to the forms of the monsters was to find it a perversion, for their limbs and shapes were terrifying to behold when seen in the world they had come to invade—but, when seen among the columns and vines of their own city, had their own certain pleasingness.

The Earl could make no such claim.

He had become enormous, towering above the two of them, with gray, rotting flesh. His bowed legs dug into the earth, cracked toenails gouging the turf. He had stooped forwards, bending nearly in half, and his head extended towards them on a long, sinuous neck. His face had vanished. Eyeless, he peered at them. Noseless, he scented them. And mouthless he howled:

"How *dare* you!"

The rest of his flesh was covered by thousands of faces, each of them the Earl's, each of them with an ugly expression. Among and between the faces sprouted long black spider's legs, and faceted black eyes, which watched them coldly even as the myriad of faces wept, and raged, and begged for pity, and smiled, and even tried to charm them.

Which was the true face? Could any of the faces be considered to be true? Were the spider's eyes which watched them, judging every reaction, the windows, it is said, of the soul?

Did the Earl have—or had he ever had—a soul?

Marcus shoved Lucy behind him. In an instant, the monster was on top of him, tearing at him with its terrible claws, pummeling his face, breaking limbs.

Lucy screamed.

That which had been Marcus lay before her, his skin splitting to reveal not meat, not blood, not bone—but the pale white flesh of one of the fungus-monsters. He had not behaved as though he were not himself, not in the slightest, and yet he had been transformed. When? Were any of them human, any longer?

The monster which had been Marcus seemed to be turtle-like, although immense, and was covered in plates of white bone, each thicker than the last. Small black eyes protruded from between the plates. The main part of his face, set deep between his broad shoulders, was a mouth whose rows and rows of teeth led deeper into a deadly maw. The outermost reach of the maw ended in a blunt and powerful beak.

The two monsters faced against each other, Marcus with his stubby legs the slower of the two. The Earl cackled as he danced around him. *"You monster! You hideous thing! What have you become? Ridiculous! You are ridiculous!"*

The Earl's voice had changed into a high-pitched, childish chanting of a thousand boyish voices, which laughed in mockery, apparently unaware of their own transformation.

Marcus's small eyes never left the Earl. As he swung his massive, slow forelegs at the Earl, missing every time and being forced to lumber this way and that to prevent the Earl's claws from catching too deeply in the cracks between the bony plates protecting him, he retreated, drawing the Earl away from Lucy, and towards the ruins of Penderbrook.

Lucy struggled for breath. She could not seem to comprehend what she was seeing, and yet it seemed as though it must always have been destined to occur. She struggled to her feet. She must do something to help Marcus, as monstrous as he had become. Perhaps with love and faith, he might be drawn back to humanity, or at least the appearance of it.

Or she could learn to accept him regardless, for even as twisted and hideous as he had become in her eyes, his actions could only be taken as kind: for she knew that he had become what he had, in order to spare her as much ill as he could.

The Earl attacked him again and again, and screeched every victory, but did not damage any of the bony plates. All of this was a game, so that Lucy might do what needed to be done.

She turned towards the boathouse, walked swiftly towards it, and threw open the door.

All was as it had been, if a little more decayed. The boats hanging along the wall were nearly in pieces.

Of Barnabas, she saw no sign, and none of the journal.

Above her, she heard some slight movement.

"Lucy..."

It was nothing more than the faintest whisper, almost lost in the screams and roars from outside.

She began to climb the stairs, careful to ensure that each foot did not fall through the rotting wood. The door at the top was open, or rather smashed from its hinges. A dark trail led from the doorway to Barnabas's work table.

It ended in a small black shape oozing along the floor, a pitiable thing.

"Lucy..."

Barnabas.

"Lucy...you must find another journal...he has destroyed the other one...this is the secret...*any* of the words will do. You must only keep reading them aloud, and all the world will shudder in horror..."

Not quite heedless of crossing the soft, rotting wood of the floor underneath her, she crossed the room quickly and took the nearest journal off the table. She opened it: the pages were moldy and black, nearly illegible—but perhaps that was for the best. She opened the book to one of the final pages and set it gently on the floor in front of what remained of her betrothed.

The small black creature dragged itself onto the pages. Limbless, faceless, and rapidly diminishing in size, it began to weep: "Oh, Lucy. He took my eyes. my eyes...I cannot read it."

"I will read it for you."

"No...you must not...it will damn you..."

They had both tried to save her: but how little they must think of her, that she would not also make the attempt? It was the way of men to throw themselves into whatever wars they might, with whatever bravery or cowardice they might possess, in order to save some shred of home, of light, of love. Did they not think that it was not also a consuming sacrifice, to rebuild oneself as a home—as a hearth—as an idol? Was it all men, all women, who played these terrible games of transformation?

Or just these two fools whom she loved with all her heart?

Gently, Lucy removed the small, pitiable shape from the page. She sat beside it with her legs curled underneath her, and pulled the rotten journal onto her lap.

The same symbol which had appeared to her previously in the nursery appeared once again before her vision. She spoke the word, and the light which pierced the shutters of the room gathered to her as if it was a small child wishing to be told a story, to be read a poem, to play a clever little puzzle-game out of a book.

She began to read.

Chapter Thirty-Four

What Is Underneath All the Faces

MARCUS DODGED; HE HOWLED in artificial pain; he attacked but missed; he drew the Earl ever onwards. He had led him all the way back to the ruins of Penderbrook. The monsters which had been brought by the fungus had retreated, or simply died; it was not clear which. The idea that any creature could simply lay itself down to death without resistance was one that Marcus could not countenance. Marcus knew that he could sacrifice himself, and cheaply at that—but that any creature of intelligence might do so as gently as falling asleep horrified him. The monsters had attacked humans out of the shadows, from secrecy, from aggression that infiltrated rather than overwhelmed. They must then be weaker than he had suspected: for would not a stronger foe have attacked them more quickly? These monsters had taken a period of decades, a slow change that was only now coming to fruition.

Even further did Marcus draw his father, all the way to the folly. Where Penderbrook had been torn down and replaced with the monsters' elegant city, the folly was untouched. It was as though the ground itself contained some poison, even beyond that of Penderbrook, and the monsters refused to approach it.

Marcus knew he had changed; he knew he had discovered himself to be other than human. He was a cousin, at least, to whatever perversion his father had become. This did not come as a surprise to him. He had always known himself for a sort of monster. If it was a monster that his father had created, well, he had long since reached manhood and independence. Was it not his own responsibility now, to have become what he had become?

As they fought, his father called him names: called him monster, fool, perversion, unwanted, unwise. That it should not occur to him that he, himself, was all that and worse, for having brought all of this to pass, did not surprise Marcus. He had often caught his father looking at himself sidelong in a mirror, and practicing his faces until he was pleased with his own appearance from every angle.

It was only in a mirror that his father could see himself.

The thought occurred to him of leading his father back to the pond, and making him look into its mirrorlike surface. But Marcus knew that even the momentary horror of his father seeing his own appearance would not make the taunting cease, but only redouble. Whatever flaws the Earl saw in himself, he would never in himself amend, but blame others for having caused them.

And so Marcus did what he had always done, which was to fight, and to endure.

He had no hope of defeating his father; he never had done. He had never expected to escape the monster his father had always been; and he knew he would never escape the monster he himself had become.

Marcus's hopes lay elsewhere: in protecting the weak, in delaying tyranny in its conquest, in drawing danger to a place where it might, as if by accident, make itself vulnerable. That he *could* endure, was the secret heart of the matter. As often as he had felt himself, as a child, on the edge of despair, he had never yet truly given himself over to it, to fall as he might.

Even in leaving home and joining the fighting in France, which he had told himself was only to spare the necessity of killing himself, he had only made himself the stronger, the more apt for his task.

He was no saint; he was no man of science. He was only a pawn, that which was moved by the chess players above, in some greater game. To know it was an unsettling thought, and yet that he was being moved about in a way that annoyed his father had its satisfactions.

His father was howling about something, ranting on and on about the injustices that had been done to *him*, the trials *he* had been through, the gratitude which was lacking, and so on, when something caught Marcus's attention.

His father cried, "And now it is all ruined, my Penderbrook! And it is all your fault!"

Marcus guffawed.

For the undeniable truth was that *Marcus was not at fault.*

And, finally, he could see it. Somehow, the cord which had bound Marcus to his father had been severed, and his father's words had no more meaning than the chattering of an ape.

It was a miracle.

The fungus-monsters had taken the perfect summer day at Penderbrook, torn down the stuffy English country house, and replaced it with something graceful and lovely, if entirely alien.

His father had even not realized that he had been betrayed!

Cruelly, Marcus said, "I did not destroy your house, Father. It was the fungus-people. They waited until you were distracted with rebirthing yourself in your glorious new image, then betrayed you."

His father howled in rage, and in pain.

A cacophony of voices rose up, each of the tiny faces stretching their jaws to cry out.

Then Marcus felt something shift within him, and felt himself being drawn backwards, away from the ruins.

Lucy had begun to read, and the world was once again beginning to collapse.

Marcus's throat tightened, and tears came to his secretive black eyes, half-hidden under his plates of bony armor. The two monsters of Pender-brook paused, one to grieve that his slaves did not love him half so well as he thought, and the other to mourn the passing of the single remaining soul which he loved.

Then the moment passed, and Marcus and his father looked towards each other, as if startled to see the other still existed.

Marcus attacked his father viciously, knocking him to the ground and pinning him there. He brought up his ponderous rear legs and began to dig away at the faces underneath him, scraping them off and scattering them. His father struggled and wept: "How *dare* you," he cried, and so on. The smaller faces, having been removed, continued to weep and cry out, although they were fainter now, their voices dwindling.

"*What...is...underneath...all...these...faces!*" Marcus roared. "What is the truth? What is under all this? Why have you done this? What drove you to it? And don't say it was my fault! You started this years before I was born! I have heard the tale from Mr. Abbott, who had once been your friend!"

"How dare you question me!" His father struggled, but Marcus kept him pinned: he had to give Lucy time to finish reading.

And Marcus found himself, at the last, truly wishing to know: *why?*

Why had his father done all this? Was it simply a flaw in his character? Was he a fool? Did he simply not care what consequences might occur? Why any of it? But particularly: why *this*?

Marcus tore and tore, until, at last, he had torn away all the smaller faces, leaving only the blank one at the end of the Earl's long and sinuous neck.

His entire body, which was now larger than most of the brick cottages in Little Millwich, was naked and deformed, covered with black, oozing sockets where the faces had been torn free.

As Marcus gazed upon that final face, he found within himself the final question, the root of it all, springing from a suspicion that he had not known that he had:

"Why did you kill my mother?"

The blank face writhed and jerked, but Marcus would not release it. He had weakened the monster enough that it could not, this time, throw him aside. The world was ending. He would never have another chance.

His father went limp, then giggled.

"It did not start with *her*," his father's sneering voice said, from deep within the monster's blank face.

Marcus snapped at it, and caught at the skin with his teeth. He tore it away and spat it to the side.

Underneath was another blank, featureless face, and for a moment Marcus could only imagine himself tearing away at it for eternity, face after face, never discovering the truth.

His father said, "It started with my brother. He asked me the same question, you see. 'Why, James? Why do you do these things?' And I answered him honestly, because he was my brother.

"He was silent for a time. And then he told me what he thought about me. He called me sordid and selfish and dull. He said I was the least interesting, most common sort of person he had ever met, and that he would have me drowned like a litter of useless kittens. And then he spat in my face and beat me until the blackness took me.

"You ask me why, but, I assure you, you *do not want to know*. You would hear my reasons and pity me. Pity *me*! You are a worm. Your brother was a worm. You are *worms* and you would pity *me*, just as *he* did! Your mother?

I killed her because I didn't need her, or her pity, any longer. I needed your brother; I could see that he would be my partner, my ally, my friend. I would introduce him slowly to that which he needed to know. I would present my case, and he—he would agree with me. *Your* only use was in showing him what was foolish, what was useless in life. You chased women in order to show him that he need not. You were a braggart, that he might remain as humble as I am. You saw no value in learning, that he might drive himself to further brilliance.

"He was *my true son*, and I killed his mother so that she might not interfere."

"And Mrs. Abbott? If you did not love or need my mother, then why destroy her friend?"

Here, the Earl bared his teeth. With sudden viciousness, he said, "Because she claimed something that was not true."

"What was it?"

There was another scuffle, but his father had lost too much strength, and could not escape. Marcus kept him pinned. Still his father resisted in saying the truth, until at last Marcus threatened to spit in his face, as his brother once had.

Wailing for mercy, his father cried, "That Harriet and Mr. Abbott had been lovers, that they had betrayed us, that Barnabas was not my child, but that of Mr. Abbott!"

Marcus shuddered. He had always felt that he, himself, had not been his father's true child. In the way that children sometimes will, he had told himself that his mother had loved another and got him of a stranger, or even—sometimes—of Barton. He had told himself that Barnabas was more like his father, although they did not appear to resemble each other in the slightest.

But now that it was said, he saw the resemblance: not between Mr. Abbott and Barnabas, but between Barnabas and Lucy. *Their* hearts beat as one, dark and inquisitive and serious. And they had almost been married.

"I killed Mary for her lies," the Earl said. Then the two of them began to slide along the ground, as if down a steep slope, towards the boathouse. "What—what is happening—why am I—"

Marcus smiled. He had played for time enough.

The end had arrived, not a victory—but an end.

It would have to be enough.

Chapter Thirty-Five

By Accident

Lucy awoke in her bed at Bramble House, her face wet with tears. She had dreamt, yet again, that Marcus had been reported missing in France, and that she was still waiting for news. All the long night she had dreamt of sitting next to a window, looking out into the gray weather, waiting. She would sometimes pace; at other times, she would dream that she wrote letters. She knew that the words she wrote were to ask if someone had news of Marcus, but, in the way of dreams, she could not read that which she wrote.

She woke to a gray day exactly as the one in her dreams. It was winter; she had overslept. She thought of the things that she must accomplish that day: to go to Penderbrook and check that the Earl had been cared for—

She bolted upright in bed, threw off the covers, and sprang to her feet. The last thing she could remember, she had gone to the library, in preparation of sitting outside the Earl's door until the morning.

This morning.

Had no one been there to watch him?

She dressed hastily. She had never been the sort of woman who wished to have a maid to dress her, and had lost whatever taste for fashion she had, when Barnabas had died. To tell the truth, it had felt like a part of her own soul had passed from this world into the next with him. That his body was missing was only a reflection of the lack he had left within her.

She was glad of Marcus's return, but sad of it, too. She knew now that, no matter how badly she had needed him to be here, he should never have come back, and she should not have asked him.

Early this morning, he and her father would have gone to Little Mill-wich. She knew they wished to examine some of the books there, and suspected that they also wished to investigate the spread of the fungus. Her father had seemed almost unnaturally grim, as he always did when there was reference to the Earl and his doings. Perhaps whatever had occurred was even larger than she herself suspected: she knew that the Earl was concealing *something* that occurred at the mill, for why else should such an unnatural number of people go to work at it? Surely Little Millwich must be the size of London by now, for all the souls it had so recently absorbed.

Her head throbbed. She looked about for the clothes that she had been wearing the previous day, but they were not to be found. Another of her mourning-dyed dresses was hanging up for her, and she dressed in that.

How had she come to be back in her own bed? And why could she not recall the events of the previous evening?

She went to her bedroom door to open it, then hesitated. Something was tucked into the pocket she had sewn into her skirt. She drew it out.

It was a slip of folded journal paper.

She nearly dropped it onto the floor. It was the oddest sensation, but the paper itself seemed to have bitten her! She sucked on her fingers, and tasted blood: it was only a paper cut.

DOWNSTAIRS, LUCY FOUND THAT her father had already left for Little Millwich. She ate breakfast and asked if there were any messages; there were none. As for news, it was said in a hushed tone by the housekeeper that Barnabas's body had not yet been found, and that it was the scandal of the neighborhood. His mysterious death was blamed on everything from illness to assassination.

If the housekeeper only knew—!

As she ate, Lucy caught the scent of smoke. She checked the chimney to ensure that it was drawing properly, and found that her hands were thicker with the scent of smoke than the chimney itself. It was as though she had just burnt something, but of course she hadn't. She washed her hands.

"What are your plans for the day, Miss?" asked the housekeeper.

"I shall to go Penderbrook and see whether the Earl passed the night well or ill, and then I shall write some letters."

The housekeeper curtseyed and excused herself.

Lucy put on a pair of stout boots against the cold and walked in the bright morning light along the path that led to the larger house. The snow had drifted in the night, and much of the path was nearly blown shut, so that she must scramble over the drifts. She crossed the little bridge over the stream at the top of the pond and thought to herself that, come the spring, the melt would surely be of unusual strength.

The sky seemed different. There was something different about the quality of light.

The year had been unusually dim and stormy, of course, and altogether too wet and cold, and filled with illness, disease, and incredible amounts of mold. She had worried over the books in her father's library. The light, when they had been able to see it directly, had had a golden, and even sometimes reddish tinge to it, especially at dawn and sunset.

Today it seemed paler; the blue sky, by a slight increment, bluer; the sun a little whiter than the sun she last remembered.

It had been said that the unseasonable weather was due to any one of a number of reasons. It was said that all the factories burning coal of late had been the main cause of it; others said the weather had come from an enormous fire in the Americas. The end of the world had even been foretold countless times.

Lucy had felt herself unaccountably saddened by the change in the quality of light, whatever the reason.

It felt as though she were finally grieving Barnabas's death. Events of late had been so strange, and had followed so close upon each other, that she had found herself unable to feel much of anything about his loss. Now, she found herself not mourning the loss of a mate and future husband, so much as she mourned the death of a brother, an ally—a friend.

For a time she hesitated upon the path, staring at she knew not what. Then she blew her nose into a kerchief—it was quite cold enough to make one's nose run—and continued onwards.

With Barnabas's death, the question of what she would do with the rest of her life had been reopened.

Marry Marcus, now that he was the heir? Become mistress of Penderbrook?

But Marcus would not have her; that much she knew. His roving eye had never come to land upon her; he had never so much as touched her, since they were innocent children.

What, then, lay ahead of her?

She would be no fine mistress of Bramble House. She could not imagine herself wed. She could not imagine a man with whom the constrictions of marriage would suit either herself, or him. No, better to give up on all that.

But what, then?

The future lay before her. She had often reviewed its dim prospect. Loveless, yet with enough of a living that she might conduct herself independently but not extravagantly, with no purpose and nothing to do.

She might take herself to London, and hire or purchase herself a house on some boundary between the world of fashion and the world of substance, and fill it with books, and read them. Perhaps she might even essay to write them—she might write them under a male pseudonym—and pit her wits against the publishers, the populace, and the press. She might establish for herself a salon, where her dark humor might be appreciated by those who enjoyed conversation more than spectacle.

She enjoyed herself in such fantasies as she crossed the grounds and wound her way back up the low hill to Penderbrook itself. The snow sparkled merrily, and frost decorated every windowpane. Her breath steamed up before her in great clouds.

She was a black raven against the snow.

She reached the kitchen door and knocked for Cook to let her in. Cook's face seemed to have lost its color, but it had seemed so on every day since Barnabas's death. Lucy stepped indoors, blinking as Cook closed the door behind her.

"Morning, miss."

"How fares the Earl?"

"Fast asleep yet." Cook nodded towards the door. "It looks a pleasant day out, barring the chill."

"I think the season has turned," replied Lucy. At Cook's questioning look, she added, "Oh, it shan't turn from winter to spring, and we shall never regain the summer that was lost. But it seems clearer out, doesn't it? As though whatever lay between us and the sun had lessened a little."

"You're talking about Barnabas's ideas, yes?"

They had been her ideas before they had been Barnabas's, but she said, "I suppose I must do."

"You don't believe that it's the end of the world, then?"

Lucy tipped her head to the side. She had long known from certain signs that Cook was a Catholic, and had pondered what that might mean—and what it meant that she, Lucy, was not. She had come to no strong conclusions, and yet she suspected that, of all who lived in the neighborhood, that Cook might understand her sentiments more than any other.

"As odd as it might sound," Lucy said, "I find that my heart feels as though it *was* the end of the world coming, and that we were all about to drown with it. But that now it has been redeemed, not by the Savior, but by some small act of decency and sacrifice, and that, although we have a great deal of work to accomplish, that we have of some great sin been forgiven." She shook her head. "Forgive me, I do not know what I am saying."

But Cook took her hands into her own. "I do not know what you are saying, miss, but I feel it.

LUCY BETOOK HERSELF UPSTAIRS to the nursery, nodding at the bustling of the other servants as she went. They still seemed to take her for the future mistress of Penderbrook, and treated her with deference—all but the ones who had known her since childhood, of course, who gave her winks and smiles. To them, she was still little Miss Lucy, following along in the two young masters' wake.

At the top of the stairs, she met Barton, whose face was likewise as drawn as Cook's had been. The pressures of Barnabas's death and disappearance, combined with the illness of the Earl, had become a sort of injury to him. Even Marcus's return had not eased it, but that was no surprise: Marcus had long been a contributor of trouble, rather than a cause of its surcease.

"How fares the Earl this morning?" Lucy asked. "And I beg your forgiveness for leaving you with his sole care last evening. I do not know what came over me."

Barton had frozen into place, looking at her with wide eyes. The strain apparent on his features was not merely the product of the worries of days past, but obviously of some new introduction.

A smell struck her, and she covered her face with her hand.

"Miss," he said. His voice trembled; his hands shook. "Miss...you must not look."

Lucy brought Barton downstairs to the parlor that she liked, and found for him some brandy that Marcus liked to keep hidden away there. Against his protests, she gave him a glass of it, and soon he had drunk it and been served another.

"What is it?" she asked. "Is it the Earl? Has he..." She disliked to ask, but it must be done. "You must tell me, Barton. Has he harmed himself? You may trust that I will carry no tales, but if some action must be taken before Marcus and my father return from Little Millwich, then I must be the one to bear the brunt of that decision."

She did not know whether that was truly the case, but it *had* been, but a few weeks before, when she was Barnabas's bride to be: she trusted Barton to be influenced by it still.

He said, "The Earl..." He cleared his throat. He could not seem to proceed.

Lucy said, "Barton, if you cannot tell me, then I shall have to look."

"You should not," he said immediately.

"Has he done some harm to himself? By intention or accident?"

"By accident," Barton was able to say. "By accident."

"Is he dead?"

Barton nodded. Silence had once again tightened his voice.

Lucy rose to her feet. "I will see, Barton, so that if it is necessary to defend you against ill-will and gossip, that my voice can be honestly used so."

A look of shock washed across his face. The idea that he might be accused of ill intent shocked him.

She added, "And, if necessary, I can defend Marcus, too."

Barton swayed, and caught at the arm of the chair, then finished the brandy and led her up the stairs.

Barton opened the door of the nursery for her, standing at the threshold, preventing her entry. Lucy smelled the death there again, more strongly than before, and locked her teeth together.

"Barton," she said, through them, "women are always the ones to have dealt with death. You think to save me from it, because I am a lady. But even ladies must wash them and clothe them, and dress them for the tomb. I washed Barnabas and helped to dress him. Do you not remember?"

He shuddered, then stepped aside.

The Earl's cot was empty. The bedding had been tossed aside. For a moment Lucy thought that she had been mistaken, that the Earl had simply vanished without a trace. Then she looked again at a half-seen shape in the darker corner of the room. The bright light coming from the window had given the corner into the deepest shadows.

She stepped towards it, dread rising in her throat.

"But what has happened to the Earl?" Barton cried. "He is gone!"

Chapter Thirty-Six

Not Who We Are

MARCUS FOUND HIMSELF WALKING along a snowy lane behind a row of small brick cottages; ahead of him was one of the two large mill buildings. Beside him walked Mr. Abbott; behind him, as he twisted to look over his shoulder, were two trails of footsteps, leading back to the square. Of Westin, there was no sign.

Mr. Abbott said, his voice strained and hoarse, "How did it go, then?"

Marcus almost asked where they were—or at least when—but, although he did not understand what had occurred, he knew the answers to those questions: he and Mr. Abbott were in Little Millwich, and they were walking towards the mill, to make their final confrontation with the monsters. Mr. Abbott would, once again, be required to speak the unnatural words that would free Marcus to try to save Lucy. It was not exactly the same situation as before, but it was similar enough.

Either they would succeed, or they would fail, and then they must make the attempt again, perhaps for all of eternity.

"I do not know if Lucy is free," he said, "and I do not know if the Earl is destroyed or all that we know, saved. But we made the attempt."

"You did not despair, then?"

For a moment Marcus almost said that they had, but then understood the import of Mr. Abbott's question. He wished to know that they had not yielded to the Earl, in the end. Marcus said, "For a moment we knelt. But we did not succumb to him. To the last we fought, even beyond death. And it may be that Lucy is free now, and that all is saved."

"But that the two of us should not know for certain," murmured Mr. Abbott. "It is not what I wanted to hear—but it is that with which I must find myself content. Tell me, were you ever able to discover what it was that he wanted? Were you ever able to find out *why*?"

Marcus said, "He told me that I would not wish to know. I asked him, to distract him from pursuing Lucy. He said that he had only told one person, his brother, and his brother had said that he ought to be drowned, for being dull. Or perhaps I misunderstood the sense of his explanation."

"If there *was* any," said Mr. Abbott. "Here, we are at the back of the tavern. Let us let ourselves in, and have ourselves a whisky before we have to face these monsters."

"But must we not go now?"

Mr. Abbott gave him a speculative look. "I have been here so long that I do not know how long I have been here. I make my way into the mill, and I read the words, and everything collapses...then I am returned to the square all over again. It is a dull way to spend half an hour, I tell you. I imagine that your loop may be a bit longer and more complicated, and yet I am sure that you will tire of it, too. Let us take our pleasures where we might. After all, there seem to be fewer and fewer of these monsters about. Perhaps, in time, we will be the only two souls remaining, and we can pass the time throwing snowballs at each other."

"Fewer of the monsters?"

"I believe the world itself is shrinking," said Mr. Abbott. "The whiteness of the snow makes it difficult to determine, but it seems—however so long it might take—that the edge of the thickest clouds slowly begins to approach the steeple of the church. The monsters flee a dying world, I believe."

"And we shall die with it," Marcus said.

"Perhaps by then we shall have bored of existence," Mr. Abbott said. "But come! A whisky, before our toy of a universe is once again upended."

And there was nothing for it, but that Mr. Abbott would take Marcus into the tavern, tracking snow all about the trackless floor.

"I must warn you that I may have become a monster," Marcus said.

"What of it?" said Mr. Abbott, who began to whistle, and soon had located a pair of bottles. "Who hasn't?"

THE DARK CORNER OF the nursery seemed to swallow Lucy up in its shadows. The scent of the room had changed, becoming chill and dead but for the slight smell of mildew. She felt closed in upon, dizzy. She reached out a hand and touched cool, rough stone.

She was underground, unable to see.

"Hello?"

Her voice echoed back to her with a mocking tone. She heard movement and turned towards it, but saw nothing. Knowing that it was a danger far beyond what was apparent, she said the word that summoned the light to her.

It came but slowly, as though from a great distance, but her eyes had by then much adjusted to the dark.

What was revealed to her was the pitiable figure of a creature whose body was covered with orifices of all types, such that a man might enjoy, but all about her flesh. She wore nothing, so that she had not even the privacy of covering them. Lucy cried out in pity, and stripped off her dress. It was cold in that place, but not so cold that she could not sacrifice comfort for the sake of simple decency.

She held it out to the figure huddled against the wall, who attempted to retreat in terror from her. In a moment she recognized her as the creature which had given birth to the Earl's golden form, which had caused her to rupture and decay, then to vanish entirely.

Where this memory came from, Lucy did not know; nevertheless, she remembered it.

Lucy held the dress out to her, but the creature would only shake her head, and Lucy worried that she had insulted her, for the creature was so foreign that perhaps she took clothing as a sort of onus rather than a gift. Lucy lay the dress upon the floor, and stepped away from it.

"I'm sorry to have startled you," Lucy said. "I was looking for the Earl."

The creature shuddered and began to keen through her orifices. Lucy pressed her lips together. She did not want to startle the creature further, but she felt as though she might scream, for the thought of what the Earl must have done to her—not least of which was causing her to be transformed into a mockery of human flesh. Lucy could not forget the creatures which had overtaken the grounds of Penderbrook, such a short time ago, and that she had found them beautiful and natural enough, when they were seen in their own right.

"I am sorry for what he has done to you," she said. "I am sure that it was unkind."

The creature's keening turned to a hiss, then a whisper: "He lies."

"I have no doubt of it. My name is Lucy. What is yours?"

"Lucy...you must leave, Lucy, before it is too late. You must fear him. There is nothing he does not touch, but it becomes sterile."

Lucy had a flash of insight: these creatures traveled in ways that spanned time and place, perhaps even identity. Today they might play at being Barnabas; tomorrow, at someone else. "My kind has not the trick of coming and going the way you do," she said. "We are trapped inside a single body, a single world. The Earl saw what you have, and wished to take it from you—but I am sure that, upon receiving whatever gifts you gave him, he cast them aside, for I know he could not possibly abide the thought of the sort of transformations that are quite usual to you."

The creature listened to her intently, her orifices gnashing. "Is this common? Among your kind?"

"I suppose it must be," Lucy replied after a moment's thought. "Although the extent of the Earl's desire, and of his fear, is unusual. He fears death, I suppose. Death, or the thought that he, himself, must come to an end."

"Fool," the creature whispered.

"I think I have seen a future where he destroys you so that he might be reborn as a sort of golden god, but he screamed at us that we had betrayed him, for he did not feel as happy about his apotheosis as he thought he would. If you can go, you must, before he uses you so ill."

The creature seemed to take what Lucy had said with great seriousness. Finally, she said, "Let us destroy him. Come with me."

She stood from the wall against which she had huddled, still disregarding Lucy's dress. She led her past a small door in the cave wall, then to a side-tunnel, at the bottom of which was a shallow grave, in which lay the form of a man, anonymous in face, a sort of half-carved statue, crafted from flesh.

Beside the grave lay the body of the Earl. A cord from one of the draperies had been tied around his neck so that the flesh bulged around it. He still struggled, his hands clawing at his neck, although it seemed certain to Lucy that he was dead, for he did not breathe—did not even attempt to breathe—past the horrific stricture at his throat.

Lucy cried out in dismay and would have gone to him, but the creature put a limb upon her chest, and held her back.

"Lucy...watch."

From the shallow grave, the figure began to move. It did not move in the way that a man might move, but instead began to sprout. Pale, lace-like fruits bubbled up from the figure's skin, then stretched into bulbous filaments dotted with beads of a clear, red liquid. These enlarged until the fruits were as large—although quite hollow—as the figure of the man underneath them.

Then the fruits burst, releasing a thin cloud of white spores, which collected about the body of the Earl. He was soon so thickly encrusted with them as to disappear within them.

The creature, who was still restraining Lucy from moving, had begun to emit a scent, not unpleasant, something like the smell of old books. The scent filled the room.

The figure in the shallow grave collapsed in upon itself, turning black and flattening at the bottom of the grave, a gray crust forming atop it.

Now the creature next to Lucy turned to her and said, "This is not who we are. We will not be this. There is no prize that is worth such perversion. I advise you to become something better—to improve your race. Such misery is not the lot of all life."

Lucy said, "What will you do?"

The creature walked towards the Earl's form, still buried under the spores, and rolled it into the grave with one foot.

Then she spat upon him, with one or another of her mouths, and a black sludge spread across the surface of the spores.

Within moments it was over: the Earl was gone, his body destroyed along with the spores, only a layer of black decay remaining.

"Be sterile," the creature hissed.

Then she pointed back the way they had come. "Turn to the right, and you will soon return to the surface."

"Thank you," Lucy said, then retreated to the branchings of the tunnels, and turned right.

Behind her, she heard the figure opening that wooden door they had passed earlier, crying, "No more shall we remain in this horror...no more."

Epilogue

The Glass Pearl

Lucy discovered herself in the folly to the north of Penderbrook, the false church the Earl had built. The sky remained of that undefinably bluer tinge, although the clouds had partly covered the clear blue sky.

She had been tempted to recover her dress before leaving the tunnel, but had dared not; and quickly she found herself frozen near to the bone.

Puffing out great clouds of breath and running as fast as her sturdy and sensible boots would allow her, she ran across the snow towards Penderbrook. She could feel the eyes of the maids and men who worked inside watching her, although no one called out to her, and no one opened a door. She crossed the entirety of the house in good time, considering the unevenness of the wind-whipped snow beneath her, and reached the door to the kitchen with her fist already raised to bang upon it.

It opened before her, and Cook drew her in.

"What is it? Where have you been? Barton has been searching for you. He said that both you and the Earl had disappeared—the Earl being gone when he reached the place, and you vanishing before his very eyes!"

"Cook," Lucy said earnestly, her teeth chattering, her throat burning from the brandy which Cook had just forced down her throat, her shoulders itching from the heavy wool blanket which Cook had thrown about her, "Cook! I have discovered everything."

The solution had come to her as she had run—not the truth, but close enough.

"What is it, child?"

"It is the fairies, Cook, the fairies! That is what these creatures are, only we have not known it! They have taken the Earl! They tried to take me, too."

Cook laughed and asked if she were mad.

"A little, I think," Lucy admitted. Then a cramp swept through her, and she bent over, gasping. At first she thought she was merely ill—ill, after what she had done and seen? how not?—but when she straightened a little, she saw that Cook suffered some sort of upset as well. Oddly, Lucy's boots had left a trail before her. She had also been drawn backwards, towards the center of the house, when she had felt the cramp.

A chill ran through her, as severe as the cramp had been sharp.

"Cook, I must return to Bramble House, and you must come with me," Lucy said, "immediately, at this moment. I..." She threw an arm over her face. "I fear that I may be..."

It was not difficult to find within herself a well of grief with which to provide a fund for tears. Cook stroked her shoulders through the blanket. "There, there, a cup of tea..."

"I want to go home!" wailed Lucy.

"Let me only get you a coat—" began Cook, and took a step towards the door leading into the house.

But as Cook began to walk, her feet slid under her, and she fell over with a thump onto the kitchen floor. She looked up at Lucy with something that was not comprehension, but not unlike it, dawning upon her face: *horror.*

"We must go," said Lucy. "Naked and barefoot if we must, we still must go, and *now*."

Within the house came a groaning and a shattering of glass, and a scream.

Lucy, clinging to the heavy wooden table upon which Cook and her assistants had once fed Penderbrook, helped the woman to her feet, and the two of them, clinging to anything within reach, worked their way to the door. Lucy had only to touch the handle for the door to fly towards them.

Spice jars few off the shelves now, tumbling across the room, casting up clouds of ground cloves, cinnamon, and thyme, only to have them whirled deeper through the door to the rest of the house. They pulled themselves, gasping for breath, along the short hallway and out the door and into the snow.

The pull here was a little weaker, although they could still feel it, and they were able to stagger, then walk, then run along the snow directly towards the pond, and, because of the unseasonableness of the weather, across its frozen surface to the other side. Soon they had reached the woods between Penderbrook and Bramble House.

Out of breath, they stopped in a clearing, and looked back.

Penderbrook was not clearly in view, but they could hear the ruination which occurred within it. No longer did they hear the sound of breaking glass, but that of wood, and stone; no longer did they hear screaming, but the cracking of ice.

"We must keep going," said Lucy.

"How far? How far must we go?"

"We may not live," Lucy said drily, "if we stop to calculate."

They ran again, this time more slowly, climbing the taller hill between Penderbrook and Bramble House. In truth they did little more than stumble forwards, Cook sobbing noisily, Lucy less so.

"What of the others?" one of them asked; the other did not respond.

They continued forwards. Suddenly, Lucy found her feet going out from under her as if pulled from behind. She landed on her face in the snow, and felt herself sliding backwards.

Cook cried out and reached for Lucy's hands. Lucy snatched them away from Cook's clumsy grasp, and allowed herself to be drawn a bit farther. She rolled onto her back. No one had hold of her; it was only some strange gravity which drew her along, in the direction of Penderbrook.

Lucy kicked at the trunk of a tree, which careened her a little in the other direction, and threw one leg around a sapling, so that she could not be pulled any further without snapping off the tree. She pressed her face against the trunk of the sapling, arms around it, and sobbed.

She was unclean. She remembered now: she remembered *everything* now, that which had occurred, that which had not, and that which might have been.

Creation itself rebelled against Penderbrook—and, possibly, her own tainted self.

She heard Cook calling to her, and cried, "Stay back! Stay back!"

Before her, a storm had arisen, silver and white. A powder which was not snow stung at her eyes. It covered the far edge of the pond and crept up the hill towards them.

The white powder seemed to be crowded with figures, ghostlike, pale, overlapping each other.

They were faceless, and more in the form of men than anything else, but she knew them to be the creatures which had come to her world, and which had been left behind, unable or unwilling to escape. Perhaps—she thought, remembering now memories that had belonged to Barnabas—or was it Marcus?—they were the last remnants of those who had been hidden or imprisoned behind that wooden door, down in the tunnel between Penderbrook and the folly.

Or perhaps they had come from the earth itself, the fruiting bodies of a fungus which had always been more hidden than revealed.

They swarmed in the snow; they were caught by it and tumbled about; they reached for her, only to be snatched away.

She prayed harder, and turned her face more firmly away. To see them was to be drawn to them, and the sapling that held her groaned against her weight.

It was no use: one leg was pulled harder than the other, and she began to slide around the tree. She wrapped her arms around it, but soon it was only her arms which restrained her from flying into the storm, and against it, they could not hold.

It would take her in a moment. The skin was torn from her forearms as she clung, bleeding, to the tree.

Then: between one heartbeat and the next, it stopped. The dreadful pulling stopped.

She fell into the snow, scraping her face against the trunk. Stunned, she rolled to the side and tried to see what had happened. Had she crossed the boundary and not known it? Or had time itself changed, as it had before, when she had discovered herself in her own bed this morning?

She could not see. The world swam before her face. And yet she must see—she must. Her forehead was bleeding where she had hit it, and she tried to wipe it clean, but her hands were run over with the streams of blood from her arms. She did not think that she was in such danger as to bleed to death, however, for the blood only ran and did not gush. She bent over and wiped herself clean with snow. She was in her petticoats and underthings, the blanket having been long since lost in the storm.

She climbed to her feet, still clinging to the tree, feeling blood drip from her arms and face down into the snow. Her eyes seemed to buzz, then slowly to clear.

Penderbrook, and all that lay about it, were gone.

She could see the edge of the lands that marked the boundary between Bramble House and Penderbrook, but there was no hillside, no pond, no stream, no grounds, no house, no ruins. Beyond Penderbrook had been a pleasant green area, with trees and great green lawns, very open. Past that ran a country lane and fields—a few farmhouses—then another village, that of Greater Waddington.

Before her she saw a road, a few farmhouses, and Greater Waddington. The land itself had bent, and buckled, leaving behind only a shortened ripple of tumultuous broken snow, and tufts of dull brown grass.

Penderbrook was gone.

But she had lived.

She shivered, and looked back to grin at Cook, then saw that it was too late: Cook was clinging also to a tree, but her face had swollen and gone blue-gray and empty, one hand clutched to her chest. Lucy checked for breath and heartbeat, but found neither.

Bleeding and on weakened legs, she began the rest of the short journey to Bramble House, where she was met by her father's servants, who cried out in terror at her appearance.

SOON, WITH LITTLE JERKS and inconsistencies, Creation healed itself. At first no one could speak of anything but the terrible events at Penderbrook, but by spring, no one recalled that anything unusual had occurred.

Spring was chill, but not unusually so; it was determined that the events of the previous year had been due to the explosion of the volcano Mount Tambora, in the Dutch East Indies.

It was widely known that Penderbrook had burnt down, and the Earl—who had been a capital gentleman—had perished in the fire. He was the last of his line (it was said), and had no heirs. The house had been pulled down. The American cousin could not be found; the property, far smaller than it had been, had reverted to the Crown. Little Millwich had burnt down in another fire on the same night. It was said that both properties had been attacked by Luddites, angered by the loss of work engendered by the mill, but no culprit was ever found.

Lucy attempted to make sketches of both Barnabas and Marcus; the sketches faded into unrecognizability, no matter how heavy the inks she used. She attempted to write a journal of what had occurred, but its writing, too, became faint and illegible. Worse, the letters began to swim before her, to twist into shapes both familiar and unthinkable. She set her pen aside.

Her father had disappeared with the others, although his memory had not been completely erased; it was said that he had recently died in a hunting accident. She wrote to the cousin who was to inherit Bramble House upon her death—she having only a life-interest in the property—and invited him to take possession of it, that the house might not wither or fester under her inattentive care.

She *had* caught from Marcus's lovemaking—which she both remembered, and did not—but had lost the child only days after her escape, and was told, very discreetly, that her womb would never again bear fruit.

Lucy tried not to write again, after the failures with the journal, but found herself drawn to pen and ink again and again, almost without thought. She found that putting down tales of one kind or another soothed her nightmares, and allowed her to sleep at night. She knew that she must not write directly upon the tale of Penderbrook, that it was an invitation to disaster. But she could pen fanciful tales of centuries past, of tall Italian castles, of German monasteries, of American farms haunted by ghosts, and the words would neither fade, nor twist upon her. When she read the tale of *Frankenstein*, she cursed and wept in jealousy, then took the best of her tales and sent them to a publisher, saying that the public might find them of interest.

It did; she moved to London, and acquired a certain amount of fame. She never wore anything but mourning again; she found that it suited her. One soul at least, she thought, should remember what dangers the Earl's vanity had spurred him to, and warn, in a little way through her stories, against its happening again.

She wrote, and lived, and went to the Great Exhibition in 1851, and finally sorted out her thoughts about all that had occurred.

It was difficult to remember that which Creation wished one to forget, but she tried.

Then, one day, late in the year 1870, an admirer who preferred to remain nameless sent her a package. Within it was a silver-gray piece of glass, a nearly perfect sphere: an artificial pearl.

The note within the parcel said that the admirer was a great enthusiast of her work, and had gone to see the house in which she had grown up, as it was near to a place that he must travel for business, and that he had walked the environs of Bramble House, admiring its beauty. The house was in excellent repair, he assured her, although the current owner had allowed the climbing roses that had given the house its name to nearly overtake the house entirely, which produced a most charming effect, as if turning the house into a sort of fairy-tale.

The enclosed piece of glass, he had found in one of the grassy fields, and said that it reminded him of one of her stories, called *The Pearl of Kearsley Green*, a tale of a lost treasure buried by Barbary pirates along Swansea Bay, which was discovered to be false, but only after a Duke had a young woman kidnapped, and her lover, a smuggler, killed. The woman had foiled the Duke's plans to wed her and take her land, and the Duke perished in a fire. Afterwards, one of his ill-favored servants found her, and left her with one of the false pearls that was at the heart of the tragedy, laughing that it was no better than what she deserved.

She held the glass in her withered old hand, and felt its pull, and knew it for no smuggler's cheat, but for a world entire: the collapsed Penderbrook. She held it up to the sun and tried to peer within it, but saw only darkness.

Her flesh rippled as she held the pearl, and her bones creaked.

Perhaps, after all, Creation was right, and it were better to forget such things.

She held the pearl for a moment longer, then sent one of her secretaries to put it away in some forgotten corner of the attic: and never saw it again.

THE END

Author Checkin!

Hi all!

This is a checkin dated from 2025, which I'm adding along with a cover and interior update to make things look a little more polished and professional.

The original release of the novel was on March 2, 2020, which—*whew*—was a bit of a stressful time, what with COVID and some other things, and I didn't think to write any kind of author's note at the time. And I'd like to remember at least a bit of what was going on in my head at the time.

I wrote *The House Without a Summer* because I ran into an anecdote, possibly apocryphal, about an author who wrote the most excessively cheesy book they could think of, and it ended up being a personal and commercial success. I won't name the author; there are actually several authors I've heard the story told about, and I suppose it doesn't much matter which.

I decided that if I were to tell the story that I thought was too cheesy to write, it would *have* to be a horror story, and moreover it would have to be a haunted house story. I love haunted houses. When I was a kid we would set them up in the basement. I adore slow, atmospheric horror: castles, mists, ghosts, plot twists.

My favorite ghost-story author is E.F. Benson, who was mainly known as the author of the Mapp and Lucia stories, about which one reviewer said, "The cosmic stakes are low, the social stakes are high, the humor is deliciously bitchy."

They sound delightful. Alas, I could never get into them.

But Benson was also a teller of ghost stories where the personal stakes are high, the social stakes are never forgotten, and the voice is *still* deliciously bitchy...until the final twists pop into place and the claws (and the goosebumps) come out. Those I love. "The Room in the Tower" and "Caterpillars" are my favorites. In both of them you know something is about to scare you, and in fact the author tells you ahead of time exactly how he's going to scare you—and still manages to breathe cold air down the back of your neck at the end.

Every time I reread one of his stories, I go, "Will I ever be that good?"

Not if I don't practice, I won't.

At any rate the story didn't turn out to be as cheesy as I thought it would be; I enjoyed writing it immensely and really enjoyed the freedom of writing "my" ultimate haunted house novel with absolutely no self-constraints whatsoever.

—And okay, I have to be honest here. The novel really started out as a romance novel about two brothers and the woman who loved them both. It was supposed to have a little electricity in it (science!) but nothing weirder than that.

I couldn't get it written.

When I reframed it as a horror novel, it practically wrote itself.

As always, the real world creeps into my stories; here I was exploring some family history that sort of blended into the first Trump presidency, the politics at the time. Who even does the sorts of things Trump does? Why does anyone get involved with that kind of person? How does that person keep the illusion of sanity going for so long? Is anyone actually fooled? From my own family history, I knew the answers; they're ugly ones.

Eventually, people like that collapse in on themselves. It's really only a question of who they take down with them.

A lesson that a lot of people haven't learned yet.

My main inspirations for *The House Without a Summer* are E.F. Benson and a lot more. *Frankenstein* and Jane Austen's *Pride & Prejudice* (I was ghostwriting at the time and had to learn her style for a project) are at the top of the list, followed by *The Turn of the Screw*, *The Haunting of Hill House*, and Richard Matheson's *Hell House*. *The House Next Door*, *Burnt Offerings*, *The Shining*, *The Graveyard Apartment*, *The Little Stranger*, *Wylding Hall*, *House of Leaves*, *The Woman in Black*, *We Have Always Lived in the Castle*, *The Amityville Horror*, *The Fall of the House of Usher*, *The Elementals*, *Ghost Story* by Peter Straub, *Rebecca*, *The Rats in the Walls*, *Heart-Shaped Box*, *Wuthering Heights*...and others.

Fortunately I haven't run out. There are always more haunted house novels to read.

The other books in the Haunted Houses series are (so far):

A Murder of Crows: Seventeen Tales of Monsters & the Macabre (featuring the house I grew up in)

The House Without a Summer (this book)

House of Masks (a sci-fi gothic with a castle)

And I'm working on a haunted Italian castle novel at the moment, because of course I am. The working title is *The Castle of Figlianza*, but I might change that. We'll see.

At any rate, thanks for taking the time to read my first experiment in writing haunted house novels, and a personal favorite of mine.

Love, De

Tampa

June 9, 2025

Acknowledgements

When I first published this book, I didn't include any acknowledgments. It was March 2nd, 2020, and I had just finished getting over the worst convention crud I'd ever had in my life, one that I picked up in October 2019 and (ironically) didn't shake off until around the time we started finding out about COVID-19. I didn't have the health or spoons to do more than the bare minimum to get the novel published at that point.

So let me add a few things now.

Thanks to the Tesla Writers, the SF/F/H networking group, mostly based in Colorado. You guys showing up to hang out and talk about All Things Writing with me helped immensely. When I moved to Tampa, leaving that group behind took a big chunk out of me, and I still miss it. You guys taught me a lot about how to put myself in front of other people and value my own expertise. Thank you.

Particular thanks to Marla Bell (M.J. Bell), who made sure I didn't chicken out. <3

As always, for Ray.

More To Read!

So *The House Without a Summer* is part of the Haunted Houses series, which isn't really a series but is a collection of stories where I explore different types of haunted houses. (I love haunted houses!) *The House Without a Summer* is the first novel in the series, but it all started with *A Murder of Crows: Seventeen Tales of Monsters & the Macabre*.

Sixteen of the stories are individual short stories with nothing really tying them together; the seventeenth is a story about a group of crows who save a kid from freezing during a blizzard, and tell her ghost stories to help keep her warm.

As you do.

Seventeen tales of monsters, memory, and the hunger that outlasts winter.

The crows are watching.

They've seen the girl. Thin. Unloved. Left outside as her home turns strange and cruel—twisting under the weight of her mother's madness.

The walls no longer hold warmth. The family's love has rotted through. And the monsters are starting to slip in.

But crows understand stories. And they're willing to share.

Out on the Great Plains, where the sky stretches cold and empty, seventeen stories unfold—dark, sharp, and feathered with dread. Tales of monsters, yes. But also of the fragile, fierce minds that endure them. Each one told by the crows, to a girl they refuse to let starve. Not just of food—but of meaning.

If her mother comes to reclaim her, it may already be too late.

And if not?

Well.

The crows have always had a taste for tragedy.

For readers of folklore-haunted horror, unsettling transformation, and the sharp bite of stories that know exactly where you live.

IN CASE YOU WERE Wondering

It was we crows who took your daughter, in case you were wondering. She didn't run away. We had—*I* had—been watching her for some time, listening to her tell stories in the grass behind the house. She would sit near the chicken coop and watch the white chickens pick at the dirt, pulling up fat worms and clipping grasshoppers out of the air as they jumped toward the fields.

Some of them were good stories. Some of them were bad. But that's what decided it, even more than any issue of mercy or salvation or anything else. Crows are, for one thing, possessive of stories. And also by then I had pecked almost all the elders into coming to listen to her at least once, except

Facunde, who was then mad and responded to nobody's pecking, not that I had had the courage to exactly take my beak to her. "She is like a daughter to me," I had pled with the others. "She *listens*." They laughed at me, they rattled their beaks, they came and heard her and were convinced, or at least bullied into pretending they were convinced.

We took her yesterday, on the same cold winter day that you traded your son to the fairies, the wind blowing in cold gray threads, ruffling our feathers. It had snowed a few days before that, a storm that had killed your husband, or so it was said. The wind had snatched the snow out onto the prairie, hiding it in crevices. It had been a dry year, and even though it was still too cold to melt the snow, the thirsty dirt still found places to tuck it away in case of a thaw.

I stamped my feet on a sleeping branch while the others argued. Some argued that we should wait for spring. So many things are different, in the spring. But old Loyolo insisted: no, if we were to take the child, we would have to take her then and there: there had been at least one death already, and no one had heard the babe's cry for hours.

We covered the elm trees, thousands of us, so many that the branches creaked and swayed under our weight. I don't know if you noticed us, before it was too late. You were, it is to be admitted, busy.

The girl played on the swings, rocking herself back and forth in long, mournful creaks. She wore a too-small padded jacket and a dress decorated in small flowers. She was so clean that she still smelled of soap. Her feet were bare under their shoes, the skin of her legs scabbed and dry, almost scaly. Her wrists were pricked with gooseflesh, and her hair whipped in thin, colorless threads across her face as the wind caught it. The house had the smell of fresh death, under the peeling paint and the dusty windows, and seemed to murmur with forgotten languages, none of which were languages of love or tenderness. Afternoon was sinking into evening. The girl's breath smelled like hunger.

"Now!" called old Loyolo, at some signal that not even I could have told you. And thousands of birds swept out of the trees toward her. From the middle of it, I can tell you, it seemed a kind of nightmare. Wings in my face, claws in my feathers. The sun was temporarily snuffed out, it was a myriad of bright slices reflected off black wings. We were no flock of starlings, hatched in formations more intricate than any weaving, just a flock of crows. Some of us were old and fat, and none of us were graceful.

We did not eat her. We did not even peck her to death, although of course there was blood. We each of us clutched her with our claws, in her hair, on her dress—and with a *clack clack caw*, we took her into the air.

She did not scream. Her eyes were wide, and all the way around they were white, but she only pressed her lips together and swallowed over and over again, even as old Loyolo practically tore her hair from the roots.

And then, as you chanted and strained over a small crib, as you hoped and prayed that your daughter would not interrupt you, we took her away so that she was no longer your problem. Although I would not be surprised if you begged me to return her, so that she could take your place, on the other side of the window, now that you realize what you have done.

WE TOOK HER TO a place hidden in a dumping ground for refrigerators and plows and empty beer cans and tangled wire. You had been there once a few years ago and shot .22sat us, hitting no one but making bright *pinging* sounds and leaving brass casings behind. We made her nest inside an overturned truck cab. We lined it with twigs and feathers and blankets and scraps of cloth and leather and tried not to shit in it. We brought her insects and mice and the last of the dried apples that hung from the branches on your apple tree. We stole for her, stole socks and jeans and too-large shirts and bright scarves with tinsel in them and rings made of pink plastic because, well, chicks will steal anything shiny.

At first she only huddled and shivered and cried. Then, as the afternoon lengthened, she began to pick her way through the garbage, looking for treasures. She found a naked human doll and wrapped it in cloth and bits of string. She tied a serrated knife to a stick. She watched the moon rise.

She did not speak.

We asked old Loyolo what we should do about that. None of us had had chicks who had been silent, and human children, well, they were a mystery.

Night fell. The snow began to come down so thick (and we had eaten so well on a dead coyote that day), that my part of the greater flock decided to spend the rest of the day with her in her nest. We pecked on her door and she opened it, and we swept in, oh, a hundred or so of us, and found places to roost before too much snow could follow us in.

She sat in the nest we had made he under the upside-down seat of the truck, wrapped herself in her blankets with a pink wool one on top, and spread it out for us to si ton. We gathered on her shoulders and all over her legs and waited, but she did not speak.

Old Loyolo coughed noisily and said, "It is time for stories."

We all looked at her expectantly, even though it's not our way to make a storyteller say anything unwilling, and with good reason.

She said nothing.

And so, after a long moment that felt like a feather caught in the throat, old Loyolo said, "If you will not tell stories, than we will tell stories. *Human* stories," he added. "So that she can remember how to be human."

It was a nice thing to say. A kind thought, for a crow. But mostly we were warm and full, and wanted to hear stories, whether they helped the girl or not.

Old Loyolo groaned to himself, jumped off the girl's knee, and hopped onto the rear-view mirror, which formed a kind of podium. "Me first, then," he croaked. "Once upon a time there was a girl who loved her father more than anything else..."

Read more here:

https://wonderlandpress.com/product/a-murder-of-crows-seventeen-tal es-of-monsters-the-macabre/

About the Author

DeAnna Knippling is a versatile author celebrated for her imaginative storytelling across multiple genres, including gothic horror, steampunk, puzzle mystery, psychological suspense, and dark fantasy. Her works, such as *A Murder of Crows* and *The Clockwork Alice*, have garnered praise for their inventive narratives and unique twists on classic tales. Readers commend her ability to blend the macabre with the whimsical, creating immersive worlds that captivate and intrigue. Whether exploring twisted fairytales or unraveling crime, DeAnna's stories linger long after the final page. Find her at

WonderlandPress.com.